Blood o

CW00404452

Old Ground

C. D. L. Watts

Text copyright © 2019 C. D. L. Watts

All rights reserved

Charles looked out of the window across a vision of Hell.

Three dismal, grey, nineteen-sixties brutalist tower blocks framed the near horizon, their walls streaked with dark stains from the rain that had penetrated the rotting concrete. Columns of gloomy, single-paned windows squinting at the low sky were hung with old, frayed, nicotine stained net curtains, not so much preserving the privacy and dignity of the residents within their prisons but rather, hiding their shame and corruption. A damning indictment of the ineffectiveness of past social housing policies. The view of the solemn trio of monoliths that dominated the skyline seemed to suck the cheer from the day. Not that there was much cheer to be gleaned from today anyway.

A deluge was falling in vertical lines and streams of water shimmered on the rusted, corrugated iron roofs of ramshackle buildings that belonged to a scrapyard and recycling company below. Each depressingly mismatched collection of structures sat in its own compound surrounded by chicken wire fences topped with spirals of razor wire with tattered rags hanging from the blades as if some poor fool had tried to escape by climbing over the top and paid the ultimate price. The muddy forecourts that more closely resembled a miniature model of the cratered surface of the moon were stacked with loosely bundled cubes of sodden cardboard and paper that fluttered in a cold breeze and rusting carcasses of cars, stripped back to their steel skeletons of any value and worth.

Charles sneered. He had worked on the force long enough to recognise the seething hole of the criminal underworld when he saw it. Unmarked vans sped along the pot-holed tracks between industrial units, no doubt carrying cargo of fake goods that had made it past the port authorities back at the dock. Hidden from view, encircled by clouds of cigarette smoke, the rulers of the underclass conducted their business. Thugs, drug dealers, con-men and racketeers. The worst kind of organised low-life. Charles had encountered their kind on many occasions before. Individually, they weren't that bright. But what they lacked in intellect, they made up for in cockiness. Of course they all 'knew their rights' and played the goddamned system like a harp, giving a wink and a semi-toothless grin as they swaggered out of the police station with no charges filed.

Scum. Every last one of them.

Charles' attention was diverted from the post-apocalyptic panorama by a shout from below. He leaned in closer to the glass and peered down the vertical face from the seventh floor of the tower block he was in. A group of five or six kids, each clad in cheap sportswear and counterfeit football kit that defined the tribe to which they belonged, had gathered around the three police vehicles parked in the street. Charles squinted through the rivulets of rainwater to see more clearly but it was impossible to make out their features from above since each of them wore a baseball cap beneath a raised hood to hide their faces. One of them had evidently grown tired of taunting the two police officers standing guard outside the building and had decided to push his luck further by hurling his half-full can of some hideous caffeine-loaded fizzy drink at the windscreen of one of the cars. The shout was from the officer who chased after him but the kids just scattered, some on bikes, others leaping over railings and running along an alley. The whole estate seemed to be a breeding ground for dysfunctional creatures.

Scum. Every last one of them.

"Chief Inspector?"

The rain seemed to intensify and the rhythmic drumming on the glass was almost hypnotic. Charles' gaze drifted upward again to the view over the scrapyard. Through the blurry lines of water he could see a couple of burly men quickly unloading boxes from the back of a van and carrying them into the scrapyard office.

Bastards. Charles thought. His teeth clenched in his jaw and he felt his pulse quicken.

"Chief Inspector Johns?"

I know what you toss-bags are up to. You parasitic leeches. Taking everything that's good in this world and turning it to shit. With your cons, your drugs and your dealings that are as dodgy as fu...

"Excuse me, Sir."

Charles snapped out of the dark visions that were filling his mind and turned his head to face the young officer who was now standing beside him. Suddenly, back in the present with senses alert to his immediate surroundings, Charles was reminded of the appalling stench in the flat. He reached into his jacket pocket and took out a small plastic tub. Removing the lid, he dipped the tip of his finger into the clear, eucalyptus infused jelly and smeared it under his nose.

"Yes?" Charles responded as nonchalantly as he could while returning the tub to his pocket.

"There's something you should see, Sir."

"Lead on." Charles gestured for the officer to lead the way back through the flat to the small bedroom off the short hallway. At the end of the hall, he saw a young female officer standing by the open front door, holding a handkerchief to her mouth and nose. He realised that she had probably never seen anything like this crime scene before. Or smelled anything like it, for that matter.

"I think we can open the window in the lounge a bit." Charles quietly said to her. "Get a bit of air in the place, eh?" He smiled as he registered the look of relief in the officer's eyes and she quickly squeezed past him to carry out his instructions.

Charles paused by the bedroom doorway. The door was hanging limply by the bottom hinge and had a hole in the middle of it big enough for a man to climb through. This was not in itself, anything to warrant attention. It was after all, how the first officers on the scene gained access. The neighbours in the other flats on the seventh floor had phoned the police earlier that day complaining of a foul smell. The truth was that the other occupants of the tower block had called the police six times over the past four days but such was the nature of the estate that sending a car to investigate had been put off time and time again. Eventually, it was decided that a sufficient number of different people had phoned, voicing the same complaint, that it required investigating. The two officers who responded to the call had no trouble in breaking through the front door but the bedroom door had proven something of a more formidable obstacle.

Charles stepped into the room and glanced at the doorframe to his left. Nine deadbolts had been fitted on the inside of the door. After the officers broke through the door, they unlocked it from the inside. And then they both ran out into the hallway and threw up. It was somewhat telling that the few remaining occupants of the block were so used to living in squalor that they waited for nearly three weeks before anyone thought to complain about the smell.

Inside the small, windowless spare bedroom, a single bed had been pushed up against one wall. In the opposite corner stood a tatty armchair with three crudely constructed corn dollies standing side by side on the seat. And on the floor in between the two was the half-rotted body of a male, of indeterminate age with a white candle laying on its side nearby. The corpse was almost completely curled up as if it had been electrocuted. The clothes were damp and stained from the putrefying juices that had seeped from decaying tissue and formed a large, black puddle of ooze on the cheap, blue carpet. What remained of the skin was in such a state of moist decomposition that it made the mummified face of Tutankhamun look like the visage of an angel and although the eyes had long since liquefied, the expression on the face was still easy to read; pure, absolute terror. Its mouth was open in an eternal scream, helped by the fact that the lower jaw was now only attached to one side of the head, and a bony hand was reaching back along the floor, clawing or grabbing, frozen in time perhaps whilst the victim was trying to escape.

Charles looked around the room again. He had inspected the scene alongside the coroner when he first arrived but the overwhelming stench coupled with the bizarre circumstances had somewhat clouded his first observations. He knew a second, more thorough examination could reveal far more about what happened.

Both the walls and ceiling were covered with sheets of plain paper, upon each of which was drawn some large, strange, archaic symbol. There wasn't a single gap between the pages. Even the inside of the door had been diligently plastered with obscure scripture, the torn edges now framing the jagged hole through which those first officers responding to the complaint had entered. Charles paused as his eye settled upon one page in particular, down in the corner to the left of the door. The upper left corner had peeled away from the wall revealing a dark, damp stain on the painted plaster. He bent to peel the page further and found that the viscous stain was concentrated only where the wall was exposed. He scowled, straightened up and went back out into the hallway to examine the other side of the wall. There was no stain. It struck him as odd that a patch of mouldy damp would be present on only one side of an internal wall but considering the overall hideousness of the building, he decided that it was of no consequence and went back into the bedroom. He felt a shudder run down his spine as he perused the other artefacts that adorned the tiny room. Secured by a single nail on every wall were wooden pentagrams of varying sizes and quality. Some, near the bed, were small and intricately carved. Others were large and rather crudely constructed. The most baffling aspect however that seemed to jar in Charles' mind was that every five-pointed star was upside down. He approached one that was closest to him and reached out. As soon as he touched it, it swung down around the nail so that it was again the right way up. He looked carefully at every pentagram and saw that each was precariously balanced above the nail at the tip of the lowest point. He reached out and gently tapped another. Just

6

like the first, it effortlessly swung round and came to a stop when the weight of the wood was again beneath the nail.

That's some freaky shit... He thought as he stepped away and took up position in the centre of the room. He turned slowly on the spot, taking in the whole, bizarre and morbid spectacle.

Door locked from the inside. He mused. *Weird magic symbols all over the place. Stars all upside down.*

He looked down at the distorted, decayed visage of the corpse and frowned.

What the hell were you up to?

"Here, Sir." Said the officer who had accompanied Charles into the room and he thrust a book forward at him.

"What's this?" Charles asked as he took it.

"It's some sort of journal or diary, Sir. It was under the bed."

Charles' eyes widened and he looked down at the book in his hands.

"Well done." He mumbled as he balanced the journal on one hand and gently opened the front cover with the other.

"Sir?"

"Hmm?" Charles replied, scanning down the first page for any clue regarding the dead man's identity.

"Do you mind if I step outside for a moment?"

Charles looked up again at the officer. He was decidedly pale. Charles nodded his consent and the officer hurried out of the room.

"Tell the coroner he can remove the body now. Or what's left of it." Charles called after him before turning his attention back to the journal. He flicked through pages and pages of detailed entries. There were drawings and sketches, paragraphs of what appeared to be research notes, book references, diary entries and strange symbols that Charles recognised from the pages on the walls. Flicking through the book, he noticed that the records only went back over the past year. He thought it strange that a journal should be so restricted in its timescale and wondered if there were other volumes that preceded it. He glanced around the room, looking for a bookcase or a stack of diaries but saw neither. Turning his attention back to the journal, the next thing he observed was that the dated entries, interspersed by drawings, hadn't necessarily been made for every consecutive day. Some were a couple of days apart, others a few weeks. Regardless of the intervening gaps, each record was on average four pages in length and highly detailed. As his eyes skimmed over the lines of handwriting, he saw names of men and women but no specific clues that would help him to identify who the body at his feet was. He flicked further and further through the book, past symbols and what seemed to be spells, and his mouth opened in surprise. Every name that he had seen earlier in the diary was now being referenced along with one other specific word; *dead.* He flicked to the final diary entry, dated three and a half weeks beforehand, and began to read intently. He looked down from the scribbled writing and hesitated as his gaze met the empty stare of the dead man. Reading on, he found the last entry was a letter, hurriedly written, not addressed to anyone in particular and without a name at the bottom. He read quickly and felt the goose-bumps rise on his skin as every hair stood on end. His mouth dropped open further and his eyes widened in horror as he read. Pausing for a moment to consider the terrifying meaning behind the scrawled writings, he held his breath as he suddenly heard a child laughing. Turning his head to the open doorway and remaining absolutely still, he listened but the sound had stopped.

He quietly made his way to the door and peered around the frame, half expecting to see a young boy standing in the lounge. But there was no-one.

You're going mad, you old bugger. He tutted and turned his head to glance down once more at the man's face.

Poor bastard. He thought and he felt a lump rise up in his throat. He coughed and flicked the pages of the journal back to the first entry in the book. He needed a starting point for his investigation. Something tangible that he could sink his teeth into. He needed a lead. His eyes settled on one word; *Exeter.* Charles snapped the journal shut and quickly turned on his heels, striding quickly out of the bedroom and past the female officer by the front door.

"Is everything alright, Sir?" She asked, noticing his pale complexion and hasty retreat from the flat. Charles stopped and looked at her.

"Yes." He stuttered. He swallowed as he collected his thoughts and his composure. "I've got to get back to the station. I – I've got to make an urgent call. I need to speak with our colleagues in the Devon Constabulary. There's a woman whose life may be in danger!"

The officer didn't have time to question him any further for, even as he was finishing his flustered explanation, Charles was striding along the corridor toward the stairwell.

1

Dillon sauntered along the quayside as the river beside him flowed gently in the opposite direction. He felt calm and content as the heat of the mid-autumn sun warmed his back through his lightweight jacket. There was no need to rush. There was nowhere else for him to be and nothing else for him to do. It was, after all, Friday evening and he had finished work for the week around an hour and a half ago, giving him plenty of time to get back to his flat, change and head out for a slow stroll by the river. He always treated himself and dined out on a Friday anyway. It had become something of a tradition, a way of marking the start of the weekend, while also ensuring his belly was sufficiently full to allow a decent lie-in on Saturday morning. It also meant he could settle down to watch a movie after dinner without the nagging in the back of his mind that he needed to do to the washing up. In truth, that was probably the most significant reason.

It never bothered him that he ate alone. In fact, it didn't even cross his mind. It was just how it had always been. He didn't feel loneliness at all. Preferring to keep to himself and harbouring a general dislike of noise and crowds, he was happy in his own company. To most people, this would ordinarily seem odd for any twenty-five year old but Dillon had always been a shy individual and the fact that he was out for a walk alone had nothing to do with the fact that he had only moved the city two months previously and perhaps hadn't yet had the opportunity to make many friends. The truth was that Dillon was happy with a simple, quiet life. He really couldn't understand the adrenaline-fuelled lifestyles that other people his age seemed to actively seek out. The thought of backpacking around the world, surfing, sky-diving, bungee-jumping and so on just made him feel anxious and if he thought about it too much, he would end up having to reach for his inhaler to stave off an asthma attack. Dillon preferred Science Fiction movies, fantasy novels, online gaming and shoegaze music. He had found kindred spirits at University on his Computer Science course but those days were long gone and now he only kept in touch with his former fellow students via social media.

His awkwardness with other people could not be traced back to any one particular negative experience when he was younger. Indeed, as he was growing up, his parents tried to get him involved in various clubs and organisations, like the Scouts and a birdwatching group for youngsters. All told, he had had a quiet but perfectly normal childhood. At school, he excelled in Mathematics, Physics and Computing. He avoided sport altogether because of his asthma in winter, hay fever in summer and besides, his skinny frame just wasn't suited for rugby. He would've been pulverised on the pitch by the bigger boys in the year group. Whilst his older brother had moved away after completing his degree and was now based in Australia, studying for a doctorate in Marine Biology and his parents had retired to a villa in the South of France, Dillon had stayed in the Home Counties where he had grown up. It was familiar, safe and, as far as he was concerned, a case of better the devil you know. With the increasing cost of living and rental prices near London sky-rocketing however, he had decided to take, what was for him, an unprecedented gamble and look for work further afield. Somewhere peaceful, picturesque and quiet. Somewhere where he could enjoy a better quality of life, even if it meant taking a hefty cut in salary from his London-based job in web design.

Four months previously he had accepted a job in Exeter, doing more or less the same work he had been doing in London but for a smaller, more entrepreneurial company. The interview had gone really well and the interviewers, one of whom was the company's Managing Director, seemed genuinely thrilled with Dillon's qualifications and experience. He was offered the position before he even left the interview and was on a high for the entire duration of the train journey back to London.

After moving to Exeter, Dillon found the slower pace of life suited him perfectly and quickly recognised that he felt totally at ease in the city. He felt safe enough to take walks after sunset without having to keep watching over his shoulder for muggers, nutters or unsociable gangs of youths who would jump at the chance to taunt a solitary, skinny, pale, bespectacled geek just for their own perverse amusement. The move had, however, been one of the more risky things that Dillon had ever done. He had never been to Exeter before and when he thought about it, couldn't recall having ever been to Devon before, although he was sure he had been on a family holiday to Paignton when he was a toddler. Moving away from the area where he grew up had been such a radical decision that it had taken a few days for the reality to sink in that this would be his new home. Such was the extent of the change that, for the first few weeks, his mind seemed to resist it and he found it difficult to shake off the feeling that he was just a tourist on holiday.

Once he had accepted that he was there to stay, Dillon set about exploring the city. The flat he was renting was only a mile from the centre and within easy walking distance from his new office. In terms of his priorities, he knew he needed to learn the layout of the shopping centre, find his local supermarket and more importantly, get his home broadband up and running. What made the relocation significantly easier was the fact that he never really had many personal possessions. All his work, music, photos, games and books were on his laptop. He didn't even need a television because all the movies and boxsets he watched were available online. It was however, during the numerous evenings of sheer frustration in the first fortnight where the broadband company had spectacularly and repeatedly failed to correctly set up his internet connection that he had started going for walks by the river. He found that he quite enjoyed it and it became something that he actively looked forward to during the day, using his lunch break to mentally plot out the route he would take.

Dillon paused outside a pub that he had walked past many times before and yet, up until that point, had not entered. He read the colourful chalk details on a blackboard tied to a bollard and felt his mouth start to water. For some reason, the thought of beer-battered fish and triple-cooked chips really took his fancy at that moment. Perhaps it was just because he was hungry. Or perhaps it was because the thought of a cool pint of beer to wash the meal down held particular appeal. He stepped into the small entrance that separated the interior of the pub from the warm breeze that funnelled along the river and stopped by a corkboard covered with flyers and posters. The leaflets advertised a variety of events in and around the city and he quickly skimmed over each one to find if there was anything that would appeal to him. He took a few photos on his phone of a poster for a free music concert a few weeks away, organised in conjunction with the University Student's Union and a big firework display to mark November the fifth. He stopped scanning the flyers when he saw one with that day's date emblazoned across the top. He pocketed his phone and stooped to read the details. It was an advert for a city Ghost Walk but the professionalism of the flyer's design was what held his attention. The tour had received high ratings on Tripadvisor and although the walk normally took place every Friday and Saturday evening, that particular Friday marked the company's tenth anniversary and all who went along would receive a free gift. He examined the contents of his wallet to see if he had sufficient cash to join the walk and, finding a folded five pound note tucked behind some old receipts, checked the start time. It was due to start at eight o' clock, leaving from outside the front of the cathedral. He glanced at his watch. He had just over an hour to eat and make his way there. *No problem,* he thought and pushed open the door to enter the pub.

Dillon reached the green in front of the impressively ornate cathedral entrance at five minutes to eight and found a considerable crowd of people milling around. There must have been between thirty to forty people, mostly families with pre-teen aged children but a few older couples as well. The sun was just setting behind the buildings on the other side of the green, creating the perfect atmosphere for a ghost walk. The air temperature steadily began to drop and shadows grew longer while the dark oranges and purples reflecting off the high, wispy clouds illuminated the carved arch of the cathedral entrance in ethereal hues. As the lawn of the cathedral green below the trees faded into a sombre grey, the twilight of the day made the autumn leaves glow as if they were on fire.

A man dressed in a monk's habit with his hood raised and carrying an old fashioned lantern approached. He stopped right in front of Dillon and looked straight into his eyes. The monk's face was covered with white make-up and his eyes had black shading around them. Dark, sunken cheeks had been painted on and his lips were painted black. He held out a gloved hand and Dillon placed his five pound note in his palm. The monk grinned and Dillon saw that he had a set of plastic horror teeth in his mouth. From a leather pouch hanging from his rope belt, he produced a sprig of rosemary which he handed to Dillon in return for the payment before he hobbled away to the next customer and repeated his performance. Dillon turned back to face the cathedral when he heard a low, tremulous voice call out. He saw a tall man, probably in his late forties or early fifties, but with the make-up it was difficult to be sure, dressed like a Victorian funeral director with a large, dusty, cob-webbed top hat. He stood head and shoulders over the rest of the crowd and Dillon presumed he must have been standing on a box.

"Ladies and Gentlemen, ghouls and goblins, welcome! Welcome to the Ghosts of Old Exeter Tour!" He held his arms out wide and Dillon saw that in one hand he had a black silver-topped cane and in the other he was grasping a sprig of Rosemary like the one the monk had handed him. There was a murmur of delight from the crowd and the man waved his cane in a circle over his head to command their attention.

"As we make our way through these dark and haunted streets, we shall meet many spirits and we shall learn of their terrible histories, their tragedies and their damnation. For some of the tales they tell will be of greed, malevolence and murder." He dropped his voice to a low growl and bent forward, eyeing up the children standing in the front row.

"But fear not!" He called out as he stood up straight and held the rosemary high up above his head. "The Rosmarinus branch you have been given will protect you from evil spirits! If you find yourself afraid or facing an evil spirit, simply wave the branch in front of you like this!" He then held the rosemary out at arm's length and waggled it around as though it were a magic wand. A number of the children copied him and seemed to feel better for having been provided with this small token of protection.

"And now!" The man continued. "We shall begin here, at the city cathedral which has a history that stretches back nearly a thousand years and we shall talk of the tens of thousands of the dead who now rest under the green, only a few feet beneath your own."

The walk lasted for just over an hour and the funeral director guide was simply excellent. He led the group through the streets from the cathedral to the entrance of the underground passages and on up to the castle before heading for the river and returning once again to the cathedral green. There was an excited atmosphere in the gathering as they marched en masse along the streets, illuminated by the lights from the shop windows. At each location where the guide stopped, he told a story of what had happened in that particular place; murders, poltergeists, hangings and the like. Dillon had no idea if any of it was true but it was certainly entertaining and he found himself being drawn in by the stories, the hairs on the back of his neck standing on end with the excitement as strange and dark images filled his mind. Along the way, other people in costume appeared from out of nowhere with the express intention of frightening the audience. The funeral director hurriedly gathered the children together and instructed them to see off the evil spirits. This provoked much waving of rosemary branches at the various characters until they ran off again. After a while, Dillon suspected that it was the same person in a variety of costumes, probably the corpse monk he had encountered at the start. He must have kept out of sight and overtaken the group by following some of the back streets. When he reached the next pre-arranged stop, he could quickly change into a new outfit before springing out, making ghoulish noises and waving his arms around.

By the time the group returned to the cathedral, it was dark. The old man stood up on his box, thanked everyone for coming, removed his top hat and bowed. He received a lengthy round of applause and afterward, both he and the monk went round handing out the free gifts; small muslin bags tied with a black ribbon that contained a variety of horror sweets, much to the children's delight.

As people began to disperse, Dillon saw a large, bald man and a woman make their way through the crowd, handing out flyers. They had definitely not been a part of the ghost walk and must have been waiting at the Cathedral for the group to return. Dillon watched them for a few moments, suspecting their flyers were simply adverts for more ghost tours but the woman caught him looking at her and she made her way over to him, holding out a flyer. She was young, probably in her mid-twenties with long, wavy brown hair. A warm, delicate smile spread over her lips as she handed Dillon the flyer with a nod of thanks before turning to supply leaflets to other members of the dwindling group. He looked down at the flyer in his hand and read the large title at the top. 'ESP: The Exeter Society for the Paranormal'. There was a grainy picture of what looked like a graveyard below the title and then a small paragraph of text. 'Genuine research into paranormal phenomena. New members welcome. No joining fee. Meet every Tuesday at the Waggon and Horses pub from seven-thirty. Come along... If you're brave enough!' It may have just been the after-effect of the ghost tour; the intrigue, the excitement and the feeling of doing something new, but Dillon found himself seriously considering going along to the next meeting. After all, what could be more exciting than 'Genuine research' into ghosts and the supernatural?

2

Dillon decided to arrive at the Waggon and Horses at just after seven-forty-five. He didn't want to appear too eager by getting there early but likewise, he didn't want to arrive too late and risk missing the meeting. After having followed the directions to the pub on his phone's GPS, he stood across the street looking at the building. It looked as though it had been recently painted white but the underlying 'House that Jack Built' appearance and the lumpy, moss covered slates on the roof hinted that it was very old, probably mid-eighteenth century at the latest. In the centre of the building was a large, curved set of black wooden doors. No doubt they had been the entrance for the carriages and horses when this was once a coaching inn, surrounded by countryside on the outskirts of the city. On the left side of the doors, half the building was occupied by a boutique women's clothes shop. On the right side of the doors was the pub. At either end of the long, wooden name-plate that bore the pub's name in black, gothic lettering were well-stocked hanging baskets. A warm glow shone through the net curtains in the pitch-framed windows and a blackboard sign next to the entrance advertised the Sunday evening pub quiz. It looked quaint and welcoming enough so Dillon crossed the road and pushed open the door. Once inside, he was surprised to find that the pub was extremely small. No more than twenty people would have completely filled it. As it was however, the place was half empty. Two men sat on bar stools chatting with the barman and a young couple, probably students, were sitting in the back corner near the door to the toilets. To his left, gathered round a table were five people. They stopped chatting and looked round at him. He recognised the bald man and the young, brunette woman from outside the cathedral so he smiled, walked over and held up the flyer he had been given as though it was a letter granting safe passage.

"Ah! Great!" The large, bald man said as he stood up from his chair. "Welcome! Welcome! Please, come and have a seat." Dillon felt his cheeks flush at suddenly being the centre of attention but another man turned and dragged a chair from a neighbouring table behind him and the rest of the group shuffled round to make room. They all smiled as he approached the chair and the large man held out his hand.

"I'm Robert but everyone calls me Bob." He said as he shook Dillon's hand, beaming from ear to ear. "And this is the Exeter Society for the Paranormal." He added as he waved his hand around the table.

"Did you get it?" The man who had provided the chair asked as Dillon sat down next to him.

"Um, sorry. Get what?" He replied.

"Exeter Society for the Paranormal... ESP?"

"Er...Extra Sensory Perception?" Dillon guessed, thinking back to where he had heard the term before in the film Ghostbusters.

"He does get it!" The man said with a laugh. "He *must* be one of us!"

"That's Frank." Bob said with a grin.

"Frank Harper." Said Frank, holding out his hand and shaking Dillon's firmly. "Retail manager." Dillon smiled and studied Frank's face for a second. He didn't strike him as the kind of person who would be a retail manager. He had something of the cheeky chappie about him. Despite his receding hairline and short beard, flecked with grey, Dillon would have guessed he was only around ten years older than he was, somewhere in his mid to late thirties. But the mischievous sparkle in his eyes made him appear considerably younger.

"Let's go round the table." Bob said. "This is Steve Hale, co-founder of the society." He nodded toward a man sitting to his left. Steve stood and reached over the table to shake Dillon's hand. He had long hair that reached down to his shoulders, a long face and his clothes had something of the alternative about them. "Steve's also a local artist and has had his paintings displayed in a few local exhibitions. Have you seen any of his work?"

"No, sorry, I haven't. Not yet. I've only recently moved to the area from London." Dillon replied. He knew that showing interest in other people's hobbies or employment was a good way of endearing him to them and avoiding awkward situations or conflict. "I haven't been to any art exhibitions yet. Are there any coming up?"

"There's one coming up in October in the Guildhall shopping centre. I'll get you tickets if you like." Steve said with an enthusiastic smile. He had a soft voice and seemed to exude calmness. He appeared to be the complete opposite of Frank.

"So what made you move to Exeter from London?" Dillon turned to face the dark haired woman on his left who had asked the question. She had what would be described as a fuller figure and her hair was jet black, cut into a well-defined bob. Her make-up and clothes immediately gave away the fact that she was a Goth. Not too over the top though, not to the extreme of Morticia Addams for instance, just enough to give a firm clue to her choice of lifestyle. She held out her hand with a smile and Dillon noticed that, like her lipstick, the fingernails that protruded from the black lace, fingerless gloves covering her forearms were also painted black. Dillon gently shook the woman's hand and was surprised at how strong her grip was. "I'm Sophie by the way. Sophie Tanner. I work in a call centre just outside town with Wendy here." She nodded to her companion to her left, sitting between her and Bob. It was the woman Dillon had recognised giving out the flyers outside the cathedral. She reached over in front of Sophie and extended her hand.

"Wendy Joyce." She said in a soft voice with a broad smile.

"Yeah, what made you leave the big smoke to move out to the West Country?" Frank repeated Sophie's question.

"Well, there was a job opportunity that came up and I fancied a change of scenery, so I went for it." Dillon explained.

"What is it you do?" Bob asked as he raised his glass of ale to his lips.

"I'm a web designer." Dillon replied. Bob nearly choked on his drink and he lowered the glass and stared at him with a huge smile on his face. The others also seemed to be quite pleased with that nugget of information. They looked almost excited.

"Web design? You mean like, web pages and web sites?" Bob asked eagerly. Dillon nodded nervously, wondering why that would be so thrilling for them.

"That's brilliant." Steve said, catching Bob's eye. They both nodded at each other.

"Certainly is." Bob continued, turning his attention back to Dillon. "We've been wanting to set up a website for the society for ages but none of us really know how." Dillon wasn't sure if Bob was waiting for him to agree to help or comment in some way but he felt like a rabbit caught in headlights. He'd only just met these people and they seemed to be signing him up for a job. He looked from one to another with wide-eyes. They all stared back, smiling enthusiastically. Dillon felt his pulse quicken and a voice started up in his mind, telling him to get out. These were the tell-tale signs of an impending anxiety attack. He knew them well and knew he had to escape. He slipped his hand into his pocket and fumbled with his inhaler. Steve must have picked up on Dillon's uncertainty because at that moment, he motioned for the barman to pour a pint for him.

"Give the man a chance." He said softly with a chuckle. "He doesn't know anything about us yet."

"True. True." Bob said and reached down beside his chair. He pulled up a black rucksack, placed it on his lap and opened the zip just as the barman brought over Dillon's drink. Dillon picked up the glass and took several large mouthfuls, instantly feeling the cool, hoppy ale calming his nerves.

"Here we go." Sophie whispered as she leant over towards him. "Out come 'The Files'. He brings them along every week just in case someone new turns up."

"Oi, cheeky." Bob said as he placed a couple of photo albums on the table in front of him. "This is what it's all about, right here." He said quietly as he patted the albums with his palm as though they were some kind of holy book. "This society was set up just over twelve years ago to investigate paranormal phenomena and document them in an effort to provide evidence for life after death and the existence of ghosts." He leant forward over the albums and lowered his voice even further, almost to a whisper, adding additional atmosphere to his words. "In these albums alone, we've collected evidence from thirty-three investigations. Be prepared to be shocked, for in these pages you will see evidence that the dead really do walk amongst the living."

"Wooooo." Dillon looked at Frank who jiggled his fingers in the air. He winked and raised his glass to his lips. Bob tutted and opened the first of the two albums. He turned the book around so Dillon could see the images. Each page had two photographs and alongside, each photo had a location, date, time and a brief description of what had been captured in the image.

"This was the first investigation we carried out back in two thousand and ten, at a church graveyard that no paranormal group had researched before." He pointed at the four photos on the first set of open pages. Dillon recognised one of them as the image that had been used on the flyer. In each picture, it was night-time. The times written next to the photos ranged from one o' clock to four o' clock in the morning. The camera flash had illuminated the old, weathered gravestones, tufts of long grass and rusted iron railings with an eerie white light. In each picture there was a localised mist.

"Those mists are the spirits that haunt the graveyard." Bob said triumphantly. "They couldn't be seen with the naked eye and they only appeared on the photos once we saw them on the computer. But they haven't been enhanced in any way.

19

That's the real deal, right there." He prodded the mist in one of the images with his forefinger. Dillon leant over to see more clearly, adjusted his glasses and squinted at the image.

"Cool." He said, trying to sound as enthusiastic as possible but in truth, he was a bit disappointed. Bob smiled with an air of satisfaction and turned the page to the next set of images.

"These three are stills from a video. It shows an object, a wooden keepsake box, flying across the room in the old pub we were investigating. As you can see, no one was anywhere near it when it took off."

"Scared the hell out of me." Steve said. "You can't see because I'm out of shot but that small box hit the wall right next to me. Shattered into a million pieces because it had been thrown with so much force."

"And these photos…" Bob continued before Frank stood up.

"You might need another drink there, mate. Looks like you're here for the long haul. What'll you have, er… Sorry, what's your name?"

"Dillon. Dillon Wells."

3

Bob spent the next twenty minutes talking through the history of the society over the past twelve years. He was a natural orator and even though the rest of the group had either been there at the times and places he described or had heard it all before, they listened intently, smiling to themselves as memories were reignited by Bob's storytelling. Throughout his narrative, he made references to past members who had been captured in photos and he knew the exact dates when the others who were seated around the table had joined the society. It was evident to Dillon that the society meant a lot to Bob and he took great pride in the evidence collected from their investigations. But there was something else that Dillon picked up on; Bob needed to be the centre of attention. It was in his mannerisms and the way he wouldn't let anyone else speak for too long. Even though Steve had been with the group from the very beginning, Bob was the leader, the organiser, the final word on decisions. It was Bob's show and, as everyone was happy to follow, the group got along just fine. Dillon wondered what would happen if anyone challenged Bob's authority.

There had been a number of member changes in the early years, 'teething problems' as Bob referred to them, until Frank joined the group four years into the society's existence. Things settled down and seemingly became more productive. The number of investigations increased and the organisation of the society records took on a more professional appearance. Both Sophie and Wendy were relative new-comers, joining only two and a half years ago. It was Sophie who had talked Wendy into becoming a member. Sophie was attracted to the idea of hanging around graveyards after dark, hunting spirits and communing with the dead. She saw it as a natural extension of her gothic lifestyle and as far as she was concerned, she was the 'Most Goth' of anyone else at the club that she regularly went to. Dillon could see that behind Sophie's bravado, there was a deep need not only to be alternative, but also to be accepted by the other members of the alternative community. Wendy on the other hand was not one to follow trends or conform to any one particular lifestyle ideology. She was happy and content with a simple, quiet life and didn't like too much fuss made about anything. She admitted that although she had been sceptical of Sophie's invitation to join the group at first, after just two investigations she was completely hooked.

"And now that we've got this veritable mountain of evidence and five key eye-witness accounts," Bob waved his hand around the table at the others as he started to wrap up the story, "We need to think about broadcasting our findings to the world. There are a lot of other supernatural societies out there and the combined evidence from all of us will certainly take paranormal investigation to a whole new level."

"Until recently, we were pretty reliant on leaflets, posters and we even tried a newsletter that could be emailed out to people who signed up on an emailing list, but that didn't really work out." Steve added.

"What we needed was to think bigger." Bob said, outstretching his arms to his sides. "We need to utilise the power of the web."

"And that's where you come in." Frank said with a wry smile.

Dillon looked around the group. During Bob's talk, he had taken the time to study the others in detail, trying to read their own personal stories, their backgrounds and their personalities. It was a habit of Dillon's to analyse other people before he involved himself with anything. It was a form of self-protection. But in this case, they seemed honest enough. He didn't get the impression that they were trying to con him or lead him on in any way for some nefarious purpose and the photos and investigations had been discussed with such enthusiasm that he felt himself being drawn in. He found a genuine interest in the 'evidence', as it was repeatedly referred to, growing inside him and filling his mind with questions. Although he had tried to mentally explain away some of the anomalies in the images; lens flares, someone's breath, reflected moonlight and so on, there were some that seemed to defy any reason. He wasn't however, quite willing enough just to accept it all as proof of the existence of ghosts. A significant and sceptical part of him wanted to confirm it with his own eyes.

"So?" Bob said finally as he closed the second album and leant back in his chair. Dillon looked blankly at him, wondering what was coming next. "You interested in joining us?" Dillon looked around at the others. They were all intently watching him.

"Yeah. Sure." He said. The group gave a round of applause which momentarily broke the calm and serene atmosphere in the pub, attracting the attention of the other patrons. Frank patted him on the back.

"Welcome to the mad house." He winked with a broad grin on his face.

"So you've managed to attract another victim then, Bob?" The barman called over with a chuckle.

"Cheeky beggar!" Bob retorted.

"Congratulations to the ESP!" The barman added. "And your next round is on me to celebrate!"

"Cheers, John!" Steve called back.

"The society's been meeting here since the beginning." Frank explained in a half-whisper. "John's seen people come and go and the society change and evolve over all those years, but there's one thing he's always relied on."

"What's that?" Dillon asked.

"The hard-earned cash of the ESP members being spent at his bar." Frank smiled and raised his glass to his lips as John approached the table with the first three pints on a circular tray.

"Do you have any more investigations lined up?" Dillon directed his question at Bob.

"Funny you should mention that." Bob smirked and leant forward, clasping his hands together on the table and lowering his voice to a whisper. The others leaned in to hear as though he was about to divulge a dark secret.

"I've recently found a place not far from Withypool in the Exmoor National Park."

"I like it already." Sophie whispered.

"Well, I don't know much about the recent history of the place just yet. I'll have to do some more research. But, what I do know is that this place, Trevalling Hall, was built in sixteen sixty-five by the Baron Trevallyn. He was greatly rewarded for being a staunch Royalist after Charles the Second was reinstated on the throne. Anyway, his wife, Baroness Trevallyn died, along with her baby, during childbirth aged only twenty-three, leaving the Baron childless."

"Aww. That's so sad." Wendy mumbled.

"Happened a lot in those days." Bob replied with a shrug. "The Hall then passed into the hands of a wealthy spice and textile merchant but after he died, his son squandered the family fortune on partying, gambling and drinking. The Hall then ends up being bought by the Montague family who occupied it right up the Napoleonic Wars in the early eighteen hundreds."

"What happens after that?" Frank asked.

"Not too sure." Bob replied, biting his lip and frowning. It's from then that I have to do more digging. What I do know is that the Hall has been empty and abandoned since the late nineteen-sixties."

"Nearly fifty years?" Frank said, surprised. "How come it's been empty for that long?"

"I suppose no one wants it. It's a big place and probably needs a lot of work doing to it. It'd be a massive project and a potential money pit. Not even the National Trust or English Heritage have taken it on. From what I can gather, it'd take millions to do it up. No one's bothered to touch it so it's just been left to rot."

"Cool." Sophie said. "A genuine haunted house."

"Exactly." Bob said with a smile. "First of all we're going to investigate to see if there is any residual spiritual energy left in the building. Who knows, we might pick up on Baroness Trevallyn herself."

"When do we go?" Wendy asked, the excitement evident in her voice.

"Not this weekend coming but the weekend after." Bob replied.

"Why the delay?" Sophie asked.

"I've got a few things to sort out before we go but I hope to have a surprise for you all next Tuesday." Bob tapped the side of his nose and winked.

"Good stuff." Frank said as he stood up and clapped his hands together. "That sounds exciting. I'm going to make a move, folks. Until next week. Adios amigos." He raised his hand to his forehead and gave a quick salute before patting Dillon on the back and heading for the door, whistling.

"Yeah, we should be going too." Wendy said as she stood and picked up her handbag. Sophie nodded and picked up her black rucksack that was studded with silver spikes. "Nice to meet you Dillon. See you next week."

"Yeah, bye." Dillon replied and gave a little wave before realising that it probably looked a bit childish and he straightened his glasses instead.

"Glad that you've decided to join us, Dillon." Bob said. Steve nodded as he drained the last of his pint.

"Sounds like it'll be fun." Dillon replied, looking from one man to the other.

"Oh, it is." Steve said. "But it'll scare the shit out of you at the same time. Better than any horror movie or roller-coaster!" He laughed.

"So, er…You up for helping us with a website then?" Bob asked.

"Yeah, I mean, if you know what you want to put on it." Dillon said with a nonchalant shrug. "The actual setting up of a website is the easy bit. It's adding all the content and the layout that takes a bit more time."

"Oh don't worry about that." Bob said with a dismissive wave of his hand. "I've got all the photos, audio and video files stored on a hard drive. Each file is kept in a specific folder for the relevant investigation. It'll be dead easy to pick out the best files from the library I've now got. I've kept everything in order and easy to access. And as far as the layout goes, Steve and I have been designing this website on paper for ages. He's got loads of drawings for the layout and artwork."

"Well, that's great." Dillon said. "Because you've already got ideas, it shouldn't be an arduous process. When do you want to start?"

"What are you doing tomorrow evening?" Steve asked with a smile.

4

"How's the website coming along?" Wendy asked as she returned from the bar and placed the two pints of ale, one for her and one for Sophie, on the table. The group had reconvened in the Waggon and Horses as they did every week but this week in particular, there was a sense of excitement in the air.

"I tell you Wendy, this man's a genius." Bob said with a broad grin as he pointed across the table at Dillon."

On both the previous Wednesday and Thursday evenings, Dillon had taken his laptop round to Bob's house, a small two-bedroomed semi-detached on the other side of the city. Steve was already there with pages of drawings and ideas for the society's website when he'd arrived on the Wednesday. The designs were very creative and beautifully drawn. It was evident that Steve had put his artistic skills to full use. Bob had so many photos and other files stored on an external hard drive that after the initial set up of the site, it really didn't take long to add the content and the layout as Bob and Steve wanted it. By the end of the session on Thursday, the website was ready to go live but Dillon advised Bob and Steve to leave it a few days and then have another look, just in case there was anything they wanted to add or change. All the while the three had been working, Bob and Steve told Dillon stories about the weird and inexplicable encounters they had experienced on some of their investigations. At no point did they categorically state that they thought the experiences were caused by ghosts. They seemed to cling on to a shred of scepticism, which Dillon found particularly reassuring. They admitted they always started an investigation with no preconceptions, so anything that happened was open for analysis.

"So when can we see the website?" Sophie asked eagerly.

"It went live yesterday." Dillon replied with a smile. He had called Bob and Steve on the Sunday afternoon to make sure they were completely happy with their work and promised he would open the site for public access on the Monday evening. Since then, it had already had sixty-four hits.

"How can we find it?" Wendy asked.

"Simple," Dillon replied. "Just type Exeter Society for the Paranormal into a search engine. It'll be the first hit."

"Cool." Frank said with a smile. "We've finally entered the twenty-first century!"

"And…" Bob said, drawing the word out as he looked around the table with a glint in his eye. "You remember I said I had something to sort out and I'd have a surprise for tonight?" Everyone nodded, including Steve which made Dillon realise that whatever Bob had been up to, Steve was as much in the dark as the rest of them.

"Is it a puppy?" Sophie asked. "A ghost hunting dog?" She leant forward in her chair and struggled to take off the leather biker's jacket she was wearing. It was a snug fit. As she pulled the jacket off, Dillon noticed a cartoon-like print on her t-shirt. The word 'Misfits', which he presumed was the name of a band, was stretched over her chest. And then Dillon noticed the straight, white scars, lined up like tally charts, on the inside of both forearms. There were a lot. He was sure that more were hidden beneath the bangles on her wrists. He hadn't noticed them before because of her lace gloves but now they almost glowed in the low light of the pub. None seemed recent however. They had all healed. But nonetheless, he felt concern for Sophie well up inside him. Not wanting to create a scene or ask stupid and embarrassing questions, he tried to not draw attention to the fact that he had seen them and instead turned his face to the others around the table.

"Don't be daft." Bob chuckled. "Frank was more in the right ball park when he said about being in the twenty-first century." He paused and bit his lip, waiting for someone to guess.

"You've got some new equipment!" Wendy said. Bob nodded proudly.

"Hallelujah!" Frank exclaimed, raising his hands in the air and turning his eyes up to the ceiling. He looked at Dillon and composed himself to explain, which he did in a mock-sarcastic tone. "Up to now, we've been doing all our investigations with the most basic of equipment. Cheap digital still and video cameras, lower end of the range dictaphones, our own torches, thermometers from a garden centre, sticky tape, cotton thread, talcum powder, you name it. As long as it doesn't cost too much, we've probably used it."

"It's all been fine in the past." Bob said.

"And I'm not denying that for a second." Frank added. "We've got some really good results in the past. But as far as being perceived as, shall we say, serious amateur professionals is concerned, we're not really keeping up with the technology that's out there."

"So where does the society get its money from?" Dillon asked.

27

"Well, we chip in ourselves. Whatever we decide we need to buy, specifically for the society, we take a vote on it, agree and divide up the cost. We get no funding from anywhere else. We're totally self-sufficient." Steve explained.

"Well…" Dillon started as an idea came to him. "Now that we have our website, why don't we start up our own Youtube channel?" The others looked at him blankly.

"What do you mean?" Bob asked.

"You've got so many videos from past investigations, it would be easy to put them online. If we agreed to let companies and products advertise on our channel, we'd earn money from them."

"Really?" Wendy asked. Dillon nodded.

"Yeah. Some people have made a small fortune on Youtube by having a load of followers and income from advertising. For some, it's a full-time job."

"That's a smashing idea!" Bob said. "And leads me very nicely on to the surprise." He reached into his trouser pocket and pulled out his smartphone. "I've got a mate who works at the university. He tipped me off that the Media faculty were looking at upgrading their audio-visual equipment and selling off some of their old stuff. I got in quick and snapped up a real bargain on this lot." He turned his phone around so everyone could see the screen. He had taken a series of photos of the equipment he'd purchased from the university.

"What did you get?" Sophie asked, squinting at the small screen and trying to make out the items that were displayed.

"Two handheld digital video cameras with night vision. Both have external ten watt infra-red lights that can be manually attached. I also got two four-track handheld sound recorders each with two built-in microphones and an extra external microphone with a lead."

"How much did they want for that lot?" Frank asked.

"One hundred and fifty. Forty-five per camera, twenty-five for each recorder and a tenner for the extra mics and leads."

"Wow. That's not bad, considering the quality of that kit." Steve said.

"Yeah. It's good innit? And just in time for our next investigation this weekend." Bob grinned as he placed the smartphone back in his pocket. It was indeed a very good deal. Each of the cameras would ordinarily be over seven hundred pounds brand new and each sound recorder would be a hundred and fifty on its own. It was probably the case that the university would've just scrapped the lot but for only twenty-five pounds per person, Bob had done an amazing job.

"Tell us more about the plan for the weekend." Wendy said.

"Okay." Bob replied. He took a sip from his pint and pushed it to one side so he could rest his elbows on the table as he leant forward. "So, you know we're heading for Trevalling Hall. We'll aim to get there for around four o' clock while it's still daylight. It'll take just over an hour to get there so we'll meet up around two. Once we're there, we'll carry out our normal reconnaissance, mapping every room and documenting everything that's there before we start. We'll break for dinner at a pub, which is a bit of a drive in itself, and then return around dusk to set up the equipment for our initial investigation. We'll give it a few hours and aim to be done by about eleven. Home by just after midnight and then we'll meet up next Tuesday to discuss what we found and whether the Hall warrants further investigation."

"Sounds nice and straight forward." Frank shrugged. The others nodded and Dillon realised that after having carried out thirty-three investigations in the past, the team were well rehearsed in terms of their preparations. He still had a few questions but decided to keep quiet and put his faith in the team's organisation. There was just one thing he needed to know.

"How are we getting to the Hall?"

"By car." Bob replied.

"That's a problem for me because I don't have one."

"No problem." Wendy said with a smile. "I'll give you a lift. I'm taking Sophie as well."

"I can't drive at all." Sophie shrugged.

"Steve, Frank and I will travel together as well." Bob said. "But we'll all meet up at my place first and check we've got everything before we set off."

"Is there anything I need to bring?" Dillon asked.

"Just a torch, warm coat and your nerves." Frank replied with a smile and a wink.

"Do you know anything else about the place?" Wendy asked Bob.

"Not really. I've only really looked into the early history of the Hall. I purposely haven't researched from the early nineteenth century, so if we do encounter anything, we can genuinely question it rather than attributing a preconception to it. The only thing I've come across that may lend itself to a supernatural presence is that Baroness Trevallyn died in the house. Anything other than her will be as new to me as it will be for you. If we do decide to investigate the Hall further, I'll do some more digging."

"So," Dillon said, trying to get a grip on the purpose of the visit at the weekend. "We're only visiting the Hall on Saturday to determine if there's anything there worth investigating?"

"Correct." Bob replied.

"What if there is something there but we don't necessarily experience it this Saturday?"

"Don't worry. If there is anything there, we'll know about it. A pin drop in the wrong place at the wrong time will be enough for us to decide to go back. We won't actually see any ghosts or objects flying around. Those are very rare events. But anything simple and often overlooked like mysterious cold spots or the unexplained flicker of a torch will be regarded as an indication of a presence."

"How often do those things occur on a recon visit?"

"More often than you think." Steve said with a nod.

"One thing's for sure." Bob said, leaning forward over the table towards me and dropping his voice to a whisper. "The dead don't like to stay quiet."

5

Dillon arrived around five minutes early at Bob's house, only to find that Frank and Steve were already there. They were like children on Christmas morning, poring over presents with an excited giddiness and fidgety fingers that wanted to touch everything. A diverse array of equipment had been laid out on Bob's dining table and the three men were busy checking that batteries were fully charged, cameras and recorders were working properly and there were enough torches, thermometers, walkie-talkies and cameras to go around. Dillon felt a little under-prepared as he mentally checked off the list of items he had brought with him in his small rucksack; a lantern type LED torch that illuminated in all directions at the same time, a second standard torch with a beam that could reach up to fifty metres, his own digital camera with video recording capability and of course, his smartphone that not only had a high definition camera function but a voice recording app as well. Once checked, the equipment on the table was packed away in a collection of rucksacks, holdalls and carrier bags and then loaded into the boot of Bob's car. As the bags were being ferried outside, Wendy and Sophie arrived.

"Is everyone ready to catch some spooks?" Sophie asked as she danced her way into the dining room to the Ghostbusters theme tune that was playing on her phone. Her level of excitement matched that of Steve and Frank. Even quiet, reserved Wendy had an energetic buzz about her. Dillon still felt a bit out of his depth, as any newcomer would, and although he offered to lend a hand, he was largely left out of the logistical operation in order to get underway as quickly as possible. It was like watching a family packing for a holiday; jobs needed to be done, things needed to be attended to, but all in an energetic, spritely fashion in the knowledge that they'd shortly be embarking on something exciting and enjoyable.

"Sure am!" Frank replied as he danced his way past Sophie, carrying a bag of kit.

"You looking forward to it?" Wendy asked.

"Yeah. Definitely." Dillon replied. She watched him for a moment, looking into his eyes for just long enough that he began to feel self-conscious. Then she smiled and nodded.

"Good. It's going to be great." She said.

"Okay everyone. The equipment's all packed up and ready to go. Are we ready to move out?" Bob called in through the open front door. He was greeted by a loud 'Yeeesss!' from everyone inside and the entourage all filed out of the building.

"Right. Here's how to get to the Hall." Bob said as he handed Sophie a printed sheet of paper with a map and directions he'd found online. "We'll see you there." He gave Wendy, Sophie and Dillon a mock salute, slumped into the driver's seat of his car and started the engine. Steve waved from the front passenger window whilst Frank, sitting behind Steve, stuck his tongue out and crossed his eyes.

"Okay, let's get going." Wendy said as Bob drove off. The three climbed into Wendy's old, navy blue Ford Fiesta and fastened their seatbelts. Sophie tossed the map and directions back over her shoulder at Dillon.

"You navigate. I'm crap at it." She said.

"No problem." He replied and studied the map. Although not being familiar with the area at all, the map was easy to follow. Bob had highlighted the route in bright orange from the north of Exeter out to the location of the Hall. Where the route ended, he'd drawn a smiling ghost in black biro over the location of the Hall. Dillon smiled and as Wendy pulled away, he started giving her directions to Trevalling Hall.

It was a simple journey after they'd left Exeter and starting heading north on the A396, past Tiverton and on toward Exebridge. Without having to keep his eyes on the map, Dillon could enjoy the view from the window of fern lined road verges, thick, green forest and mile after mile of quintessential English countryside. The smell of fresh air, with the hint of warm vegetation wafted in through the slightly open window that Sophie had the tips of her fingers poking through as she rested her elbow on the door. The sunlight on the fields made them appear to glow in a kaleidoscope of green and yellow hues, and he felt relaxed and happy as he watched the beautiful vista roll by. When they reached Exebridge, Dillon told Wendy to head for Dulverton and continue north on the B3223, which would lead them on to Exmoor. The road at that point was a lot narrower than the A396 and Dillon felt a little uneasy with the speed that Wendy was driving around blind corners. In places the drop from the side of the road was disturbingly steep and he feared at one point that should they crash and plunge through the trees and undergrowth, they may never be found. Eventually, the road exited the woods and crossed on to the moor. Clouds had gathered overhead and although they were too light to threaten rain, their sombre grey seemed to sap the life from the landscape. Vast swathes of open moorland with clumps of sedges, gorse and bracken stretched as far as the eye could see. It was a strange, morose landscape that extended beyond the ridge of the horizon, where the dark earth merged with the brooding sky. The gently undulating ground was punctuated here and there by the silvery reflection of small, dark, shallow pools. A few weather-weary sheep fled from the roadside as the car passed, only to stop and stare as it drove away, as if to question the noisy blue monster that had disturbed the death-like silence of the moor.

"There should be a crossroads somewhere ahead and then we turn off to the left." Dillon called forward, not taking his eyes or forefinger from the map.

"Up there. I can see it." Sophie replied, pointing ahead through the windscreen. Wendy slowed the car down and turned on the indicator although she didn't need to bother as there was no other vehicle in sight.

"Are you sure?" Wendy asked as she gazed past Sophie along the single track road that snaked away into the distance.

"Yeah…I'm sure." Dillon answered, double checking the map just in case he had made a mistake.

"Okay then." Wendy said as she turned the car to the left and began to accelerate along the road which, Dillon noticed, didn't even have a name.

"You could get seriously lost out here." Sophie mused as she studied the bleak landscape that now surrounded them. Even the trees looked forlorn, their leafless, craggy branches reaching out as if imploring the travellers for help.

"I think we're here." Wendy said thoughtfully as she slowed by a pair of grey, stone gateposts. There were no gates between them and the stone had eroded to such an extent that with a casual glance, they could have been a pair of Neolithic standing stones. Only one of the gateposts still had a carved finial on top although that too had fallen victim to the ravages of the weather and its original form could no longer be discerned. Nevertheless, it still gave some indication of the gateposts' former splendour.

"Really?" Sophie asked hesitantly. Wendy looked at her and nodded. She turned the car off the road, through the gateposts and on to a broken, overgrown track. The car bounced around as the wheels dipped into a multitude of unavoidable potholes and Wendy slowed the car to a snail's pace to prevent any damage to the already old and worn suspension.

"Christ almighty!" Sophie exclaimed as she held on to the door handle for support.

"Sorry." Wendy whimpered.

"It's not your fault. This road's bloody awful."

"I don't even think it's a proper road and judging by all the weeds growing out of it, it doesn't look like anyone's been along here in donkey's years." Wendy replied, her voice breaking from a succession of jolts.

They continued on for around five hundred yards beyond the gateposts, following the twisting track through dense thickets of overgrown shrubs and trees. As they came round the final bend, the track entered a vast clearing, in the centre of which was the most astounding ruin Dillon had ever seen.

Wendy pulled up next to Bob's car and the three got out whilst simultaneously staring up at the front of the long building that faced what must at one time have been a grand gravel driveway, but was now virtually unrecognisable as such. Behind them, on the other side of the drive, was a weathered set of stone steps that led down to an overgrown lawn area. The weeds had grown tall but it didn't take much imagination to envisage what the lawn would have looked like in its heyday; a pristine, manicured green carpet, stretching away to the treeline. The building that loomed over the drive had a long frontage. On either side of the columned entrance, a row of tall ground floor windows ended at both corners in a large angled bay window. A long row of smaller windows filled the first floor from end to end. It was an impressive structure. Or at least it used to be. The once majestic walls were now weathered, dull grey and spotted with orange and white lichens. Streaks of rusty orange ran down from hidden pockets of iron in the stone, creating the illusion of blood seeping from the very fabric of the structure. Most of the glass had gone from the window frames and only shards clung on to the rotting wood, glinting in the pale light. The few time weathered, opaque windows that were still intact reflected the low, grey clouds and it seemed as though pale faces were peering out at the onlookers from the dark depths. Jagged cracks in the masonry ran from the tops of the walls to the ground, splitting elegant curved sandstone lintels. They looked like bolts of black lightning, frozen in a snapshot. Where the dark grey, slate roof had collapsed at one end of the building, daylight could be seen through a few first floor windows, revealing the rotten, skeletal structure of broken roof timbers. The light that could be seen through these apertures made the lower line of windows seem dark

34

and foreboding, the outside world held in stark contrast with the impenetrable void that filled unseen rooms. Peering into the gloomy interior generated a distinct sense of unease that sent shivers down Dillon's spine and he felt as though dozens of hidden eyes were watching from the shadows.

"Welcome to Trevalling Hall!" Bob said cheerfully as he stepped out from the doorway and started down the steps. "I heard you pull up. Frank and Steve are just inside having a look at some of the rooms and deciding which ones should be out of bounds for safety reasons." He turned to look up at the building. "It's in a worse state than we thought in there. You can see where the roof's collapsed in this near corner and that's had a massive effect on the rooms in that wing of the building." He looked back at Wendy, Sophie and Dillon, and shrugged. "I suppose you'll be wanting to have a look inside yourselves?"

"Hell, yeah!" Sophie exclaimed and practically leapt up the steps toward Bob.

"Let's go." Wendy added with a clap of her hands. Bob grinned and turned around, leading the way into the building. Dillon paused at the base of the steps and breathed in the silence for a few seconds to get a feel of the place. Slowly scanning the windows along both floors, he tried to see if he could pick up on any 'vibes' that the building could be giving off. He held his breath and listened. The breeze whispered through the long grass and the tree canopies behind him rustled. Aside from that, there was nothing. He tutted at himself for being so ridiculous and climbed the steps to enter the building. As the cooler air from within caressed his cheeks, a thought crossed his mind; *What the hell am I doing here?*

6

"Okay folks." Bob said as everyone gathered in a semi-circle in the entrance hall. It was a large space that bounced echoes of Bob's voice off the bare, peeling, mouldy walls. There was a strong smell of mildew and damp and, as Dillon's eyes adjusted to the poor light, he started to make out what a mess the room was. The floor was covered in dirt, dead leaves and bits of plaster that had fallen from the ceiling. The paint on the walls had mostly flaked away, disintegrating into grey dust on the floor. In a number of places, huge areas of bare brick could be seen where the plaster had completely crumbled away. Mould stretched up the walls in large streaks, like black, withered fingers that infected everything they touched. The room was a manifestation of decay; dank, dark, rotten and diseased. At either end of the wall opposite the entrance was an open doorway that led to the back of the building. One still had a fragment of the door which hung limply from the lowest hinge. The other didn't have a door at all and the darkness beyond seemed impenetrable. On both the left and right of the entrance, more doorways granted access to the rooms that ran along the front of the manor. Through these, the grey light from the outside world could be seen, trying desperately to penetrate the gloom but to little effect.

"First things first." Bob said, producing a notebook and pencil. "Let's do a walk round and draw up a map of the place. That way, we'll get a feel for the lay of the land and, more importantly, know where we all are for the initial vigil. Based on the results of that, we can determine where we set up the equipment later after dinner." The others nodded.

"Vigil?" Dillon asked. Bob looked at him, seemingly unaware of the reason for his confusion.

"What we tend to do in the first instance is split up and just spend some time in different areas of the site we're investigating to see if anyone experiences anything." Steve explained. "Then, we all meet up, share our experiences and determine if the location is worth further investigation." Dillon nodded and smiled at Bob to show that he understood and he could continue.

"We try to conduct all our investigations as scientifically as possible." Bob added, remembering that this was Dillon's first excursion with the group. "We assume nothing when we go into a property or visit a site and anything we do experience has to be rigorously recorded and backed up with some kind of evidence."

"Right." Dillon said. He was impressed by the team's approach. But then, he thought, if they wanted to be taken seriously by parapsychologists and the scientific community, they needed concrete, irrefutable evidence. Without it, their experiences wouldn't count for anything. It then became clear why Bob had such a vast computer library of video and sound files at his house. The team had been collecting evidence for years. Dillon momentarily wondered why none of the evidence to date had been accepted by the scientific authorities but he put the thought out of his mind as Bob led the way through the first door to the right.

The group, shuffling forward in single file, entered a room that stretched back a surprising distance from the two tall windows at the front. At the far end, the room curved and there were the remains of some kind of low wooden platform or dais set into the curve. At the front of this stage, two columns reached up to the ceiling. The walls and ceiling were in a similar state of decomposition to the hall they had just left but there were a couple of pieces of old, broken furniture; a long, wooden table that had collapsed at one end where the legs had rotted away and a wooden bench of comparable length.

"Looks like this was some kind of dining room." Wendy suggested. The others nodded as they surveyed the room, pointing at where they believed another table and sideboards may have once stood. Because the room was empty save for a few subtle clues regarding its former purpose, it was relatively simple to superimpose the scene in its hey-day as a dining hall or perhaps as a ballroom. During mealtimes, the Baron and his wife may have sat here together for dinner, attended by a small army of servants. Maybe when they hosted parties or masked balls, a string quartet could have occupied the space on the dais. It was easy to imagine if Dillon closed his eyes. But the reality when he opened them again couldn't have been further from the dream.

"Might have been." Bob muttered as he sketched a bird's eye map of the building the group had seen so far. "But I'll tell you what's not sitting right with me." He added, frowning at the table and bench. "Those things there." He jabbed his pencil in the direction of the dilapidated furniture and the others studied them carefully.

"What about them?" Wendy asked.

"Well, I accept they're not from the time of the Trevallings. They're much more recent. What do you think Steve? Post Second World War time?"

"Yeah. They do look like they're in the style of the forties and early fifties." Steve replied thoughtfully.

"So they're our first clue as to what this place was used for in more recent times." Said Bob. "And if we imagine more than one bench in here, I reckon you could easily see how this place could've seated about fifty kids. What do you think, Steve? Orphanage? Boarding School? Outdoor pursuits centre?"

"Could be any of those things." Steve replied thoughtfully, looking around the room. "We need to see more and do some more research when we get back, but at least we've made some observations that could guide us."

Bob nodded as he finished sketching the shape of the room, adding in the positions of the table and the bench. Dillon noticed that in between several pages of his notebook, he had inserted sheets of carbon paper, ensuring that everyone got a copy of the map when he had completed the drawing. Dillon smiled at this ingenuity. It was a crude but effective way of photocopying in the field.

"Whatever it was, we'll call it the Dining Room for future reference." He said and then carried on through a second door to the right, opposite the doorway they had entered by.

A large room opened out before them that obviously occupied the corner of the building. The angled bay window afforded views out to both the front and side and next to the window on the far wall was a tall wooden frame with the tattered remains of a rolling blackboard hanging in it.

"No prizes for guessing what this room was used for." Sophie said.

"Indeed." Bob mumbled thoughtfully. If the hypothesis was correct and the previous room had been used as a dining space for a group of children, then this object significantly narrowed down the possible reasons why the children were there in the first place.

"Considering the location of this building," Bob added, "It's highly unlikely that the students would've travelled here every day for their lessons and then gone home in the afternoon. I think this must have been used as a boarding school after the War."

"That's a reasonable theory." Steve said. "And if you're right, then we should expect to see some kind of accommodation for the students upstairs."

"Agreed." Bob said and completed his sketch of the room.

"Shall we call this one the Classroom?" Frank asked, pointing at the derelict blackboard.

"Yup." Bob muttered as he added the label to his sketch. "Right, on we go." He turned and marched through the room to a doorway at the back which led to the rear of the building.

"Library." Frank stated as they examined the derelict, rotten and broken shelves, that lined the wall on the left, opposite the window, now empty of books. At either end of the shelves was another opening, the closest of which led back into the dining room. Bob added to his sketch and nodded for the group to continue. Through the library was a room in the back corner of the building that was virtually identical to the classroom at the front, except this room didn't have a bay window. It didn't have the remains of a blackboard either although there were a couple of old, broken wooden chairs scattered around.

"We'll have to go back." Steve said. He had seen there was only one way in or out of this second classroom. The group turned and went back to the library, turning immediately right and exiting through the second door.

"Okay." Bob said slowly as he surveyed the dark space they had entered. There were no windows and they soon worked out that they were, more or less, in the centre of the building, behind the dining hall. Steve and Frank switched on their flashlights and illuminated the space. At the back was an opening that Sophie poked her head round to see what was there. A window in the room beyond must have allowed in sufficient light for her to see the furniture that remained, for she quickly returned and said she'd found the kitchen but added that you'd need to be at death's door from starvation before considering preparing a meal in there.

"Wonder what's down there." Steve said as he pointed his flashlight at a set of stone steps that descended into a pitch black hole.

"Buggered if I'm finding out." Frank laughed. "You can go first."

"It's probably just a cellar or storeroom for the kitchen." Bob mused as he added to his floor plan. "There won't be any windows down there so we'll explore it later."

"Phew." Frank said, mockingly wiping his brow with relief.

"Looks like this corridor runs through the middle of the building, behind the dining room and entrance hall." Wendy said as she peered along the dark passage behind the stairwell to the cellar.

"Yeah, look. There's a door back into the dining room." Steve said as he joined her and pointed his flashlight along the corridor. They all filed out and past both a door to the dining room and another to the entrance hall. A short distance further along on the right was an opening into the creepiest part of the house so far.

"Jesus Christ." Frank muttered.

"I don't think he's here anymore." Bob whispered back.

The six investigators stood in a line with their backs to the wall and surveyed the room they had entered with a morbid fascination. The wide space occupying the middle of the rear of the house, behind the entrance hall, must have once been used as a chapel. The decorations that remained on the walls and ceiling were unmistakably religious; painted murals on fractured plaster that had crumbled and discoloured, plasterwork on the ceiling that had cracked and fallen to the floor in pieces and dust. The disturbing effect of the ravages of time and decay on the images was that many of the painted people, presumably figures from the Bible, had no faces or were missing limbs. The scenes that once portrayed a sacred serenity now looked like a storyboard for a zombie apocalypse movie. Broken and rotted wooden chairs were scattered around, some on their sides and some still standing upright as though an invisible worshipper was still present in silent prayer. Underneath the shattered windows on the outer wall of the room were the remains of an altar; a table, split in two, with a rotting, algae and moss-stained lectern standing to one side. It filled Dillon with a sense of eerie disgust. He would never have described himself as a religious person but nonetheless, the chapel's state of decay was nothing short of an abomination.

"Let's move on." Bob suggested, seeing the others were all standing open-mouthed at the spectacle before them. They didn't need to be told twice and they quickly left, continuing along the corridor.

"We'll have to go up." Steve said as they reached the main staircase beyond the chapel. "Frank and I have already seen that the rooms at the far end on this level have been totally mashed where the first floor fell in when the roof collapsed"

"Okay. No problem". Bob said as he scribbled out the space at the far end of the building. "Did you go upstairs?"

"No, not yet." Steve answered as he peered up the stairwell to the landing above.

"Lead on." Bob said with a nod and Steve carefully mounted the stairs, one softly planted footstep at a time, pausing whenever one step creaked unexpectedly to make doubly sure it was safe to continue.

"We'd best get a move on if we're going to get the recce and vigil done before tea." Frank said as his stomach rumbled.

"It looks like there are fewer rooms up here." Wendy said reassuringly as they climbed the last of the stairs and stepped into a long corridor that seemed to run from one end of the building right through to the other.

"Let's forget about that way." Bob said, pointing his pencil at the end of the corridor where the utter carnage wreaked from the collapsed roof was clearly visible in the light that fell between broken timbers and crumbled walls. "Let's start over there."

Bob led the way across the corridor and down a short passageway. A window at the end looked down over the main entrance. The passage turned to the right and ran along the front of the building. Opposite the line of windows, a number of small, empty rooms lined the corridor.

"They must have been offices or something. They're virtually identical, even though that one at the far end near where the roof collapsed is bigger." Frank said as he peered into each room in turn.

"Righto." Bob said. "Makes sense that the front of the house and the far corner on the ground floor and this floor were used as staff quarters. It's just a shame that some are so badly damaged and unsafe that we can't get into them."

"Never mind." Wendy said, making her way back to the staircase. "Let's try the other end of the house."

To the right of the stairs, the corridor forked into two and both passages ran to the far end of the house. The windows looked out from the side of the building over the grounds that stretched around the back. Walking along the first passage running parallel to the front of the house, the group entered a long room with a number of windows along the front wall and an angled bay window in the far corner.

"We must be over the dining hall and classroom." Bob explained as he studied his floor plan of the ground floor. "Looks like this was some kind of dormitory." He pointed at a couple of rusted, skeletal bedframes that stood to one side of the room. There were more at the far end near the bay window but they had been turned over and piled on top of each other in a confusing, twisted heap of scrap metal.

"Looks like we've found the accommodation you'd anticipated." He said with a grin and a wink in Steve's direction.

"There's some kind of washroom on the other side of the corridor." Sophie said as she came into the dormitory.

"Let's go and have a look." Bob replied and led the way in to the long washroom. A single window on one side illuminated the dirty tiles and grimy sinks that lined the walls. Black cobwebs sagged between the pipes beneath each sink and dead insects littered the dirty tiled floor.

"Yuck." Wendy mumbled, wrapping her arms around herself for fear of being contaminated by the filth in the room. She hurried through a doorway on the opposite side and the others followed quickly.

They crossed through the second long corridor into another dormitory running above the kitchen and rear classroom at the back of the building. This one had a few more metal bedframes and even a couple of battered and rusted lockers. The line of windows offered views across the overgrown rear gardens. Not far from the back of the hall was a circular fountain. In the centre stood a tall plinth with a stone urn on top. One of the handles had broken off and the whole sculpture was weathered almost to the point of being unrecognisable. The shallow, circular pool was now filled with dead leaves, a multitude of spiky weeds and a few puddles of black, brackish, stagnant water. It was a sad sight and the fountain must have once looked beautiful as water ran over the rim of the urn, glistening in the sunlight. Before the decay. Before it went to ruin.

"Right then. I believe that's Trevalling House mapped out." Bob said triumphantly as he carefully tore out pages of the notebook with the carbon copies of the floor plans and handed them round. He closed the notebook and clasped it in front of him with both hands, drumming his fingers on the cover and grinning at each member of his team in turn. "So, who's going to be first to decide where they want to be for the vigil?"

7

"How long do I have to stay in here?" Dillon asked, trying to hide the nervousness in his voice.

"Let's see." Bob mumbled as he checked his watch. "It's nearly half past five so we'll give it about half an hour and then we'll reconvene and head off for dinner." He smiled and gave Dillon a wink.

"And I've just got to sit here and see if anything happens?" Dillon hadn't expected this to be what a typical ghost hunt was like. He had enjoyed the initial exploration of the building and was anticipating everyone sticking together on a second walk-round, asking questions into the darkness to see if they were alone in the house or if any spirits were present who wished to communicate. He felt a bit foolish at his own naivety. He realised his expectations had been based on what he'd seen in films and television programmes. He didn't think he'd be left on his own.

"Basically, yes." Bob replied with a firm pat on Dillon's shoulder. "Just pay close attention to your surroundings and try to commit to memory everything that seems out of the ordinary; any noises, changes in temperature, anything that stands out as a bit weird."

"Okay." Dillon nodded. He looked around the room that he had been assigned to as Bob left and closed the door after him. It was one of the office spaces at the front of the first floor, along the passageway from where the roof had collapsed. This particular office opened inward from the passageway and therefore didn't have a window. Dillon wasn't worried though because he had both his lantern and another flashlight to keep the dark at bay. He strained his ears to hear Bob's footsteps growing fainter as he went off to check the others were in position before taking up his own station in the library downstairs. As Bob's footsteps died away, Dillon suddenly felt very alone. His senses were heightened by a mixture of fear and excitement. His skin tingled and his ears picked up every subtle creak and groan of the old building, his eyes darting around the room to where the sounds seemed to originate.

Dillon was the last to be escorted to his room by Bob, so he knew where each of the others had been stationed. Wendy and Sophie both had a dormitory each. Steve was in the Dining Hall and Frank had bravely opted for the old chapel. As he had cheerfully explained before he was left in the dim, dank previous place of worship, it was one of the few rooms that still had chairs in it. Looking around the empty box room that Dillon now found himself in, Frank's words echoed in his mind and for a moment he regretted not having a room with a chair. He sighed loudly and made his way over to the wall facing the door where, in the circle of light cast on the floor by his lantern, he used the side of his shoe to scrape away the dust and bits of paint and plaster that had fallen. Turning and sitting with his back to the wall, he placed the lantern on the floor next to his left leg. And then, in the silence, he waited.

After a while, Dillon's mind began to wander. He took stock of his absurd situation, laughed to himself and wondered how the hell he had ended up in a dark, derelict room in a ruin in the middle of nowhere. Of course, the chain of events that led to his situation were perfectly normal and logical but in the silence where time seemed to lose all meaning and the walls were unchanging, his brain filled with other theories. What if this was part of a grand prank? A rite of initiation? What if the others had all quietly met up outside and, sniggering to themselves, had made off back to Exeter, leaving him there in that cold, stale room for hours, or days even? Just as those thoughts crossed his mind, the door slowly creaked open and he watched nervously, wide-eyed and frozen to the spot, waiting to see what was going to happen next.

"How are you doing buddy?" Frank whispered as he poked his head round the edge of the door. Dillon breathed an audible sigh of relief and nodded that he was okay. Frank ventured into the room and held out a walkie-talkie.

"You forgot this. We've all got one. If something really freaky happens, give us a holler on this." He handed Dillon the walkie-talkie and turned to leave.

"Only about quarter of an hour and then we'll go and get some grub." He said with a smile as he closed the door behind him.

'Another quarter of an hour?' Dillon thought. 'I've only done half the time?' In the silence, the seconds seemed to have stretched into long, tedious minutes. Time seemed to pass in slow motion. But then, when you're alone with only your thoughts for company, even a few minutes could feel like an eternity. He settled himself back down and placed the walkie-talkie near the lantern. Every so often, it hissed and crackled. Because this happened on quite a frequent basis, he didn't attribute the random static crackling to anything out of the ordinary.

Just as he felt he was reaching the end of his vigil, there was a burst of activity on the walkie-talkie. Amidst the hissing, cracks, pops and squeals, he heard

Sophie and Bob speaking to each other, followed by Steve. Then Frank joined in and finally Wendy. They were excitedly, almost hysterically, chatting about changes in temperature in their respective rooms and a feeling of 'presences'. They used a lot of acronyms that only they seemed to understand. Dillon listened intently, trying to piece together what they were talking about. He felt somewhat left out. The room he was in was comparatively dull and he was dismayed that he wasn't sharing their experiences. Still listening to the conversation on the walkie-talkie, he waved his hand despondently in the air. The room he was in wasn't undergoing any temperature fluctuations and there were no 'presences' that he could detect. He was totally alone. He scanned the room in the light of the lantern, peering into the darkest corners and recesses. And then he noticed something odd.

On the wall directly opposite where he sitting was a slim column of shadow. It had been there, halfway between the door and the corner of the room, ever since he sat down. He hadn't really paid much attention to it because it was there when he started his vigil. It was merely a feature of the room he was in and therefore didn't qualify as a change or environmental alteration that would have attracted his attention. Nevertheless, as he studied the shadow further, the more he noticed there was something not quite right about it. The only light source in the room was his lantern and there was nothing between the light and the wall that could cast the shadow. He wiggled his outstretched left foot to see if that was responsible but the shadow didn't move. He leant forward, waved his hand in front of the lantern and watched the resultant large, blurry shadow dance across the wall. From the appearance of the dark column, it looked as though there was something standing in the middle of the room, blocking the light. But there was nothing in the centre of the space other than air and no matter how heavy that felt, there was no way air could be responsible. He couldn't understand or explain what he was seeing and then his heart almost leapt out of his chest as the shadow moved.

To try and describe fear in words simply doesn't do it justice. There are simply no words, nor a combination of them that can capture the full intensity of horror. The panic that gripped Dillon's body in that instant was beyond description. Every muscle in his body tensed and all he could hear was his rapid breathing and heartbeat throbbing in his ears. He stared, unblinking at the column of shade on the wall, wondering for a moment, or at least maybe trying to convince himself, if he had imagined it. And then it moved again. He held his breath and stared as the column seemed to turn and drift slowly across the surface of the wall towards the door. He watched in terror and awe as the shadow reached the door and disappeared, melting through the old wooden panels. At the same moment, the door banged softly against the frame as though someone had pushed against it from inside the room. He waited for a few long seconds, still holding his breath and staring at the door. The walkie-talkie crackled next to his leg and roused him from his petrified state. He quickly leapt to his feet, grabbed the lantern and walkie-talkie and left the room, peering out into the passageway through a crack in the door before he was satisfied it was safe to leave.

"There he is." Frank said with a grin as he saw Dillon coming down the main staircase. The others had already gathered at the foot of the stairs. Bob and Steve were concentrating on a video that Sophie had captured on her mobile phone.

"You're not going to believe what I just saw." Dillon said shakily as he approached the group. Bob looked up from the phone with a huge smile on his face. He turned the device so Dillon could see the screen. The image was dark and fuzzy but he could clearly see the dormitory where Sophie had been stationed for her vigil. A number of small, spherical, translucent objects floated wistfully across the screen, changed direction, floated back and vanished one by one. Dillon looked at Bob, hoping he would explain but he simply beamed with a smile so broad, it must have hurt his face.

"Oh, I think we will." He nodded.

8

The group left the old manor and made their way back across the moor to the main road. A short drive further in the direction of Withypool and they came to a country pub on a crossroads. It was the first such building they had seen and, knowing they couldn't spare the time to search the area for anywhere else, it was unanimously decided to just go with it. A few cars in the car park and a faint orange glow from the windows was sufficient to show the place was open so they pulled in. It was evident from the moment they walked through the door that the pub didn't get a lot of business, just enough to keep it running. The decoration was, to say the least, out of date with nicotine stained walls and a carpet that had been dragged kicking and screaming from the mid-eighties when all it wanted was to be rolled up and left to die. It was one of those places that seemed to have been adopted, rather defensively, by the locals, few in number though they were, and outsiders were considered not so much with suspicion but surprise.

"We'd like to order food please, if your kitchen is still open." Bob took the lead and approached the portly, middle aged barman who leaned on the counter and eyed his new customers with a puzzled expression.

"Yes, yes it's still open. All our meals are on the blackboard on the wall there." Came the reply with a hint of astonishment. As soon as he realised these strangers were paying customers and not merely lost tourists asking for directions, the barman's demeanour changed immediately and he gave them a broad, courteous smile. He pointed toward the far wall where, above the 1970's style wooden mantelpiece that somehow clashed with the grand old stone fireplace, the menu blackboard was hanging at a slight angle. The choice of meals was both limited and rather basic but then, no one in the group had really been expecting too much. They made their choices, most opting for ham, egg and chips whilst Steve chose sausages in onion gravy with mashed potato. The barman scribbled the orders on a crumpled notepad that he produced from beneath the bar and rushed it through a doorway to the kitchen before returning and serving drinks.

"Well, well, well!" Bob said triumphantly as he placed his pint on the table and wiped the froth from his moustache with the back of his hand. Although the pub was largely empty, except for the four older gentlemen propping up the bar, the group had instinctively chosen to sit at a round table in the corner, subconsciously mirroring their seating arrangement back in the Waggon and Horses in Exeter. They even sat in the same order around the table; Bob with his back to the wall, Steve to his left, then Frank, Dillon, Sophie and finally Wendy. As they waited for their meals to arrive, they sipped their drinks gingerly as the adrenaline from their first experience at Trevalling still pulsed through their veins. They were all wide-eyed and quietly giddy with excitement.

"We've never had such a response." Steve mused thoughtfully while staring wistfully into the middle distance. A grin tugged at the corners of his mouth. "Some ghost hunters could wait their entire lives to witness a mere fraction of what we've experienced this evening."

"True, true." Bob replied with a confident nod. "We seem to have stumbled on a supernatural goldmine here." He prodded the table with his forefinger. "So it's absolutely vital that we document everything with the utmost care."

"Good thing you've got all that new kit then." Frank said with a smile. He winked as he lifted his glass to toast Bob's lucky foresight.

"Hell, yeah!" Sophie exclaimed. "Just imagine the cool videos we can put on our new Youtube channel! We'll be famous!" She looked at Dillon and gave him a huge smile as she fluttered her overly long, black eyelashes.

"We still need to maintain an air of professionalism." Bob warned. Dillon sensed a hint of nervousness in his tone although it was totally understandable. Both he and Steve had been involved with the Exeter Society for the Paranormal for so long that he wouldn't dream of doing anything rash that might jeopardise the integrity of their work. Least of all reduce their investigations to nothing more than cheap streaming internet entertainment. Dillon recalled what Bob had said about approaching investigations from a scientific perspective. It had given him a sense of confidence that the motivations for their paranormal research were honourable. Bob's insistence that everything be conducted as scientifically and professionally as possible was essential, in light of the fact that no-one in the group actually was a professional paranormal researcher. In order to gather evidence that could withstand the scrutiny of the academic elite, there was no room for sloppiness.

"Agreed." Steve said. "If we want to be taken seriously by both the scientific community and society at large, we need to ensure our evidence is absolutely irrefutable."

"We also don't want to put up a half-arsed attempt at an investigation and then risk other groups swooping in and conducting their own research which could yield better results than ours." Bob added.

"So," Wendy took the opportunity to speak during the brief moment of quiet contemplation that followed Bob's statement. "What's the plan for this evening after dinner then?"

A hint of sunlight was all that remained to illuminate the edges of clouds high up in the west. They glowed with a reddish tinge that contrasted with the deep indigo in the east that was gradually spreading to consume the entirety of the sky. Once the headlights of the cars parked in front of the ruined building had been switched off, all colour was drained from the landscape and the site became the grey domain of shadows.

The group of investigators gathered in a huddle in front of the entrance and switched on their torches. Small, dancing circles of light picked out the cases and bags of equipment, methodically checking every bit of kit was accounted for. The beams were then turned to slowly sweep the wider area. Sophie and Wendy aimed their lights across the long grass toward the treeline as if to check there was no-one who might have followed them and was now watching, hidden in the shrubs. Aside from the branches and leaves gently swaying in the cool breeze, the only discernible movement was from restless rooks vying for the most comfortable roosting position. Meanwhile, Frank, Bob and Steve directed their torches on to the building. They discussed the location of the rooms from the earlier vigil and pointed them out by shining the beams into the relevant windows. It may have just been nerves from attending his first full-on investigation, but Dillon felt he was the only one to notice how the darkness in each gaping hole seemed to swallow the light and utterly consume it.

"Ok folks," Bob said cheerfully. "Grab a bag or a box and let's get this kit into the building." Frank gave a mock salute, held his torch in his teeth and grabbed the first two bags closest to him. He jogged up the steps and disappeared into the void, closely followed by Steve, Sophie, Wendy, Dillon and finally, Bob.

It took a few trips back and forth between the cars and the building to get all the equipment into the entrance hall and unpacked. On the last run, the group commented that it had become somewhat lighter outside than before. The detail in the trees was now clearly discernible and the shadows across the long grass had retreated. The outer walls of the old hall had become eerily luminescent with a bluish milky glow that was mirrored by the sky overhead. Finally, the source of the extra light made itself apparent as the moon rose up over the trees. It was a welcome addition to the torches that the team were reliant on but, as Wendy had pointed out, the moonlight did nothing to penetrate the all-encompassing darkness of the building's interior. Dillon mentally noted that the contrast between the faint glow of the moon and the dark interior was now even more marked, the ruled lines along the thresholds of doorways or windowsills further emphasising the stark division between light and shadow.

"Right then." Bob murmured thoughtfully, shining his torch upward to the ceiling and partially illuminating his face in the process. "We'll split up into pairs as we discussed and share out the kit, so each team has sufficient technology to capture anything that happens. Sophie and Wendy, you've got the dormitories upstairs. Frank and Dillon, you're in the old chapel. Steve and I will be in the classrooms. Any questions so far?" The others shook their heads but because Bob couldn't see what they were doing in the low light, he checked each person's response by momentarily directing his torch beam at each in turn.

"Okay. Good. Now, let's get tooled up and get to work."

Dillon shuddered as he and Frank stood in the doorway of the old chapel and scanned the room with their torches. In the blackness, the space was even creepier than before and the darkness masked the edges of the room, making the chapel feel vast. A cold, silent emptiness. Frank took the first steps into the space, swinging his torch from side to side. He pointed the beam towards two chairs that, although lying on their sides, appeared to be intact.

"Here, let's grab those and set up by the back wall under the window." Dillon walked forward, picked up the two seats and set them side by side where Frank indicated with his torch. He held his own torch in his teeth as he pressed firmly on the dusty wooden seats to check they were safe to sit on.

"Give 'em a wipe." Frank said. "I don't want a few decades worth of crap all over my arse." He put down his bag of equipment, reached into his pocket and handed Dillon a crumpled paper napkin from the pub. Dillon smiled and used it to brush the layers of detritus from the seats. They sat down and opened the bag of kit that Bob had issued them with.

"What's that?" Dillon asked. He'd recognised the video camera with night vision and infrared lamp as well as a small pocket-sized audio recorder. But he was unfamiliar with the black box with an external speaker plugged into it that Frank removed from the bag and rested on his knee.

"It's a Spirit Box." Frank said proudly. "It scans radio frequencies like five per second or something daft like that, but spirits can speak through it. You can actually hear them talking and it's not a radio station because the frequencies are scanned at random. So if you hear a voice that's speaking, even if it's just one word, you know it can't be radio because that one word would have to be broadcast over several random frequencies at the same time."

"Have you ever heard anything through it?"

"Um… Once, yeah." Frank bit his bottom lip. "I mean, there were other times when we got something but we couldn't understand what was being said."

"So what did it say on that one occasion?"

"Well, we were in an old pub in Somerset and we were all sitting in the bar when we felt there was something with us. So we asked what its name was." He paused and Dillon watched as Frank looked down at the Spirit Box, turning it over in his hands, examining it as though he was still a little bit dubious about it.

"And what was the name?" Dillon asked after a few moments.

"Well," Frank's response was long and drawn out. Almost like a sigh. "It's difficult to say if it was actually a name or not…"

"What did it say?"

"Angel."

"Seriously?"

"Yeah. There was a woman who was with us at the time. A bit odd. Wore loads of tie-dye and had a couple of dream catchers as earrings. You know the type. Typically hang around Stonehenge and 'commune with Gaia'. That sort of thing." He rolled his eyes dismissively. "And anyway, she got really excited about it and started banging on about guardian angels and all that jazz. Even started pulling out a deck of angel cards there and then in the middle of the investigation. Kind of made a joke of the whole thing if I'm honest."

"So you don't really trust this Spirit Box then?"

"It's not that I don't trust it. It's just a machine after all. But I think you have to stay objective with what you hear. You can't afford to interpret what comes out. It's either clear as day or it's just noise."

Dillon liked Frank's matter-of-fact perspective and he peered into the bag to see if there were any other toys that Bob had given them.

"What else is in there?"

"Not a lot." Frank replied, reaching down and pulling out a walkie-talkie and a collapsible tripod for the camera. "Here, hold this." He said as he held out the walkie-talkie and stood to set up the tripod. He placed the video camera on top of the tripod and switched on the infra-red light. Although Dillon couldn't see the beam, he saw the small LCD screen light up with all the detail of the chapel that the darkness was hiding.

"Right then." Frank said as he sat down. "Now let's see if anyone's at home."

Bob and Steve walked cautiously from the entrance hall into the old dining room. They slowly scanned the space with their torches and the video camera that Bob was holding in front of his face. His eyes were fixed on the small screen, watching for the slightest movement that could give away the presence of a ghost. They placed one foot carefully in front of the other, avoiding making excessive noise and if the sole of their shoe crunched on a piece of debris, they would quickly lift it off again and find another place to step. Because they had been doing this kind of work for so long, they knew they had to account for every noise they made. Footsteps, scraping sounds, knocks or voices could easily be masked by a clumsy approach. Steve crept forward towards the end of the dining hall, his torch in one hand picking out where he should tread and a voice recorder held out at arm's length in the other.

"If there is anyone here who wishes to speak with us, please come forward. We mean you no harm." Bob said gently. They both waited. Outside, the breeze rustled through the tall grass.

"Please, if you can hear me, come forward and speak with us. Tell us your name. Tell us your story." Bob slowly panned the camera around the room. The infra-red light penetrated the dark emptiness and on the screen, Bob could see a black and white image of Steve, holding his recorder out in front of him and listening intently to the silence.

"Whoah!" Bob suddenly said.

"What? What?" Steve whispered as he turned his head to face Bob.

"Seriously! A bright orb appeared out of nowhere to your left and passed, like right behind you!"

"Where did it go?" Steve remained glued to the spot but his head was turning as he looked around him. The fact was, beyond the reach of his torch beam, he couldn't see anything.

"I dunno. It just kind of went behind you, up a bit and then faded."

"Perhaps something's trying to come through?" Steve wondered.

"Let's go next door. It looked like it was heading in that direction." Bob led the way into the first classroom, following the image on the camera screen. Steve followed close behind, peering at the screen over Bob's shoulder.

"It's definitely colder in here." Steve mumbled.

"Yeah. And there's a weird feeling in here too."

"I've got goosebumps." Steve said.

"Me too. But not because I'm cold. There's something in here with us." Bob whispered. He made his way to the centre of the room and stopped. Steve stood beside him and they panned the camera around the space.

"Is there someone in here?" Bob asked. He waited for a reply.

"Did it just get even colder?" Steve asked quietly.

"Sure felt like it."

"Maybe something's trying to gather energy to manifest?"

"Could be. Let's see if it can do anything."

"If there's someone here, please make your presence known. Move something or speak to us. Anything that can tell us you wish to communicate." Steve said into the blackness.

From the bowels of the building ahead of them, there came a loud, hollow knock.

"Shit." Bob muttered as he instinctively swung the camera in the direction of the sound.

"That's great." Steve said as he reached further in front of him with the recorder. "Please do that again so we can find you."

They both jumped as they heard another deep knock. And then another.

"Sounds like it's coming from the back of the building. It's not in here." Steve said, pointing at the wall toward the back of the classroom to where the noise seemed to come from. Bob took a step forward.

"Yeah. Let's go."

"Is anyone up here?" Sophie asked. She and Wendy had made their way up to the dormitory at the front of the building. The long room stretched ahead of them and in the gloom, the far wall seemed a great deal further away than it had been on the first walk around. Wendy stepped forward into the room, slowly moving her torch around in an arc, picking out the old rusted bed frames that resembled a post-apocalyptic art installation.

"Hang on a minute." She said as she fumbled with her torch. She switched it off and for a moment, the two girls were plunged into darkness.

"What are you doing?" Sophie asked.

"Wait." Wendy said calmly. Switch off your torch and just close your eyes for a few seconds and then look again."

Sophie did as she was told and turned off the light. They both stood absolutely still and closed their eyes. There was only the silence of the room and the sound of their hearts beating in their ears. Then they opened their eyes again.

"Oh, wow." Sophie exclaimed.

"See? We just needed to acclimatise to the light that was already in here." Wendy said with a smile. Without the artificial light of the torches, their eyes could adjust to the blue-white glow of the moonlight that poured into the room through the old upstairs windows. The moonlight that fell in glowing rectangles on the floor reflected upwards and lit up the dormitory with an ethereal hue. It felt ghostly. It felt as though, if there were ever a time and a place to make contact with the other side, then this was it.

"Is anyone here with us?" Sophie asked again. She panned her camera around the room but nothing appeared on the screen.

"Is this where you came to school?" Wendy asked softly. They listened again. And again there was only silence.

"What was that?" Sophie whispered as she wheeled round and pointed the camera back at the doorway where they had entered the dormitory.

"I heard it too." Wendy replied.

54

"Footsteps?" Sophie asked.

"Yeah. Small footsteps. Like a child. Running along the corridor."

"Let's go and take a look." Sophie tip-toed toward the door as she stared unblinking at the screen, watching for any sign of the child that they had heard running behind them. Just as they reached the open doorway, they both stopped dead in their tracks and a shiver ran over their skin.

"Holy shit! Did you hear that?" Sophie whispered excitedly behind her to Wendy.

"Yeah. Sounded like a kid giggling."

"But there aren't any kids here!" Sophie exclaimed.

"Or are there?" Wendy mused. Sophie stepped through the doorway into the corridor and pointed the camera along the passageway back to the stairwell.

"What's your name sweetheart?" She asked. They both waited. From their right, they heard another pattering of feet echoing in the corridor on the other side of the washroom.

"Shit!" Sophie exclaimed. "Quick, I'll go around the end and you go through the washroom. We'll meet up in the other corridor and see if we can make contact!"

Sophie started off along the corridor, using the infra-red image on the camera screen to guide where she was going. Wendy turned, switched on her torch and headed into the washroom. She didn't stop and passed straight through into the corridor on the other side. Looking along the passage, she couldn't see anything or anyone. Sophie clearly hadn't yet made it around the end of the washroom. Wendy looked around and saw the doorway into the dormitory at the back of the building. She hurried into the second, long room and waved the torch around to see if anyone was in there. It was darker than the dormitory at the front but she could see the moonlit landscape through the windows along the back wall. She slowly walked over to the nearest window, looked out and her breath caught in her chest.

A young boy was standing just in front of the old fountain, staring up at her. The shadow of the building formed a straight line on the ground right in front of his feet and Wendy could see both the fountain and the child in the moonlight as clear as day. His hair seemed unkempt and matted and chunks were missing, revealing bone-white patches of skull. His face had the features of an old, sick man; long drawn out lines, sunken cheeks and thin, pursed lips. His nose was missing in its entirety, revealing two gaping holes from which a black viscous fluid ran down and around the down-turned mouth, dripping onto the almost concave chest. The clothes loosely covering the emaciated and crooked body were nothing more than rags; dirty, stained, torn and shredded. The limp hands that protruded from the tattered sleeves were bony with long fingernails where the flesh had receded. The bare feet of the sorry spectre were gnarled, cut, bruised and blackened with filth. But Wendy couldn't feel sorry for this child. At first, she didn't feel pity or anything that would be a natural, human emotional response to such a vision. She felt only fear. The unflinching gaze that met her own was from empty eye sockets. Black recesses where sparkling children's eyes had once looked in awe and wonder at the world were now pits of despair. Wendy had never seen such sorrow and her bottom lip began to quiver. As if it could sense her emotional torment, the boy slowly lifted his thin arms up toward her, his palms facing upward as if begging for help. Wendy's heart suddenly filled with pity and as she let out a soft whimper, the boy took a step forward into the building's shadow and vanished. Wendy let out a scream and dropped her torch as a hand landed on her left shoulder from behind.

"Is anyone in here with us?" Frank asked. Both he and Dillon sat motionless, listening. "You try." He whispered and gave Dillon a nudge with his elbow.

"Me?" Dillon retorted.

"Yeah. You've gotta start somewhere, kid. Just ask a few questions. See if we get a response."

"What shall I ask?"

"Whatever you want!" Frank chuckled. He found Dillon's reticence amusing but also recognised that if he was going to seriously get into ghost hunting, then Dillon would need to get over feeling daft about talking into thin air. "Remember, if there are any spirits here, they were living, human beings once. For all we know, they're probably just as eager to communicate with us as we are with them. We've just got to let them know that's what we're here for."

Dillon thought about Frank's logic for a few moments. It did feel absurd but Frank was right; if there was anyone or anything in the old chapel with them, then the only way to know would be to ask them.

"We're not here to hurt you." Dillon started. "We just want to talk. Please, let us know you're here… somehow."

"That's good." Frank whispered. "Leave it a few moments to see if we get a reply and then try again."

They waited.

"Is anyone here with us who wants to talk?" Dillon asked. Again they waited.

"Do you feel that?" Frank whispered.

"What?"

"It's getting cold."

"Yeah, I feel it. But is that really a sign of a ghost?"

"Absolutely. They need energy to come through into our realm. As they draw energy, the space will get colder. Something's trying to communicate with us."

"Look!" Dillon said suddenly and pointed to the corner of the chapel to the left of the door.

"What?"

"I'm sure I saw something move in the corner. It looked tall but I couldn't make it out. I only saw it out of the corner of my eye."

"Christ!" Frank said. "Over there, in the other corner. I saw it too!"

"It's still there!" Dillon said, the pitch of his voice rising through excitement, or fear, or both. "But I can only see it if I don't look straight at it."

"Me too! I can only see it as a shadow in my peripheral vision."

"Wait…" Dillon said. "Is the one you can see still there in the corner on the right?"

"Yeah."

"The one I'm looking at is in the corner on the left!"

"Bloody hell! There's more than one!"

"What about the camera? What can you see on that?"

"Nothing." Frank said as he craned his head to see the screen.

"Nothing?"

"Yeah, literally. That whole end of the chapel is filled with like, a mist or fog or something. I can't see anything!"

"But it's still there… Wait… oh my god… There's another."

"Shit! There are more in the other corner as well!"

"There must be about a dozen of them!"

"Yeah… Christ… There's a whole group of them!"

Although they stayed seated, Dillon and Frank turned their heads from left to right. It was only in the in the edges of their vision that the forms were visible. A group of featureless, humanoid shadows was gathering in each corner at the far end of the room. The walls behind them seemed to shimmer, dematerialise, becoming increasingly transparent and opening up to reveal an emptiness that conveyed a foreboding sense of a barren eternity. The vision was blurry and slowly oscillated as though the shapes were being seen underwater. They faded in and out of sight like smoke dissipating on a breeze as they tried to come forward. Stretching back in to the void, the gathering of shadows seemed endless, each one slowly gliding forward as if to speak and flickering in and out of existence as transient as a spark,.

"Let's get the Spirit Box going." Frank said as he fumbled it in his trembling hands. He handed Dillon the speaker to hold as he flicked the switch and turned up the volume. A hiss of white noise emanated from the speaker.

"We know you are there." Frank said, raising his voice over the hissing and crackling from the speaker and directing it toward the shadows in the corners.

"Please, talk to us." Dillon pleaded. He no longer felt daft for speaking out loud to the nothingness. His pulse was racing and his mind was being pulled between feelings of terror, curiosity and excitement. His skin prickled with fear as the hairs all over his body stood on end. Part of him wanted to run, screaming from the old house and never return, while another part of him wanted to stay, to explore, to push the boundaries of his experience and understanding.

"Tell us who you are." Frank said. The Spirit Box continued to randomly scan through frequencies but the hissing and crackling from the speaker remained a continual din.

"Is there something you want?" Dillon asked. "Something that we can do for you?"

Frank almost dropped the Spirit Box and the pair both leapt to their feet as a single word, crystal clear and unmistakable, suddenly came from the speaker.

"*Run.*"

Dillon let out a cry as the walkie-talkie in his pocket suddenly burst into life. He reached into his pocket and retrieved the device as Frank scanned the corners of the room for signs of the congregation of shadows. He glanced at the clear image on the camera screen.

"They're gone."

"Sorry. I didn't mean to scare you." Sophie said, smiling apologetically.

"Jesus... You almost gave me a heart attack!" Wendy responded, gasping for breath and clutching her chest.

"Well, you were just standing there, like, frozen. I called your name but you didn't even turn around. What's going on?"

"There was a boy standing down there." Wendy turned back to the window and pointed at the fountain.

"A boy?" Sophie asked excitedly.

"Yeah. Probably about eight or nine years old, at a guess. But you should've seen the state of him. I've never seen anything like it. Not in my worst nightmares."

"What did he look like?"

"Like the dead. His clothes were all torn, his skin was rotting and his eyes... Oh god, Sophie... His eyes."

"What about them?"

"He didn't have any."

"No shit! Wow! What happened?"

"Nothing. He just reached out his arms to me and stepped forward into the shadow there," She pointed at the line of shade cast by the roof of the building. "And then he just disappeared."

"Cool. Did you get any footage?"

"No. You had the camera."

"Oh, shit. Yeah. Sorry."

"It's okay... If he really wants help, then he'll be back, I'm sure."

"Is that what you think? He really wants hel..." Sophie was cut short as the walkie-talkie in Wendy's jacket pocket crackled and a muffled voice broke the quiet of the room.

"I'm sure that knocking sound came from through here." Bob said thoughtfully. He had led Steve through from the first classroom at the front of the building to the library in the middle. But it didn't feel as though the sound they heard had originated from this room either. When he heard the last two knocks, Bob had pointed the camera at the wall of the first classroom. In his mind, he pictured where the line of sight would have continued through the wall. It was at a diagonal to the room they now found themselves in.

"Yeah. You're right. It sounded like it came more from the left." Steve said, waving his arm in the general direction from where he believed the sound came from.

"Let's continue." Bob said, leading the way through the doorway toward the kitchen.

"Do you hear that?" Steve asked as they paused in the dark room beyond the doorway.

"Yeah." Bob replied, straining his ears to hear. It was a sound that was difficult to make out. Faint and yet close. A dull, rattling sound. But hollow. Like old wood on stone.

"It's not coming from the kitchen." Bob said as he panned the camera round and turned his head from side to side to pinpoint the direction of the noise.

"Down there." Steve said flatly. Bob turned and pointed the camera at Steve. He was standing with his arm outstretched, pointing at the stone staircase that led to the cellar. His torchlight illuminated the gaping hole. Bob wandered over, aiming the camera down into the pit and stopped.

"Bloody hell. The door's shaking."

"Christ. It is as well." Steve added, shining his torch on the old, rotten door. The sound they could hear was coming from the decayed planks gently banging against the stone doorframe. It was as though someone was on the other side rattling the door against the frame as if they were trying to escape from a subterranean prison. Suddenly the rattling stopped.

"Call the others. We all need to go down there." Bob said.

"Thank god you said that." Steve said as he pulled the walkie-talkie from his pocket.

"Why?" Bob asked.

"Because there's no way I'm going down there on my own."

9

The six investigators stood in a semi-circle around the hole. They trained their torches on to the wooden door and listened as Bob recalled what he and Steve had seen.

"There's obviously something down there." Bob reasoned. "And it's the only place in the whole building that we haven't explored. This will be the final part of the investigation for this evening, although I have a strong feeling we'll be coming back." He looked at the others and they all nodded. They had all experienced something in the few hours they had been in the house and what they had seen was a great deal more than any of them had ever witnessed before. It would have been idiotic to have left the house after just one evening's investigation when it promised so much more. It was a no-brainer; of course they would be coming back.

"Okay." Bob said as he handed his camera to Steve. Stepping slowly down the staircase and keeping his eyes firmly fixed on the door, he reached the bottom step and stopped. He gently reached out his trembling hand and took hold of the latch. He wrestled with the mechanism and tugged on the handle but the door remained closed. Leaning in, he examined the way the door sat in the frame. It seemed as though it would open inwards, away from him. He stepped back, turned side on to the door, braced himself and barged against the door with his right shoulder. He grinned as he heard a splintering, cracking noise from around the lock.

"Won't be a sec'." He said as he rubbed his hands together. Bracing himself for a second time, he charged the door and almost fell through as, with a sickening crack, the wood shattered around the lock and the door swung violently open. A draft of stale, damp, mould-infused air rushed out. Trapped in the cellar for countless years, the air had become stagnant. It was virtually unbreathable. Bob covered his mouth and nose with his hands as the cold, musky miasma drifted up to the others.

"Fuck!" Frank blurted and instantly turned his head away. He quickly smothered his face with the sleeve of his jacket. Dillon, Steve, Sophie and Wendy all followed suit, screwing their faces in disgust.

"It'll clear in a minute." Bob said through his fingers. He turned his attention to the space that had opened up beyond the door. "Steve, chuck me a torch." He caught the torch that Steve tossed down and swung the beam into the void. Though it was a sizable space, it appeared to be a single room. The walls were composed of rough-hewn stone blocks, stained by damp and mildew. The ceiling was low but not low enough that he had to stoop. Stepping forward, he almost fell down the single step he hadn't noticed on the other side of the door. His foot landed on the soft, dusty earth floor with a muffled thud. Turning in a semi-circle, he scanned the whole cellar. Ordinarily, it wouldn't have required any more than a cursory look, a quick scan on a camera, a few photos and perhaps a couple of minutes of digital voice recording. But, aside from the mystery of the door shaking in its frame, Bob knew there was something else about this room. It had an atmosphere. A feeling that he couldn't quite put his finger on.

"Come on down." He called back. "But watch out for that step behind the door." The others filed down the staircase and stepped into the room. Sophie and Wendy were still covering their faces but Steve, Frank and Dillon were overcome with curiosity to the extent that the odour didn't bother them anymore.

"There's not much in here." Bob said. He glanced around at the rest of the group.

"Yes there is." Wendy muttered behind the sleeve of her jacket.

"Yeah. Definitely." Steve added.

"It feels…" Sophie started but broke off as, like Bob, she struggled to explain the atmosphere in the room.

"Go on." Bob encouraged. "What do you feel?"

"It feels old." Wendy said. "Like, really old. Older than this building."

"Yeah." Sophie added. "But like, a kind of powerful old."

"I can feel suppression." Steve said. His eyes were closed beneath a deep frown as he tried to tap into the energy of the space. "It's negative. It's strong. It's…"

"Evil?" Bob asked.

"I don't know." Steve replied, shaking his head. "This feels like it's bigger than good and evil. Older than good and evil. It feels like there's no boundary between the two."

"Look at that." Frank interrupted. He was pointing his torch to an iron ring on the side wall. Hanging from it was the rusted remains of a black iron chain.

"There's another one further along." Dillon said.

"And there's two on this side." Wendy added.

"Strange." Steve mumbled as he shone his torch from one ring to another in turn. "They're all directly opposite each other. I wonder what they were for. There's no way they would've kept animals down here." He stepped forward to the centre of the room to gauge a mid-point, equidistant from each of the four rings when he suddenly tripped and stumbled.

"You alright?" Bob asked.

"Yeah, fine." Steve replied. "Just tripped over something stuck in the floor." He turned and pointed his torch at the earth and found an object sticking up. He bent down and pulled it free of the dirt. It looked like the top edge of one of the oblong links in an iron chain. Pulling the link free of the soil, he saw it was still attached to the rest of the chain. He pulled harder and the length sprang up in the direction of one of the rings on the wall. He turned and pulled the chain out towards the centre of the room but stopped as he felt resistance.

"There's something on the end of this." He said thoughtfully. The others watched in silence and anticipation, shining their torches at the chain and the spot where they felt sure something was about to emerge from the ground after its entombment in the soil for generations. Steve grasped the chain with both hands, near where it disappeared into the earth. He pulled and a mound of soil rose up at the end of the chain, cracking as it bulged. Suddenly, the surface of the earth exploded in a puff of dusty clods and the object at the end of the chain came into view, landing on the ground with a thud.

"What the holy fuck is that?" Frank asked flatly. His question was rhetorical. He knew exactly what it was. They all did. They just didn't want to admit it. The shock on the faces of everyone was clearly visible, even in the low light and their wide, unblinking eyes were fixed on the rusted iron manacle attached to the end of the chain.

Without a word, Bob stepped over toward one of the other rings and kicked away at the dust until he found an end of another chain. He freed it from the ground until he too pulled out an iron manacle. Steve and Frank both repeated the discovery of manacles from the last two remaining rings until all four rusted iron shackles lay exposed on the earth. The group stood around with their backs against the walls, staring at the scene before them.

"This was no cellar." Frank said. Both shock and disgust were audible in his trembling voice. "It was a dungeon."

"But who was it a dungeon for?" Sophie asked.

"Looking at the size of the space in the middle of these, I'd say it must've been someone small." Bob said solemnly.

"Someone small." Wendy mumbled. "Like, a child."

The team stood in silence, staring in disbelief at their discovery.

"I think we're going to need some help on this one." Bob sighed.

10

The team gathered for their weekly meeting at the Waggon and Horses the following Tuesday, where they eagerly recounted their individual experiences of the visit. The discussion was animated and excited. There was a collective sense of pride at having gathered so much evidence, the edited highlights of which Bob had been only too happy to share on his tablet. He had combined the footage captured by each of the sub-groups into a video collage and the result was undoubtedly spooky. Strange, disembodied noises could be heard echoing along corridors or emanating from empty rooms. Orbs and other mysterious floating light anomalies zipped across the field of view and that, at the time, had been invisible to the investigators. But the most thrilling highlight was the voice, recorded on the video camera from the Spirit Box that Dillon and Frank had in the chapel. Although there was no accompanying image recorded, the ethereal voice telling the pair to 'run' was creepy but, more importantly, irrefutable. When it came to discussing their discovery in the cellar however, the mood in the group changed dramatically. There was a sombre tone in the voices of those who spoke, trying to offer some kind of explanation that didn't involve their worst fears. Deep down, they all knew that they had uncovered the relics of past barbaric and inhuman activities, even though they had no idea what those atrocities were. But that made it all the more difficult to reconcile. Their imaginations, fuelled by speculation and envisaging the most depraved and sadistic acts, ran wild. There was a palpable reluctance to mention the presence of the manacles and what diabolical purpose they had been used for.

The shackles just didn't seem to fit with the history of the house which, to the best of their knowledge, had been the country seat of Baron Trevallyn and then the Montague family. But what had happened to the hall after the Napoleonic wars? That was still a mystery. The group concluded that the story of the dungeon in the cellar must be hidden in the later, unknown history of the house during the nineteenth or twentieth centuries. To that end, Bob promised the group that he would carry out more research through the rest of the week before they returned to the site. Proposing that they go back the very next weekend, Bob called for a vote and smiled with a glint of satisfaction in his eyes when everyone raised their hand in favour of the suggestion.

He already knew that the others wouldn't be able to turn down another opportunity to investigate Trevalling. Calling for a vote was simply a surreptitious way to get the rest of the team to admit to themselves that they wanted to be part of the group. Of Bob's team. His paranormal society. Of course, it hadn't always been that way. When he was bought a Ghost Hunter experience for a birthday present by friends at work, he had attended with his wife somewhat reluctantly. But the evening had totally converted him and made him a staunch believer in the afterlife. Every knock, bump, whisper or cold patch of air was interpreted by the experience leader as evidence of a ghost. And Bob had lapped it up. Afterwards, he became obsessed. Intent on setting up his own Paranormal Society to capture evidence of life after death, he joined forces with Steve and the pair of them spent night after night exploring graveyards, old churches, castle ruins and anywhere that they thought might be haunted. Even when he wasn't out investigating, he'd carry out research, spending hours in the library or on the internet, finding other sites to explore or other groups' evidence. And after a while, the arguments with his wife started. Then she found someone else. And then she left. But Bob was okay. He had his new family. Both living and dead.

It was mid-afternoon by the time Wendy, Sophie and Dillon arrived at Trevalling. Both girls had to work the morning shift at the call centre so they'd arranged to pick Dillon up after lunch. Bob, Steve and Frank had gone on ahead, setting off for the hall at around ten o'clock. Although all the equipment fitted neatly in the boot of Bob's car, they couldn't collect Dillon because the passenger seat had been reserved for a special guest. No one would tell Dillon who the mystery person was. They just smiled and winked at each other. All Dillon knew was that this individual was called Jackie.

For most of the journey, Sophie and Wendy complained about their jobs; the incompetent management, the lack of resources, people who had obviously phoned in sick so they didn't have to work a Saturday morning and so on. Some of the stories they regaled Dillon with were genuinely amusing and he found himself feeling guilty for laughing at the tales of the customers and some of the amazingly stupid things they would come out with. Dillon was under no illusion that whenever he called a helpdesk or call centre, his enquiry would be investigated with the maximum of efficiency and respect, but he was nevertheless shocked by the way Sophie in particular referred to the customers. He was surprised by how cutting her remarks were. Particularly because, as is the way with call centres, she had never actually met any of them. They were just voices at the end of a phone line. And yet, her descriptions of fat, spotty chavs or decrepit miserable old people, based on nothing more than her own imagination were harsh. But Dillon reasoned that when you have people phoning you all day, every day, predominantly with the express intention of complaining or shouting at you, you need a coping mechanism. Taking the mickey was evidently how Sophie dealt with what must be a poorly paid and unsatisfying job and Dillon wondered if this coping mechanism was actually more of a defence. Perhaps it was a way that she kept her confidence, her self-belief. Maybe belittling others gave her the edge that she needed, or craved, to ward off feeling downtrodden, useless and depressed. He remembered seeing the scars on Sophie's arms and her somewhat rebellious and unique choice of dress made him question if it all was just a way of attracting attention; perhaps a cry for help. On the surface, she seemed too bubbly a personality to have a genuinely tortured soul but there was still something about her that Dillon couldn't quite put his finger on. A deeper level of melancholy. A darkness that she wanted to keep hidden and was in a continual battle to prevent it from taking her over.

"Oh, look." Wendy pointed as the car bumped along the old driveway toward the house. "They've started without us."

"Well, they have been here for a while now." Sophie said.

Dillon leant forward between the two front seats and took in the scene through the windscreen. Although he was far away, Bob was easy to identify by his shape. He was on the grass beyond the far right end of the building with a long orange ribbon that he was periodically staking into the ground. He was following someone who Dillon couldn't quite make out. He presumed that this stranger must be Jackie and she seemed to be holding a couple of rods in front of her. They were swinging to and fro and crossing over. Wherever they crossed, Jackie would walk in that direction and Bob would follow with the ribbon. Another two ribbons had already been staked into the ground, one running directly up to the front of the house and the second from the end wall to the left. Both ribbons met the walls of the building slightly off centre. Frank and Steve were sitting on a couple of camping chairs by the back of Bob's car. They had a flask of what Dillon presumed was tea and were eating some sandwiches. When they saw Sophie's car approaching, they stood and came over to meet them.

"Nice of you to join us." Frank said with a sarcastic grin as the three emerged from the car.

"You keep that up and we'll piss off again." Sophie retorted.

"What? And miss all the fun? You wouldn't." Frank smirked. "Here, have a pork pie." He pointed to the bag of food in the boot of the car.

"What's been going on then?" Wendy enquired, waving her arm at the orange ribbon that stretched from the front wall straight out to the treeline.

"Oh, you wouldn't believe it if you couldn't see it for yourselves." Steve replied, his eyes wide with amazement.

"Tell us everything." Sophie said as she slumped in Frank's camping chair. Frank shrugged and perched himself on the edge of the open boot. He thrust his hand into a plastic pot in the food bag and pulled out several cocktail sausages, popping them one by one into his mouth as if they were sweets.

"It's been incredible really." Steve began. He took a sip of tea from his plastic cup and paused for a second as though composing himself before telling a story. "We got here at around eleven. As soon as we came on to the site, Jackie said she felt strange. When she saw the house, she went pale and started to feel dizzy. She said she wasn't picking up any spirits but that she could feel a powerful energy. We parked up and walked around the outside of the whole building and Jackie told us where she could feel the energy was strongest. Bob suggested we used the divining rods to trace any lines of energy and well, you can see for yourself." He nodded toward the orange ribbon.

"The weirdest thing is," Frank continued, "that there are two lines of energy that pass through this site. And they cross right under the hall."

"No shit!" Sophie said.

"What are lines of energy?" Dillon asked.

"They're Ley Lines." Steve answered. "No one really knows what generates them but there are hundreds that criss-cross the countryside, running under sites of special historical significance like burial mounds and stone circles. They link up these sites and where they cross, it's a really powerful place."

"Like at Stonehenge." Frank added.

"Really?" Dillon asked. He looked round at the ribbon, and then up at the house. It suddenly felt much more than just a ruin. It now felt as though it was hiding a much more ancient secret.

"So Bob and Jackie are finishing tracing the last line now as we speak." Steve said.

"What, so there's one around the back as well?" Sophie asked.

"Yup. And it's a continuation of this one at the front, so the line actually runs straight through the building." Frank replied.

"It's not dead centre though, is it?" Wendy pointed out.

"No. I noticed that too." Steve said. "The line here passes through the dining room and out the kitchen at the back. The line at the side seems to be more toward the rear of the building. It's difficult to tell where it goes in on the left because of the collapse but I reckon when Bob and Jackie are done, they'll find the line goes through the back of the library and then through the chapel."

"But the chapel isn't where the lines cross?" Sophie asked, leaning forward in the chair.

"No. It's not." Steve responded quietly.

"So…" Sophie prompted him.

"Based on the maps that Bob sketched and where the lines are…" Steve broke off as he fumbled in his pocket for a copy of the map. He mentally drew two lines through the rooms where the ribbons were entering and exiting the building.

"Well?" Sophie pushed. Steve took a deep breath and let out a long sigh.

"It looks like the lines cross under the cellar."

"Dillon, I'd like you to meet Jackie." Bob said proudly with a broad smile. The pair had returned to the car after they had completed siting the final ribbon. Dillon instantly felt nervous of Jackie. She looked rough. She was short, probably only five foot two, but she had a sturdy frame and was definitely not someone you would lightly pick a fight with. Her tight, pink leggings and grey leopard print top clashed in a way that made you want to wince. The gold rings, multiple bracelets, thick gold chain with a horse pendant and enormous gold hoop earrings also did little to compliment her pale skin tone. Her dyed black hair was slicked back into a ponytail that jutted out from the crown of her head and the heavy application of makeup failed to hide the deep lines on her face. She had piercing eyes that gave you the impression she was looking for an argument and a deep voice that sounded as though she gargled with gravel.

"It's a pleasure, my lover." She rasped in a thick West Country accent and grinned. Dillon tried to avoid noticing the gaps in the nicotine yellow teeth that adorned her thin-lipped mouth. One gap had been filled with a gold tooth. She held out her hand as her bangles jingled together and gripped Dillon's hand like a vice. He could feel every ring on her fingers digging into his skin. She held his hand firmly and the smile dropped from her lips. She stared into his eyes as if she was staring into his soul and after a few moments, she smiled again and released his hand.

"Likewise." He said meekly with a weak smile. Jackie turned and tossed the two metal divining rods into the boot of the car before fishing into a beige, leopard print handbag for a packet of cigarettes.

"We've known Jackie for a number of years and she's been very kind to help us with some of our more significant investigations." Bob explained. Jackie blew a plume of grey smoke up into the air above her head and nodded.

"She is one of those rare people who have the ability of being able to communicate with spirits." Bob continued. "It's a gift she's had all her life, since she was a little girl and she's learned so much about the Beyond from her contact with the departed."

"So, you can actually speak to spirits?" Dillon asked. He still felt uneasy about Jackie and thought that by showing interest, she would warm to him and not threaten to break his legs, or worse.

"Oh, yes." Jackie replied in a drawl as she exhaled another lung-full of smoke. "But not just speak to 'em." She continued. "I can see 'em as well."

"Really?" Dillon asked. That comment really did grab his attention. Jackie nodded. "So, what do they look like?"

"Like you an' me, love." Jackie shrugged.

Dillon immediately noticed a flaw with Jackie's answer.

"But, if they look like us, how can you tell the dead from the living? What is it about them that tells you they're spirits?"

"Well," Jackie took a drag on her cigarette and allowed the smoke to slowly billow from her mouth as she smiled, the clouds drifting through the gaps where teeth used to be. "You see, love, they're not like us. They sparkle."

"So, I said I'd do some more research on the house during the week and I've got some things I found here." Bob said as he retrieved a notebook from the glove box. By this time, everyone was taking advantage of the opportunity to tuck into the sandwiches, pork pies, snack-size Cornish pasties, sausages, bread rolls and crisps that Bob had brought along. He positioned himself in the centre of the semi-circle of investigators and held the book open in front of him as though he were about to deliver a sermon.

"So, we already knew that the hall was built in 1665 by Baron Trevallyn. He was given a significant sum of money by Charles the Second as a reward for his support during the English Civil War. This house was built using that money but as far as I can tell, Charles the Second never visited. The hall took three years to build and not long after moving in, the Baroness, who was called Alice, died during childbirth. The Baron never remarried and so after he died in 1697 with no heir to inherit the estate, the whole lot was sold to a wealthy merchant who had trading links with Venice and Amsterdam via Bristol and Plymouth. His son, who inherited the estate after his father's death in 1732, was a bit of a wild-child and blew the family fortune on a rather hedonistic lifestyle. He went bankrupt and the hall was bought for a fraction of its value by the Montague family in 1737, in whose possession it remained until 1804 when the Earl's son was killed in the Napoleonic Wars. The Earl retreated to his family home in London and in honour of his son's sacrifice, handed the hall to the military as a hospital for troops injured in the wars that claimed his son's life. When the war was over and Napoleon was exiled to St Helena in 1815, the number of troops cared for at the hospital diminished and in 1817, the hall was transformed into an asylum."

"An asylum?" Frank interrupted. "What, like, for insane people?"

"Absolutely. And I did wonder if the chains we found in the cellar were linked with that. But it seems that there were never that many patients cared for here and because of the tremendous rise in the population during the Industrial Revolution, the hall was repurposed as an orphanage. So that means, as a result of the remodelling, any artefacts or structural features associated with the asylum would have been removed." Bob studied his notes and turned a page. "In 1914, with the outbreak of the First World War, the hall was taken over by the military and reinstated as a hospital for troops and sailors who came back to England via Plymouth. The hospital was then turned into a Tuberculosis Sanatorium but in 1939, with the start of the Second World War, the military took it over again as a hospital up until 1947. I found some old black and white photos in the museum archives from the time when the hall was a TB sanatorium and a war hospital in both wars." Bob slid a few folded sheets of paper from the notebook and handed them round. In one photocopied image, a line of beds on wheels had been positioned in front of the building. Between each bed stood a nurse and the patients were propped up on pillows staring at the camera with gaunt expressions. The nurses were smiling and the patients still had a look of hope in their eyes; hope that they could be saved from their affliction by the curative properties of fresh, country air. In the other two images, two rows of beds in one of the dormitories were occupied by men with bandages round their heads or their arms in slings or in a couple of cases, with limbs missing altogether. These were the casualties of war. They didn't look at the camera. Unlike the Tuberculosis sufferers, they had seen so much horror and death that they no longer had any hope.

"Now, this is where the records get a little bit sketchy." Bob continued. "It's like, we have a pretty good picture of what went on here up until the middle of the twentieth century but then the hall kind of goes into a Dark Ages sort of period."

"Even though it's a lot more recent?" Wendy asked. Bob nodded. "That's strange isn't it? I mean, you would have thought that records would have been more complete in more recent times."

"Tell me about it." Bob mumbled. "I had a hell of a job trying to find information. I tried the internet, Exeter library, parish records held at the Cathedral, the Council archives. You name it, I looked. I've got the museum archivist digging around through their records a bit further. She said she'll get back to me at some point this week coming."

"So what did you find out?" Steve asked.

"Well, in 1947, it was turned into an orphanage and boarding school. That makes sense considering the layout we've found; the large dining room, the dormitories, the classrooms and the library. Everything seemed to be going well and things were pretty quiet up until 1956 when the headmaster retired and a new guy turned up. All I know is that the new Headmaster's name was Alexander Curwen-Oakes and he ran the place up to when it closed down in 1969."

"Closed down?" Frank enquired.

"Yeah. Sounds a bit suspicious doesn't it?" Bob closed his notebook and folded his arms. "I'm hoping that we'll get some more information from the archivist this week about what happened during those last thirteen years."

"Well, be that as it may," Frank said, rubbing his hands together. "What's the plan for this evening, Boss?"

"We're going to focus our investigation on the chapel and whilst we have Jackie with us, try to make contact." Bob explained.

"Cool." Sophie grinned.

"So, we'll get the cameras and digital recorders set up in strategic positions in the chapel and see what we can capture."

"Right." Frank said and turned to haul a canvas bag of equipment out of the car. He passed it back and went fishing for more kit. After a few moments, Bob, Steve, Wendy and Frank were making their way up the steps of the building, carrying bags and boxes of equipment. Jackie followed behind, after having first stubbed out the butt of her cigarette with the toe of her shoe.

"Is Jackie, like... For real?" Dillon quietly asked Sophie as the pair of them picked up the camping chairs.

"Oh, totally!" Sophie exclaimed. She immediately placed the chair back on the floor and looked round to make sure the others had moved far enough into the building to be out of ear-shot.

"What she's told us is, like, totally amazing!" Sophie continued. Dillon was taken aback by the excitement in her voice.

"She said that the realms of the Beyond cannot be conceived or imagined by the mind of humans because no human could ever even hope to comprehend them. They're dimensionless, timeless but eternal. Realms inhabited only by ethereal beings. Life, she said, was merely an aberration. A transient period of existence bound by space and time. I mean, isn't that cool?" Dillon could only nod.

"It's like, because of the restrictions of dimension, the living realm is the smallest and most inconsequential. No matter how big you thought the Universe was, or even the potential of the Multiverse, it pales into insignificance compared with the other realms." Sophie waved her arm dismissively at everything around her. "Spirits can occupy a body, whether it be a plant or animal, in the material realm for only a short time. And they're the unlucky ones. They experience pain, sorrow, the inevitability of death and decay. But they're us! WE are the spirits trapped in this wasting flesh!" She prodded at her forearm and Dillon's attention was drawn back to the lines of white scars.

"Those spirits that never pass through the living realm will never know such horrors. And those that were unfortunate enough to live and then pass on to other realms after their material body died, took with them the pain, sadness and memory of death." Dillon found Sophie's reference to life as being 'unfortunate' disconcerting and he felt uneasy with the way the conversation was going and how Sophie's excitement and conviction were growing by the second.

"Sometimes, those who have lived and died will push back at the tenuous membranes separating the realms to try and communicate with their fellow spirits still trapped in life. And you know why? Out of pity. They are the 'ghosts' that we see out of the corner of our eye or who we communicate with during a séance." Sophie's voice dropped to a whisper. "I don't know about the others but I am so into what comes after this. You know, like, knowing that there's something after this shitty existence and it's so much better than anything we can ever imagine." She picked up the camping chair and gave Dillon a huge smile, to which he could only meekly smile back, captivated as he was by the maniacal look in Sophie's eyes.

"I don't know about you, but after everything Jackie's told us, I almost can't wait to fucking die." She chuckled and turned to make her way into the hall.

"Wait," Dillon said, his voice trembling. "Aren't you afraid of death?" Sophie looked him straight in the eyes with a wry smile tugging at the corner of her mouth.

"Absolutely not." She said sincerely and then carried on toward the doorway.

Dillon stood for a few moments, his mouth open in shock at what Sophie said. Was she joking? Was she having a laugh at his expense? He couldn't tell.

One thing he did know was that it scared the shit out of him.

11

Dillon carried the chair up the steps and entered the gloom of the building. He paused next to Sophie who had come to a halt just inside the doorway. Squinting, he quickly tried to adjust his vision to the low light levels in the old hallway and, as the room became clearer, he saw Jackie. Bob, Steve, Frank and Wendy were standing almost to attention behind her, the boxes and bags of equipment still in their arms. They didn't move a muscle. Jackie stood facing the back wall with her eyes closed, her chin slightly lifted and her hands held up in front with both palms facing outwards.

"There are many here." She whispered without opening her eyes. Her brow was furrowed in deep concentration and the tips of her fingers twitched as though sensing the air around them.

"How many can you feel, Jackie?" Bob asked quietly.

"Too many to tell." She replied. "I feel sickness, healing, hope, despair and death. The gathering amongst us are from ages past that reach back many centuries. They are not all from the same time. They cannot sense each other here. The departed from each age are alone." She lowered her hands and turned to face the others. A quizzical expression passed over her face. "With so much energy here in this place, I don't understand why they can't leave. But I can feel their entrapment. They can't find the way to cross over."

"That's strange." Bob mumbled. From everything he had read, all his research over the years, everything that Jackie told him and all that he had observed, he assumed that once a spirit was freed from its corporeal host, it would seek either a portal or fissure between the realms to cross back to the Beyond. The hauntings he'd witnessed and read about were traditionally the result of spirits pushing through into this world from the other side at those points of weakness. But here, in this old ruin, it seemed as though the spirits of the departed couldn't leave. Or didn't want to. It was something that Bob had never encountered before.

"What would you like to do, Jackie?" Steve asked softly. Jackie turned to him and thought for a few moments. "Show me the whole building." She replied confidently.

The group left the equipment in the entrance hall and followed Jackie around the building. Frank was filming everything on a camcorder and both Bob and Steve were clutching digital voice recorders to capture everything that Jackie said and any potential responses. Bob had deliberately held back from giving her any information in advance that might have influenced her 'insight' but every time Jackie explained what she could feel or see, he looked at the others in amazement and mouthed the word 'unbelievable'. Comparing what she said with what the team already knew about the building's history, the accuracy of the details she gave was astounding. In the classrooms and library downstairs, Jackie reported hearing children and seeing them outlined against the light entering through the windows. Upstairs, she sensed the presence of soldiers and, without Bob having given her any context before the visit, she was confused by the range of different uniforms. There was no doubt in Bob's mind that she could see the troops of the Napoleonic as well as the First and Second World Wars when the building was utilised as a military hospital, milling around for eternity but completely unaware of each other. Then, just as they were about to leave the second dormitory, Jackie stopped.

"I'm sorry, my dear. I cannot help you." The others froze immediately and stared at the doorway where Jackie's gaze was fixed. Bob and Steve both crept forward, flanking her on either side while holding out their voice recorders. Bob held out a digital thermometer close to the doorway and waved it gently in the air just beyond the frame.

"It's colder there." He whispered as he looked at Steve. Steve held out his free hand, fingers outstretched and nodded as he felt the cooler column of air in the doorway. Bob glanced back at Frank who had trained the camcorder on the empty space. Frank shook his head to acknowledge that he wasn't seeing anything on the small screen and Bob nodded to train the camera on Jackie instead. Frank slowly tip-toed to Jackie's left and stopped behind Steve. He turned the camera towards her and saw that she was looking slightly upward, as though to meet the eyes of someone taller, standing in front of her. The others could see nothing.

"I'm afraid I don't know where your sister is." Jackie said calmly. She wasn't in the least bit afraid. She had seen many, many spirits over the years, and some in a worse state than the man who now stood before her. He was dressed in a green uniform with metal buttons, but it was far from neat and tidy. The thick fabric of his jacket was torn and bloodstained. His right arm was in a sling, the soiled, triangular bandage supporting his forearm. His left leg was missing below the knee and a wooden crutch wedged under his left armpit supported his weight. Half his face was badly burned, the flesh blackened and raw. The wound extended from the top of his head, where a bloodied bandage circled his temples, all the way down the right side of his neck. His uniform was torn and charred all down his right side. Over his right eye, medical tape held a cotton pad in place, the pure white of the pad now stained red with blood and yellow from tissue fluid that seeped from his injured eye socket. His right ear was completely missing and when he spoke, the sinuous structures in his throat could be seen moving, like the strings on a puppet, through a hole that disappeared beneath his collar.

"When did she say she was coming to visit? Tuesday? Well, I think Plymouth was badly bombed and the roads might be blocked. I'm sure she's just been delayed. She'll be here just as soon as she can. You never know, she might have sent you a letter in the meantime. Won't that be nice? Oh, don't cry, dear. I'm sure she misses you too. Why don't you go back to bed and rest? Perhaps see what the postman brings, hmm?" Jackie smiled and gave a gentle, reassuring nod to the wounded soldier as he faded into the darkness.

"Temperature's rising." Bob whispered. Steve nodded his agreement.

"He's gone." Jackie said. Dillon thought he could hear a tone of sadness in her voice. She sighed before she left the room and everyone else followed. Dillon realised that the dead soldier had been trapped in the hospital where he had finally succumbed to his injuries for around seventy years. Utterly alone. Reliving his last few, painful moments of life, again and again. And now completely beyond any help. He wondered if the man's sister ever did make it to the hospital. Even if she had been too late.

Back in the entrance hall, everyone waited to hear Jackie's report. She insisted on a cigarette break before going any further but, after she'd had time to think, she agreed with Bob's plan of trying to communicate with the spirits in the chapel, since that was where Frank and Dillon had experienced the most promising contact.

12

Pale sunlight illuminated the old chapel through the broken windows. The group sat in a circle, some on old wooden chairs that were still intact and others on camping chairs. Jackie sat beneath the window, facing the door. She had been intrigued by the account of Frank and Dillon's experience in this room. She believed they had witnessed the opening of a portal to another realm. Her curiosity was magnified when Bob played her the recording of the voice captured on the Sprit Box. She had never heard anything like it before. And over the years, she'd heard a great deal from the Beyond. She spent most of her time in the area around her home in West Cornwall, communing with spirits associated with the many Stone-Age sites. They were ancient spirits. They had crossed over a long time ago and had a wealth of knowledge to pass on. That was how Jackie had started. When she was a little girl, she was often visited by spirits who just wanted to talk with her. They somehow knew that she could hear them and they came flocking in their hundreds. There was no way that the knowledge she picked up from the dead could be tested by any conventional examination. It was beyond the reach of any branch of science to prove. As the years went by, Jackie not only heard the truth of the spirit realms from the various entities she encountered, she saw them as well because the spirits taught her the art of astral projection. Most of the time when Jackie had spoken with those who had passed on, they had words of comfort or wisdom to share. But Dillon and Frank's experience was odd. It was something new. Something she had never experienced before. She had never heard the dead telling the living to 'run'.

Before she began trying to contact the spirits who were present, Jackie explained that portals, like the one Dillon and Frank had seen, can be found in sites where there is a high level of energy. Exactly like the kind of site where two Ley Lines cross. The energy can be 'tapped into' by spirits. It serves as a pan-dimensional force that provides pathways, openings and places of transcendence for beings to cross from one realm into another. The drop in temperature normally associated with the manifestation of a spirit is because it needs to use some of the ambient energy to make its presence known. They need energy to move from one realm to another. Of course, where the energy is strongest, it is easier to cross over and these inter-dimensional spiritual highways are the portals. It is through the portals into the living realm that spirits can enter the vessel of an unborn child. Once inside the foetus, a spirit would then be trapped for the duration of the lifetime of that human being. Those who would be still-born are the lucky ones, spared the sorrow and pain of life. For them, transcendence came early. And they were thankful for it.

For a few moments, the group sat listening, holding their breath and waiting for a sign that there was someone else present with them. Not daring to move or create a sound, their eyes flitted from side to side, trying to pick out forms within the shadows. But nothing happened.

"Please, do not be afraid." Jackie called out. "We have come to hear your stories. Please, share with us what you will." She lifted her arms out in front of her and held her hands flat, her palms facing upward. Again, everyone waited.

"Oh, there you are." Jackie said finally. She lowered her arms and placed her hands on her knees. She smiled at something past Wendy, outside the circle of investigators. Something that only she could see.

"Come forward, dear. Don't be frightened. We're your friends. Tell me, what's your name?" She paused and leant forward in her seat slightly, enticing whatever was outside the circle to approach.

"George? That's a handsome name for such a strong young man. How old are you George?" Again she waited and the others sat motionless, their eyes dancing from the space beyond Wendy to Jackie and back again.

"Six? Well, well. That is a good number. Come closer George and tell me who your friends are back there behind you."

Wendy was the first to turn. Then Sophie looked round. Dillon, Bob, Frank and Steve all turned their gaze to the front of the room. But they saw nothing.

"How many, Jackie?" Bob whispered almost imperceptibly.

"Lots." Jackie replied with a smile that spread over her face. "All the children have come to see us." She held out one hand as though she were offering it and she gave a sigh as the spirit of George stepped forward into the circle and placed his hand in hers.

"I felt that." Wendy muttered. "Did you feel that?"

"Yeah." Sophie said, her eyes wide and a huge grin on her face. "It's like something passed right between us. Must've been George."

"I've got goose-bumps!" Wendy exclaimed, rolling up her sleeves and studying the skin on her forearms.

79

"And who's this?" Jackie said, turning her eyes from where George stood on her left over to her right. "Come on closer. Don't be shy. George and I are friends. Would you like to be my friend as well?" She held out her other hand and Sophie gave a squeak of delight as another cool breeze passed between her and Frank.

"Bloody hell!" Frank couldn't contain his shock and he studied his right arm closely before looking up at Sophie who simply nodded and grinned like a Cheshire cat.

"What's your name, my darling?" Jackie whispered as she leant to her right. She now had both hands held out in front of her and her thumbs were moving back and forth in the air as though she were caressing the backs of the hands that were in hers. "Robert? That's a lovely name. And how old are you, Robert? You're six as well? Well now, isn't that nice." She paused and appeared to be looking Robert up and down.

"Tell me, Robert, how did you get those cuts on your wrists and ankles?"

Bob's eyes widened suddenly. He looked at Steve and saw that Jackie's question had shocked him too. The realisation of what Jackie was seeing quickly dawned on the investigators. Their mouths dropped open as their worst theories about the manacles in the cellar made sense. And so it was true. The chains and manacles they had discovered in that dark, dank hole had been used on children. And as young as six years old. Each of them felt a knot tighten in their stomach. Dillon was glad he couldn't see the atrocities inflicted upon the flesh of the young boy. He took some small comfort in being spared that horror.

"Chained up?" Jackie asked. The expression on her face turned to one of shock and concern. Her thumbs stopped moving, no longer stroking the small ghostly hands that still held hers, the first human touch they had experienced in decades. "Tell me, sweetheart, who did this to you?"

The others all leaned forward to hear the answer. They held their breaths and stared, unblinking at Jackie.

"Headmaster?" She asked quietly. Bob sat bolt upright in his seat, his eyes flicking excitedly from one investigator to the other. They shared his surprise. It was plainly written in their expressions.

"But, why would your Headmaster do..." Jackie broke off mid-sentence and her head suddenly lifted. The frown on her face vanished, replaced by a look of confusion and, Dillon thought, a touch of panic. Her eyes flitted across the end of the room and her hands suddenly dropped.

"Wait!" She exclaimed hurriedly. "Don't go! George, Robert, what's the matter? What's wrong?"

"What the...?" Frank said, his voice full of alarm. The air in the chapel suddenly changed. It felt charged like it was full of static. The team grew fidgety in their seats, turning quickly and looking around as draughts of cool air swept past them.

"Did you hear that?" Sophie asked, her voice trembling. "There! There it is again!" She turned her head in the direction of the sounds she heard; soft cries and whimpers of fear and trepidation, the sounds of frightened children fleeing something terrible.

"I heard it!" Dillon said. "But I heard it over there." He pointed to the opposite side of the room from where Sophie had heard the cries.

"It's all around us!" Frank said as he twisted in his seat, trying to pinpoint where the sobs and cries were coming from.

"Jackie," Bob leaned forward to attract Jackie's attention. "What's happening?"

"I don't know." She replied uneasily. "All the children are afraid. They're running away." She looked from Bob back into the centre of the circle. "George. Tell me, what's wrong? What are you afraid of?"

Dillon felt a shudder run through him as he saw Jackie's eyes widen and then she clasped her hands to her open mouth.

"Shit's proper going down now!" Frank said as he and the others swivelled round in their seats and looked around the chapel. Their breath billowed in front of their faces as the temperature in the room plummeted.

"What are they saying, Jackie?" Bob demanded. "What's happening?"

"They're all gone." Jackie said as she rose to her feet and looked around her. "There are no more here."

"But why's it got so cold?" Wendy asked, folding her arms across her chest. Jackie walked to the centre of the circle and held her hands out, palms facing outward, in an effort to sense what was going on.

"There's something else…" Jackie's voice trailed off into a whisper and the others leapt to their feet, knocking their chairs over as three loud bangs echoed throughout the building as though three doors had slammed violently in their frames.

"What the…?" Frank stuttered.

"Get the cameras!" Bob ordered. Steve and Frank grabbed a camera each. Wendy and Sophie picked up the voice recorders and Dillon trained a torch on the chapel doorway. They all waited as if something was about to enter the room, but as the echoes of the bangs died away, the room fell silent.

"Shit a brick." Frank mumbled as he pressed his free hand into his temple. "I've just got a splitting flash headache."

"Me too." Wendy said, wincing as the pain in her head throbbed.

"The air feels really heavy." Steve remarked. "It feels like it's…pulsing."

"The energy has grown strong. The portal is open." Jackie muttered, her hands still held out in front of her. She sounded concerned and Dillon noticed the deep frown on her face, her eyes staring, unblinking at the doorway.

"Can you see it, Jackie?" Bob asked. "Can you see the portal?"

"No." She replied flatly. "It's not here."

"Where is it then?" Bob turned to face Jackie and tracked his camera round on to her.

"In there." Jackie turned her head to face the wall of the chapel and pointed. The others needed no further explanation. They all knew where she meant. Shivers ran down their spine and their skin tingled. But it wasn't because of the cold.

"God, it's really strong here." Frank said. He rubbed the side of his head with his left hand and winced. The team had gathered at the top of the cellar steps. The cold air felt leaden and pulsated as though a low, inaudible bass frequency was being played through a PA system at full volume. Below them, the old wooden cellar door was shaking in its frame.

"Are we really going down there again?" Wendy asked meekly.

"This is where the Ley Lines cross." Jackie explained. "The energy is strongest here. This is where the spirits can cross over."

"Yeah…" Frank said. "So, like Wendy said, do we really want to go down there?"

"This could be the best thing we'll ever document." Bob replied. "It's not a question of if we want to go down there, it's a matter of need; we simply have to."

"You first then, Boss." Frank gave a nervous laugh.

"I'll go first." Jackie said and she took the first step down toward the door. The cameras followed her every movement and the group watched as she reached the door, held up her hand and gently pushed. The door swung open and a rush of warm air swept out, up the steps and washed over the others.

"Jesus, what was that?" The shock in Steve's voice was unmistakable.

"Well either we just got blasted by a phantom hairdryer or I just had a hot flush." Frank replied.

"Come on." Bob said and followed Jackie down the steps. The others followed, tentatively stepping down, one stair at a time, never taking their eyes off the dark doorway below.

"The walls are shaking!" Sophie exclaimed. She had reached out and placed her hand on the wall to give herself more balance as she descended the staircase and noticed that the stone was vibrating.

"There's a lot of power here." Steve said as he looked round at her. "Can you feel it in you? Going through you? It's like every cell in my body is vibrating. I've never felt anything like it before."

"It's like a static charge." Dillon added. In his mind, he likened the sensation to the tingling feeling in his fingertips that he remembered when he touched the family's old fashioned television screen as a boy. But this feeling wasn't just in his fingertips. It was through his entire body.

"Mind the step." Bob called back as he disappeared into the darkness. The others followed and allowed their eyes to adjust to the low light in the cellar. Even with Dillon's lantern, the room was unbelievably dark.

"Look." Wendy finally said and pointed at the ground. "The floor's moving!" Steve crouched and aimed the camera along the floor. On the small screen, he could see the dust dancing, rising and falling in time with the vibration that filled the room.

"Turn the light off." Jackie said.

"Really?" Frank asked. He wasn't too keen about being plunged into complete darkness but Jackie looked him straight in the eye and nodded. Dillon switched off the lantern and the group were plunged into blackness.

"Wait..." Wendy was the first to speak. "I can see."

"Me too." Bob said. Dillon looked round to where Bob was standing and was surprised to see Bob lifting his hand in front of him and turning it over, testing his sight.

"There's a light coming from somewhere." Steve said as he turned on the spot where he was standing and, looking at the screen on the camera, tried to find the source of the faint, bluish glow.

"I can't tell where it's coming from. It's all around us." He said, obviously confused.

"It's pure energy spilling through the portal." Jackie said. Everyone turned to look at her.

"But, where is the portal?" Bob asked.

"All around us. We are in the midst of it." Jackie replied. "Can't you feel it?"

"Yeah." Frank grumbled. "My head hurts."

"Exactly." Jackie smiled. "But did you notice that it's warm in here?"

"Oh yeah." Sophie said. "You're right. I'm not cold anymore."

"We are experiencing the infinite." Jackie said quietly. "Now, everyone be silent and we may hear them speak to us from the other side."

A few, tentative minutes passed as the group stood in complete silence, bathed in ethereal light, their eyes and cameras trained, unflinching, on Jackie. As they watched, she closed her eyes and turned her head slowly from side to side.

"There are voices." She whispered. "They know we are here now. They can sense us. They're coming forward. Closer. I can feel them now. They are afraid. But not of us. They're trying to speak to us but they're still too far away. They're getting closer. The voices are muddled. They're speaking over each other. It's difficult to understand. Wait… One has come forward from the others. I can hear her more clearly. She's frightened. I think… she's trying to warn us. She's telling me something. The Fallen? Yes… that's what's she's saying. The Fallen are coming. The Fallen are coming."

"Who are The Fallen, Jackie?" Bob whispered.

"I don't know. The Fallen are coming. The Fallen are coming. That's all she's saying. Wait. She's going away. They all are. But she's still saying it. The portal is closing. It's getting dark. Dillon, it's time to turn on the light."

"My headache's going." Frank said as Dillon switched on the lantern and bathed the room in a yellow glow.

"And the humming has stopped." Steve added, placing his hand on the wall and feeling that the vibrations were receding.

"Who are The Fallen, Jackie?" Bob asked again.

"They didn't tell me." Jackie sighed.

"Well, they don't sound nice whoever they are, so I think we'd best scarper before they get here." Said Frank.

"I don't think that's going to be possible." Jackie said. The others all stopped and looked directly at her.

"What do you mean, Jackie?" Asked Steve.

"The Fallen aren't coming through the portal."

The others watched and waited, a feeling of trepidation growing in their chests.

"They're already here."

13

"I'm still not sure I get it." Sophie shook her head.

"It's exactly like Jackie said in the car on the way back." Replied Frank as he swallowed a mouthful of ale and placed his pint back on the table.

"Yeah, but we weren't in the same car, were we?" Sophie replied, a hint of annoyance evident in the tone of her voice.

"Fair enough." Steve said softly. He crossed his arms and leant back in his seat. "So, we know that the building is located on the junction of two ley lines. Yes? However, this may have been a complete accident."

"How do we know that?" Sophie interrupted. "I mean, perhaps that was deliberate by Lord what's-his-face."

"I doubt that the Baron Trevallyn had the mystical nature of the site in mind when he built his manor." Steve replied. "For one thing, the ley lines don't cross right under the centre of the structure. It's off by about five or six metres. And secondly, if the intention was to build something over a site of such mystical power, then don't you think he would've gone for something a bit more extravagant than the larder?"

"Maybe." Sophie shrugged and sipped at her drink.

"So, let's assume for the moment that the location of the hall is purely coincidental. Now, imagine that nobody picks up on the power underneath it for all of its history, right up until the mid-twentieth century when it's turned into a boarding school. The first Headmaster retires and someone else comes in to take his place."

"Alexander Curwen-Oakes." Dillon said.

"Exactly. Well remembered." Steve smiled. Dillon felt proud but soon felt his cheeks flush as he noticed Wendy smile at him and give him a wink.

"Now, Mr Curwen-Oakes and his wife rock up out of the blue and take over the running of the school. He's there for, what was it, twelve or thirteen years before the school is closed down in 1969."

"Okay, I get all that." Sophie exclaimed. "But what does that have to do with what Jackie was saying?"

"Well, the spirit of the little boy, Robert, told Jackie that it was the Headmaster who had chained him up in the cellar. It's too much of a coincidence that Alexander Curwen-Oakes is chaining up young children in a cellar, right over the site of a trans-dimensional portal. So Jackie hypothesised that maybe Mr Curwen-Oakes knew about the ley lines. She thinks it's possible that he took over the running of the school for his own spiritual purposes."

"What kind of purposes?" Dillon asked.

"He could have been a student of the Occult, so it's possible that he wanted to open the portal to invoke spirits." Steve sighed.

"But why?" Wendy asked. "What could he hope to gain from that?"

"Have you ever heard of John Dee?" Steve asked. He looked around the faces of the group. The blank expressions were sufficient for him to guess the answer. "He was an advisor to Queen Elizabeth the First and dabbled in the art of Black Magic; sorcery, astrology and the like. One of the things he's apparently known for is necromancy which is raising the spirits of the dead to ask questions about the future."

"What do you suppose the link is with Curwen-Oakes?" Sophie asked suspiciously.

"Jackie has inferred that those kind of practices are only attempted by experts in the Black Arts and if she's right and suspects that Alexander Curwen-Oakes may have been a practitioner, he could very well have used the power within the building to contact the dead through the portal in the cellar."

"But why was he chaining up children?" Frank asked. The expression on his face was one of the utmost seriousness. Gone was the happy-go-lucky cheeky glint in his eye. This was a subject that did not lend itself to jokes and he feared that he already knew the answer to his question before he had even finished asking it.

"Well," Steve started. He sighed and unfolded his arms, placing his hands in his lap and interlocking his fingers. "Unless you have a gift like Jackie, it's very difficult to communicate with spirits. The simplest way is to give them a voice so they can speak."

"And in a school, there were plenty of victims." Sophie finished Steve's explanation and said exactly what the others were thinking. An uneasy silence descended over the group. Even the other sounds in the Waggon and Horses, people chatting and laughing, glasses clinking and pumps gushing seemed very distant all of a sudden.

"How many do you think he mistreated?" Dillon asked quietly.

"Over thirteen years? God only knows." Steve shook his head and reached forward for his drink. He lifted the glass to his lips and swallowed several large mouthfuls.

"We definitely know of one." Said Frank. "Don't forget Robert had the marks of the shackles on him. He didn't just tell Jackie it was the Headmaster who chained him in the cellar, she saw the wounds on his wrists and ankles for herself."

"Yeah. And it was probably the last thing that happened to him." Sophie said.

"Well, she did say that whatever happened to Robert in the cellar, it was what killed him." Steve added.

"He could've murdered dozens." Frank muttered, his eyes fixed in an empty stare on his pint glass.

"Very possibly, yes."

"So why doesn't anyone know about it?" Dillon asked.

"Think about it." Frank answered. The look in his eyes was one of shock and disgust. "You've seen how remote that place is. When Alexander Curwen-Oakes took over as the Head, it wasn't just a boarding school, it was an orphanage as well. If the kids he used were all orphans, who would ever go looking for them? Who'd know when they went missing? Who cared? The bastard could get away with anything. He probably drugged them and then when they were asleep, carry them down to the cellar where they'd be chained up and the one adult they thought they could trust would use them as vessels for his own sadistic rituals. If they survived, then great, he could use them again and again. But if they died, well, that was just tough shit. He probably got rid of the bodies somewhere where they'd never be found. Out on the moor probably. No-one would ever know. And that fucker would just move on to the next kid. And the next after that. And so on. Christ, it makes me so angry." Frank folded his arms and Dillon could see his fists clenched so tightly that the knuckles had turned white.

"What happened to Curwen-Oakes?" Sophie asked. Dillon could hear anger in her voice, tinged with a touch of vengeance. He knew that if she had her way, she'd hunt him down and make him pay for his heinous crimes.

"He's dead." Bob replied flatly. Up until that moment, Bob had been very quiet. He'd just been listening to the others talking about what had happened to the children at the school. He had barely even touched his beer and that was most unlike Bob. Because of his sheer size, he could easily hold his drink and he was normally on his third pint whilst the others were still finishing their first. But not now. His first glass still sat in front of him, with only a few mouthfuls consumed.

"How do you know?" Sophie demanded. Bob leant to one side and picked up his bag. He rummaged inside and pulled out several sheets of folded paper. Pushing his glass into the centre of the table, he unfolded the pages and laid the stack down in front of him.

"After what happened on Saturday, I was keen to get back to the research, to see what else I could find." He said as he flattened the crease in the paper with the palm of his hand. "I called the archivist at the museum yesterday morning and she said that because I'd asked her about a specific, short period of time, she was able to focus her search much better. She'd managed to turn up a number of newspaper articles from between 1964 and 1969. These are photocopies."

"What do they say?" Frank asked. He uncrossed his arms and leant forward, peering at the photocopied columns of newspaper print and photographs.

"The earliest of these six is about a boy who went missing from the school. Apparently there was a huge search out on the moors for him but he was never found. He had allegedly run away from the school but the weird thing the police noticed was that he hadn't taken any of his belongings from the dormitory. His clothes and few personal possessions had been left behind. It seemed strange, even at the time, because if you were going to run away with the express intention of never going back, you'd take everything you owned with you."

"Perhaps he never left." Sophie suggested.

"That's what I was thinking." Bob nodded slowly. "Even though there was a statement from the Headmaster that said he just vanished one night, there's not really any evidence that he did actually run away. But who was going to doubt the word of a Headmaster, eh? A respected member of society. A pillar of the community. He could've weaved a web of any old lies and the authorities would've taken his word as gospel."

"Does it mention who the child was?" Steve asked. There was a pause. Everyone looked at Bob, waiting for an answer. He sat with his eyes closed for a few moments. He didn't need to look again at the article to double check. He already knew. The name was burned into his mind.

"Robert."

"Fuck!" Frank exclaimed.

"I knew it!" Sophie shrieked. "What a bastard!"

"You said there were six articles." Steve said in an effort to quieten the group. He was well aware that the other customers in the pub had all stopped what they were doing and were looking at the small gathering in the corner.

"The next one is from about eight months later." Bob said as he removed the first page and slid it under the pile, revealing a second article. "It reports that a young boy committed suicide in the changing rooms. He hung himself from the pipes in the showers."

"Wait." Frank frowned. "We didn't see any showers."

"The changing rooms were in the end of the building that was destroyed during the collapse." Bob explained.

"Don't tell me that the name of that kid was George?" Frank added.

"No. This boy was eleven and his name was Jonathan. George was only six, if you remember." Bob replied.

"But we're sure that George was one of the boys who died in that place?" Sophie asked.

"Pretty certain, yes." Bob nodded mournfully.

"And the other articles?" Steve was keen to see what other details Bob had uncovered.

"Well, the next three all follow a similar pattern. Boys go missing from the orphanage and they're never found. Despite extensive searches of the moors. In these later cases however, the boy's belongings were missing as well. Seems that Curwen-Oakes and his wife learned from their first mistake with Robert."

"You think his wife was in on it?" Steve asked, the surprise evident in his voice.

"Absolutely." Bob replied confidently. "There's no way she couldn't have known about it. There were only the two of them there."

"No other teachers?" Frank asked.

"Doesn't appear to have been. There were a couple of others from the days of the previous Headmaster but by 1963, they'd both left. Curwen-Oakes and his wife didn't advertise for any more staff. And now we know why."

"So what happened in 1969?" Steve asked. Bob turned to the final article which had two long columns of text and a black and white photograph of the front of

Trevalling House. The gardens looked unkempt and overgrown and in front of the building were a couple of police cars and a police van.

"One more boy went missing in 1969. Or at least that was the last of the ones that the authorities and the press knew about. But when word reached the authorities of yet another runaway and they visited the building, they found it going to ruin. Obviously, Curwen-Oakes and his wife couldn't manage the upkeep of the building and the grounds by themselves. By this point, there were only a handful of kids there. But when they were found, they were all dressed in clothes that were nothing more than rags and they were emaciated. On the brink of starvation. The authorities closed the place down with immediate effect, sent the boys to other institutions and arrested Curwen-Oakes and his wife. He committed suicide in his cell before his trial."

"And his wife?" Sophie asked.

"Weird one, that." Bob frowned. "Seems she had already gone completely barking mad. It was suggested that she had gone insane a couple of years before. Her husband must've just been using her to do his evil will and her mind just couldn't hack it. She spent the last of her days in a lunatic asylum. She died in 1983."

The group went quiet. Bob handed round the photocopied articles and they were read with keen interest.

"Do you think they're still out there? On the moors?" Wendy's voice was weak and tinged with nervousness.

"Who?" Frank asked as he placed his pint on the table.

"The children."

"You mean the ones who ran away?"

"Yes. Well. No. At least... The paper says they ran away, but what if Jackie was right and they died during Curwen-Oakes' rituals? He probably buried them out there. Where no-one would find them."

"Who's to say they're buried on the moor?" Dillon said thoughtfully. The others all glanced round at him. He felt his cheeks blush and he straightened his glasses and cleared his throat. "I mean... It's a bit risky to say the boys had run away over the moor and then allow a search party, probably with dogs, to go looking. The police know how to look for things. If there were bodies out there, they would've been found."

"What are you getting at?" Bob asked.

"Well, all I'm saying is that... If I were thinking like Curwen-Oakes, I would've reported that the boys had run away and sent the search party off over the moor looking while at the same time, I would've..."

"Buried them in the school grounds!" Sophie exclaimed. She clapped her hands and made Dillon jump. "Wow, so you do have a dark side to you after all. I love it!" She leant over and stroked Dillon's shoulder and upper arm. He felt his cheeks blush again.

"It's a possibility." Bob mused. "If they are buried in the school grounds, then that might go some way to explain why they can't leave and cross over to the other side. They're trapped there."

"Or, as we thought before," Steve interrupted. "They *won't* leave because they're warning others about The Fallen."

"Yeah. That's right." Frank joined in. "Jackie said that all the children were running away from The Fallen. They were all, like, keen as anything to talk to us beforehand and then as soon as this dark entity turns up, they all scarpered. Maybe they *are* trying to warn others."

"Did Jackie have any idea what The Fallen is?" Wendy asked.

"She wasn't a hundred percent sure." Bob replied. "The energy was dark. Very dark. But she said it was from a different place than where the children are now. A different dimension. A place where no earthly spirit would ever want to go."

"Sounds like the kind of place an expert in the Occult would love to hang out." Frank mused.

"Well, our best guess is that The Fallen is Alexander Curwen-Oakes. Or at least his spirit. Perhaps he's become something else on the other side, a vengeful, evil spirit that verges on demonic."

"But why's he come back?" Wendy asked. Bob shrugged but Steve cleared his throat to answer.

"In many of our investigations, we've communicated with or gathered evidence that spirits are earthbound because they have unfinished business. Take the soldier who Jackie met in the upstairs dormitory for example. He was obviously waiting for his sister to visit. And we can assume that he died from his injuries whilst he was still waiting. That's unfinished business. He's back, trapped in an endless loop, wandering the dorms of the old hospital, forever waiting for his sister to visit. Perhaps he knew he was dying and he just wanted to say goodbye. It would have been the most important thing for him. And now he's back, called by that compulsion. But we know he will never be able to say goodbye. So he's trapped there forever."

"That's so sad." Wendy mumbled. She reached forward for her drink and lifted it to her lips in an effort to prevent the others seeing them quivering. She blinked quickly to drain the tears that were forming in her eyes. But Dillon did see and he felt his heart wrench. Wendy was such a quiet, sensitive soul. A rare example of a truly lovely person. And to see her upset was almost too much. He felt a desire well up inside him to hug her, to hold her close, to share his warmth with her and let her know that everything was okay. But he resisted, conscious that this was neither the time nor the place.

"So what kind of unfinished business could Curwen-Oakes have?" Sophie asked.

"I'm not sure." Steve sighed. "I mean, he is dead after all. And if the objective of all of his practices was to conjure the dead, then there's little point coming back for that now."

"Maybe he's trapped there as well." Frank suggested. The others looked at him and waited for him to elaborate. "Killing kids has got to have some effect on you. Even if you're a sadistic bastard to start with. I mean, his missus went bonkers, didn't she? So it would be daft to think that murdering children wouldn't have had some impact on his mind as well. Perhaps he went crackers as well?"

"It's possible that the killings and the rituals may have warped his brain." Bob said thoughtfully. "And the effect on his spirit would have been just as extreme. So perhaps he's back like a junkie looking for just one more fix? Maybe he's drawn to the place where he wielded such power. And if the children really are buried in the school grounds, unable to leave, then he's still the Headmaster."

"Even after death he still has a hold on them." Sophie said through gritted teeth.

"And they'll never be free." Wendy shook her head.

"Well, we've got to do something about that then." Frank said assertively. "We've got to find them."

"You mean, find where they're buried?" Steve asked.

"Yeah! And then we'll dig them up, take them away from that horrific place and give them a proper burial! That will stop the old bugger bothering them for the rest of goddamned eternity!" Dillon was surprised at Frank's enthusiasm for his new idea. If he had half the chance, he would've gone high-tailing it back to the old ruin at that moment, a torch in one hand and a shovel in the other. And he would've dug up the entire garden until he found the children.

"Let me think for a second." Said Bob and everyone turned their eyes toward him and waited. He sat with his arms folded over his broad chest for a few moments, his lips pursed and his eyes, set under a deep frown, staring up at the ceiling.

"Now, hear me out." He started, lowering his eyes and looking at the rest of the team, studying their faces one by one. "This could be an excellent opportunity for us, as well as doing something truly remarkable for those children."

"What do you mean 'opportunity'" Sophie asked.

"If we go digging around in the grounds, we may or may not find something. If we don't find anything, then our suspicions were wrong and it was just part of the investigation. If however, as we presume, we do find something, like children's skeletons, then we will have to go to the police. That's not something we can keep to ourselves. But it should make the local news, or even the national news. And that would be excellent publicity for the Exeter Paranormal Society. We would have uncovered some truly awful crimes. There'll be journalists wanting to talk to us, there'll be an official investigation into the children's murders, hell, there might even be a documentary!"

"We'll be famous!" Frank said excitedly and lifted his arms up in the air. The excitement quickly spread throughout the group. At last, they could do something that was worthwhile and wasn't merely collecting evidence of ghosts, but actually *using* that evidence for a greater good. To help free the children from their eternal prison in that hideous ruin, under the evil watch of *him,* their old Headmaster. And if they achieved some fame along the way, then all the better.

"So when are we going back?" Wendy asked. The tears had gone and she was now just as keen as the others.

"What are all doing this weekend?" Bob asked with a smile.

"Well, I don't know about everyone else, but I'm going to Trevalling Hall to go rescue some lost children!" Frank said enthusiastically. The others all agreed and raised their glasses to commit themselves to the weekend's venture.

"Well that settles it." Bob said with a laugh. "On Saturday, we go back to Trevalling Hall."

14

Daylight didn't illuminate the morning of Saturday, so much as merely skirt round the edge of the horizon. Low, gun-metal clouds blocked what little warmth could have been gleaned from the Sun and the landscape seemed like it had been painted in varying sombre, shades of grey. It was dull, misty and generally dismal. The air was filled with the kind of fine drizzle that is barely noticeable on your cheeks but manages to soak every item of clothing you're wearing in seconds. Since their previous visit, Exmoor seemed to have mutated into a barren, threatening wilderness and Dillon found the views during the drive to the Hall both bleak and depressing. All the life had gone. All colour, vibrancy and joy had been bled from the world, leaving a deathly anaemic, silent facsimile, suspended in perpetual dusk.

The Hall too had been morphed into something more sinister. The windows were darker and streaks of rainwater that permeated the stone intermingled with rust-red stains, giving the impression that the whole building was bleeding. The long grass, heavy with rain, was hunched over, the seed-heads bowed as if in mourning. Wildflowers had either closed or shed their petals as if they had given up the will to live and were resigning themselves to death. Once colourful autumn leaves, under the extra weight of water, had fallen during the night, leaving bare skeletal branches of trees silhouetted against the slate sky. Rooks, with their feathers puffed in a desperate effort to try and preserve a modicum of warmth, watched from their perches on the boughs as the cars arrived in front of the Hall and the team of investigators clambered out, each pulling up their collar to keep the cold mist from seizing their neck in an icy grip.

Wendy and Sophie made a dash from the car to the doorway of the entrance. Frank and Steve sauntered up the steps, seeming unfazed by the weather. Dillon followed after Bob and Jackie but as Jackie entered the building, she stopped and tottered to one side. Bob caught her arm and steadied her.

"Are you okay, Jackie?" Wendy asked, rushing forward and taking her other arm.

"Yes, yes. I'm fine. But..." She left the sentence hanging in mid-air and stood up straight. Bob and Wendy let go of her arms and took a step back. Everyone watched as Jackie took several long, slow, deep breaths and closed her eyes. Her jet-black, perfectly painted eyebrows twitched as though she could hear something.

"What is it?" Bob asked.

"There's a lot of energy here today. The place has come alive. It's almost as though…" She stopped again, frowned and then opened her eyes. She looked at Bob.

"It's almost as though we were expected." She said solemnly. Although Bob maintained his calm and strong composure, he felt his stomach tense. The look in Jackie's eyes coupled with what she said sent a shudder of trepidation through his body.

"Do you wish to start indoors, Jackie?" Steve asked. "You know, to see if we can contact the children? Maybe they can guide us to where we'll find them."

"Yes." Jackie replied after a few moments' thought. "But not in the cellar. I fear the energy there will be too overpowering. I have a suspicion that the portal is already open. If The Fallen were to use that energy, I don't know what could happen. It would be best to try and make contact somewhere more directly linked with the children."

"What about the dormitories?" Sophie suggested.

"That's just what I was thinking." Jackie grinned. "You must be psychic." She let out a low, rasping laugh. "But nothing before I've had a fag." She turned and took a few steps back to the open doorway where she fumbled in her handbag for her cigarettes and a lighter. She lit up and blew white clouds of pungent smoke up into the air where they were lost in the mist.

"In the meantime, let's get the kit from the car." Bob said.

"What have you brought?" Sophie asked.

"Well, we've got a couple of cameras, same as always. But there's the shovels, trowels and divining rods that we're probably going to need today."

"Okey-dokey." Frank said, rubbing his hands together and striding back out to the car. Steve followed and a few minutes later, they returned, Steve carrying the camcorders under his coat and Frank with three shovels and two trowels across his arms.

"Done, Boss." Frank said triumphantly as he stood the shovels up against the wall. "And now?" He saw Bob glance over at Jackie who was leaning against the door jamb, gazing out across the glistening grass, enveloped in wisps of smoke.

"Now, we just need to wait."

"It feels different up here." Wendy whispered as the group entered the dormitory at the front of the building. Aside from the cameras that Steve and Frank now operated, the rest of the equipment had been left in the hallway and the team had headed straight upstairs. Jackie led the way, her hands in front of her and her fingers outstretched.

"Yeah, I feel it too." Sophie whispered. "It feels kind of...edgy."

"There's definitely a heaviness in the air in here." Bob said. "It's not that it's particularly cold or anything. It just feels kind of oppressive."

"We're not alone." Jackie said. "There are entities here that are using the energy to manifest. What you can feel is the drain of that energy from our realm. Keep an eye on each other. Some may try to use your energy directly. If you suddenly feel freezing cold, it could be that something's trying to latch on to you."

"Something?" Frank asked. He had the camera focussed on Jackie's face and he felt uneasy from the way she said the word. "I thought we were going to contact the kids up here?"

"That's the idea." Jackie replied. She turned her head slightly so she was looking directly into the camera. Frank stopped and stared into Jackie's eyes on the small screen. "But I'm not sure that it's only the children who are with us right now."

"Is it The Fallen?" Wendy asked while looking around the room. "Is it Curwen-Oakes?"

"Whatever it is, it's keeping its distance for the time being." Jackie said. She turned her head back to the room and closed her eyes. She raised her hands higher in front of her. The tips of her fingers twitched. "We're being watched. There is a dark force here. But it's curious. It doesn't know what to make of us." She opened her eyes and turned to the rest of the group. "It could turn at any moment. I suggest we try and communicate with the children quickly before it learns what we're here to do."

"Okay." Bob said decisively. "Let's do it." Jackie walked into the centre of the room and knelt on the floor, placing her hands on her thighs. The others stood in a semi-circle near the doorway, watching and waiting.

"Robert? George? Are you here?" She called out. "Come on sweetheart, let me know if you're here. I just want to talk with you."

"What the...?" Frank exclaimed as he wheeled round to face the doorway. There was a loud bang from somewhere at the other end of the building, as if a door had slammed. Frank stepped out into the corridor and swung the camera from side to side, looking for something that would account for the noise. He listened and could swear that he heard whispering from the bottom of the staircase. He turned back into the room and trained the camera back on Jackie.

"Come forward, little one." Jackie said as she held out her hand.

"Jesus, it just got really bloody cold in here!" Sophie said as she tucked her hands beneath her armpits.

"Yeah, I can see my breath." Dillon added as he blew out a cloud of vapour.

"Come on, my darling. I won't hurt you." Jackie continued. The whole group flinched as, from downstairs, they heard two bangs in quick succession and what sounded like someone running.

"Shit." Frank said. "Come on. Let's go see." With his free hand, he grabbed Dillon's sleeve and the pair of them went out into the corridor.

"It's got darker in here." Frank said as he mentally compared what he was seeing along the passageway with the same view just a few moments earlier.

"Listen." Dillon hissed and grabbed Frank's arm to halt him in his tracks. They both froze. Although they couldn't see around the corner down the staircase, they could hear footsteps coming up.

"Wait." Frank whispered. "Watch." He pointed the camera along the corridor toward the top of the staircase, half expecting someone to come into view. Both he and Dillon jumped as they both heard and saw a door at the other end of the corridor swing open and then suddenly slam shut.

"That wasn't the bloody wind!" Frank said. He was answered by a sudden chorus of frantic whispering that crept up the stairwell. They heard scratching noises either on or under the floor and the walls made cracking sounds like they were being pushed from the inside. An ethereal half-scream, half-whine echoed through the building and the pair quickly turned and went back in to the dormitory.

"Tell me how I can help you." Jackie said. She was still kneeling on the floor with her hands in her lap but her gaze was focussed on a space just in front of her.

"What's happening?" Frank asked.

"She's made contact." Bob whispered. "But it's neither Robert nor George. It's a new one. A kid of about the same age we think, maybe a bit older. And it sounds like there are others but they're hanging back."

Jackie studied the poor creature that was standing in front of her. Her heart was full of pity for the boy. He was definitely one of the most heart-breaking apparitions she had ever seen. The dirty, ragged clothing hid a body that was in a severe state of decomposition. Stick-thin limbs protruded from tattered sleeves and trouser legs. Brown, putrefying flesh barely concealed the bones that in places protruded from tears in what remained of the skin. The filthy, matted hair, some of which was missing from areas of the skull where the scalp had rotted away, did little to soften the image of the child's face. The shrunken features of the boy framed the black, empty eye sockets and absence of a nose like a hideous expressionist painting. The thin lips curled back from discoloured teeth as the spectre spoke.

"Buried... Prison... Release."

"Christ, did you hear that?" Sophie asked. Her skin shivered and the hairs on her arms stood on end. Although the rest of the group couldn't see the boy, the voice entered their heads like a faint sound at the end of a breaking phone line.

"I heard it." Dillon replied.

"And me." Said Wendy. "But I couldn't make out the words."

"What do you want us to do?" Jackie asked. "How can we help you?" The room seemed to fill with whispering as though a thousand voices all tried to talk over one another in a desperate effort to be heard.

"This doesn't feel good." Wendy said. "There's something wrong here."

"Bloody Hell." Both Dillon and Frank swung round to face the doorway behind them as a scream echoed through the building. The scratching and whispering intensified.

"Something just grabbed my sleeve!" Steve wheeled round and looked behind him but saw nothing. "I swear it, something just grabbed my sleeve and tried to tug me away."

"I'm getting a headache." Wendy said and she held her hands over her ears. As she did so, her eyes widened and she looked round quickly at the others. "Put your hands over your ears." She ordered. "You can hear them much clearer."

"God, you're right." Bob replied as he closed his ears with the palms of his hands. "I can hear them. All of them. I can make out a few words. 'No' is being shouted a lot."

"And 'Fallen' as well." Wendy added. She turned to look at Jackie. "Jackie, is The Fallen coming?"

"Show me, dearest. Show me where." Jackie leant closer to the boy. She became aware of a smell of damp earth and rotting flesh that appeared to emanate from the wraith-like figure. There was no doubt in her mind that this boy was one of the ones who had been murdered by the Headmaster and buried somewhere close by. "Please, show me." She pleaded. The boy turned his head to face the back of the building and then he raised a bony arm to point to the grounds at the back. An anguished howl rang out in the room and the pile of twisted bedframes in the far corner toppled forward, crashing to the ground and momentarily drowning out the cries that filled the air.

"In the other room." Jackie said as she rose to her feet and strode past the group. She led the way through the washroom to the second dormitory and the rest of the team quickly followed, their eyes flitting around in the direction of the myriad noises that seemed to come at them from all sides. Wails and crying could be heard from downstairs. Pleas of 'No' and frantic scratching in the walls seemed to follow them. Their clothes were tugged by unseen hands. Their hearts pounded, their breathing was quick. Fear gripped their minds and every shriek, every bang made their insides somersault.

"In here." Jackie commanded as she led the way across the second corridor into the dormitory at the back of the Hall. The room was full of whispers, a cacophony of anguished, babbled voices.

"I think The Fallen is coming." Wendy said to Jackie. All the voices she had heard in her head seemed to be screaming that The Fallen was coming. A hundred voices crying out in fear, crying out in unison, warning them, pleading with them to flee.

"No, my dear. It was here all along." Jackie said. "It's been with us from the moment we set foot in this place."

"We'd better be quick then." Bob said. "We need to find these kids and call in the police before anything seriously bad happens." Jackie walked to the centre of the room and knelt on the floor again.

"Come back, child. Show me outside where I can find you." She looked around the room for the boy as the whispers, howls and cries intensified. Three bangs echoed along the corridor followed by footsteps running. The air in the room became almost too heavy to breathe and the temperature fell lower.

"Look!" Wendy cried and pointed out the window she was standing near. The others rushed to her side and Jackie rose to her feet. She jogged back to the window where the team were staring in disbelief at the faint spectral form of a boy. He stood in front of the fountain looking up at them.

"That's the same boy I saw when we were here before." She said, her voice breaking.

"Are you quite sure?" Jackie asked, not taking her eyes from the corpse-like vision standing on the wet grass.

"Absolutely. I'll never forget those eyes."

"Or lack of them." Frank muttered, his unblinking stare fixed firmly on the apparition.

"Well, that's the same spirit I was just talking to in the other room." Jackie said.

"What was it that he said in there?" Bob asked. "We couldn't quite make it out."

"He said 'buried, prison, release'." Jackie answered.

"And now he's showing us where he was buried." Sophie said. "He was asking us to find him and release him from his prison in the ground. We gotta get down there and get digging!"

"Yeah, and quick before The Fallen catches up with us. Old Curwen-Oakes is gonna be pretty pissed when he finds out what we're going to do." Said Frank. He looked at Bob and Jackie for agreement. They were both still staring out the window at the boy.

The team jumped and turned their attention from the window to the end of the room where several doors on the old metal lockers slammed shut and bounced open again. A shriek rang out through the room and a blast of cold air swept through the space and out the door. The whispers grew in intensity and the words 'No' and 'The Fallen' could be heard as clear as day.

"He's gone." Dillon said as he glanced back out of the window to where the boy had been standing. The others looked out and scanned the overgrown gardens for any sign of the child.

"Right. That's it. Let's get the hell out of here." Frank said, raising his voice to be heard over the noises that filled the room. He turned from the window and made for the door.

"We're not leaving, are we?" Sophie asked, surprised at Frank's rapid decision.

"No. Not yet." Frank replied as he reached the doorway. "We've gotta find that kid first."

The group paced around the building to the fountain at the back. Bob, Frank and Dillon were each carrying a shovel and Sophie had a trowel in each hand. Steve had both camcorders and was using them simultaneously to record everything that was happening. Although it was still misty and the drizzle was falling in waves on the cool breeze, the air was lighter and somewhat warmer than in the Hall. Everyone felt a sense of relief to be out of the building but they hadn't escaped it completely. Cries and loud thuds could still be heard echoing inside. The myriad spirits that were trapped in the ruin were shaking the walls and pleading with the group to turn and run. Their shrieks were warning the team about The Fallen and the group were paying full attention to the fact that time was not on their side.

"He was standing right here." Frank said as he halted on the very spot where the boy had stood. He looked up at the window from where they had seen him and at the broken fountain behind him to double-check his bearings. Jackie nodded.

"Yes. This is the spot. I can feel…" She stopped mid-sentence as an expression of concentration came over her face.

"Well, we'd better get started." Sophie said and pointed to the shovel that Frank was holding. Frank looked at Bob for his consent and as Bob nodded, Frank plunged the edge of the shovel through the blades of wet grass and into the earth beneath. Bob and Dillon stepped up and joined in. Soon a pile of sodden earth had accumulated by the side of a wide hole. The screams and noises from the building continued all the while and as Wendy looked up at the windows, she gasped and felt as though her heart skipped a beat. In every dark window, she saw misty white forms sweeping back and forth. Sometimes one would stop and appear to look down at her from the window, before it evaporated back into the darkness. It seemed as though every spirit in the entire building had manifested to warn them of The Fallen. Their sobs, whines and howls reverberated through the empty rooms.

"Quick." She said as she turned back to the three men digging. The fine rain had soaked their hair and clothing. Mud was forming clods on their boots. Bob had to keep stopping to wipe the droplets from his glasses. They worked to the horrific accompaniment of the departed spirits of the Hall wailing and thumping.

"Whoah." Frank barked as his shovel hit something solid. In the split-second the shovel came to a halt, all the noise from the Hall stopped abruptly. Bob and Dillon stopped digging. A deathly silence descended over the site.

"They've all gone." Wendy whispered as she scanned every window for a sign of the ghostly white spectres.

"It's quiet." Steve whispered. The group stood still and listened. He was right. There was no sound. No breeze rustling the vegetation. No screams or noises from the building. No birds. The only thing they could hear was their own heavy breathing and their heartbeats drumming in their ears.

"There's something here." Frank said as he scraped the shovel against the object he had hit.

"Pass me a trowel." Bob said as he held out his hand to Sophie.

"Please." Sophie said, passing one of the trowels to Bob. He smiled.

"Thank you very much, Sophie dearest." He replied before turning his attention back to the hole. He knelt in the mud and began scraping the earth from around the end of the shovel that Frank was still holding.

"It looks like a slab of slate." He said as he continued to carefully remove the soil from the smooth, dark grey surface.

"There's an edge here." Frank said as he moved the shovel back and felt it slip down into earth again.

"Follow it round." Bob instructed, waving the blade of the trowel to illustrate his order. He stood up and stepped back from the brink of the hole as Dillon and Frank both traced the edge of the slate slab with their shovels.

"There's a break here but it looks like it's just a corner that's broken off." Dillon said as he identified a cracked section of the slab.

"That's it." Frank stepped back from the hole and looked down at the square line that he and Dillon had traced in the earth, following the outline of the slate. The slab measured around a metre square. A large enough piece of slate but relatively thin. One or two people at the most could easily lift it. The group stared at the stone for a few moments. They half-anticipated what they would find beneath and they each felt a conflict of intrigue and fear well up inside them.

"Okay." Bob said finally. "Let's lift it." He walked round the hole to join Frank and the pair slid the edges of their shovels under the lip of the slab.

"Ready? One, Two, Three." Bob said and they both levered the shovels against the ground. There was a sucking noise as the slate peeled away from the earth beneath and both men pushed down on the shovels as hard as they could. The slab slowly lifted upward and then, as if it was suddenly released, it was freed from the grip of the underlying earth and it rose freely.

"Grab it." Bob said as he and Frank held their shovels steady. Steve handed the two camcorders to Wendy as he and Dillon stepped forward and grabbed hold of either side of the slate. With Bob and Frank's help, they tilted the slab upright and then swung it back where it landed on the grass with a thud. A sudden rush of freezing air washed upwards from the hole like a tide and surrounded the members of the team, encircling and caressing each person in the group. They each reeled backwards from the icy draught but soon regained their composure and looked down into the pit.

"Oh my god." Wendy muttered. She raised her hand to her open mouth.

"Jesus Christ." Sophie mumbled. Her eyes were wide and fixed on the spectacle at her feet. The others gathered round the two women and stood, solemnly looking down at their discovery. The hole was full of bones that partially protruded from the soil but they seemed to be arranged in parallel lines. The onlookers could make out arms, legs and ribs but the most shocking thing they saw were the foreheads of three small skulls that emerged from the ground. The tops of eye sockets were visible and the three faceless skeletons seemed to gaze upwards at their discoverers.

"There are three of them." Steve said. No-one else said anything. They stared at the bones as they began to glisten in the rain that was washing them clean. The feelings that welled up as they looked upon the small skeletons were a mixture of shock, sadness and grief. But above all, they shared a sense of relief and achievement. They had fulfilled their objective. They had succeeded in rescuing these forgotten children from their eternity in the black earth, trapped in the grounds of the school where they had been murdered. And now, they could be given a proper burial. The team had granted freedom to the spirits that had spent decades tortured by the Headmaster in whom they had placed their trust. In the end, the children had won. Now the world would know what happened at this horrific place all those years ago. The children would be heard. At last, they would have a voice. People would learn of the horrors, the torture, the murders, the loss of innocents, the deceit and the death. The children would be nameless and faceless no more. They would be remembered.

Caught up in the rollercoaster of action and emotion, no one seemed to notice that Jackie had not said a word since Frank, Bob and Dillon had started digging. She had stood by at a distance, watching with a deep frown on her face and biting her bottom lip. She couldn't tell the others what it was that was troubling her. It escaped words. It was a general feeling of unease that she couldn't pinpoint the cause of. The only thing she knew was that it had something to do with these children buried by the fountain. Even as she looked down into the pit of bones, she couldn't express what it was that she was feeling. But she knew it was dark and very, very frightening. She stared into the eyeless faces and wrung her hands together.

"We'd best call the police." Bob said finally.

15

The police arrived at the Hall within an hour after Bob phoned them. The first car that arrived had two officers who, upon seeing the skeletons in the hole, immediately called for assistance. Three more cars then arrived, followed by a van and an unmarked vehicle, from which two detectives in suits emerged. The whole site was cordoned off. The hole too was surrounded by blue and white Police tape and a tent erected over the pit. After around an hour and a half of questioning, the detectives were happy to let the team of investigators go home. But only under the strict condition that they would remain in the area, should there be further questions. As far as the detectives were concerned, the discovery of these skeletons by supernatural means wasn't a particularly satisfactory explanation. But, for the moment at least, there didn't seem to be any other explanation for how the team had 'stumbled' across the three bodies.

Whether it was because of a tip-off or simply the result of a diversion of police resources to the site, the local media soon received word that something was happening at Trevalling Hall. The first reporters for local newspapers arrived in time to see three black body bags being carried from the tent to a waiting black van. The footage that appeared on the local news was grainy, having been filmed from beyond the boundary wall of the Hall, the camera crew hidden from view by the trees and thick undergrowth. Then, the story exploded and made the national news. A statement was released by the police which confirmed that the skeletons of three unknown males aged approximately nine or ten years old had been discovered at Trevalling Hall and that the remains had been taken away for forensic analysis. With an increase in public awareness of the case, the police knew that they were under pressure to produce results, so a team from the University of Exeter with ground penetrating radar equipment was brought onto the site to determine if there were any more hidden graves. In the meantime, the press learned who had made the discovery and the Exeter Society for the Paranormal was suddenly thrust into the limelight. Each member of the team was involved in interviews for newspapers, local television news and magazines such as Fortean Times who quickly latched on to the idea that the discovery had been made using contact with ghosts. Dillon and Wendy were somewhat reticent to appear on television and preferred to remain anonymous, but Bob and Steve lapped up the attention. It was what they had been working on for over the past decade. Bob especially. At last, his paranormal society had finally made a name for itself. He felt vindicated. All those people in the early days who mocked him should be laughing on the other side of their faces now. Particularly his ex-wife. And the parasite of a man she was with now. Finally, he had the last laugh.

After a couple of weeks of publicity, hype and local celebrity status for the Exeter Society for the Paranormal, the story gradually lost its vigour. No further graves were identified on the site. The public grew increasingly sceptical about how the bodies had been found. Obscure questions and even stranger answers and conclusions began to circulate on social media. Some of the comments turned nasty. Some people even said the whole thing had been a hoax. The newspapers and magazines lost interest in the story. After all, the old Headmaster and his wife were both dead. No trace of what became of the last cohort of students at the school could be found. But above all, no one knew who the children from the grave were. They had no families. No descendants. They were faceless. Nameless. And even though in the beginning when they were first discovered, the public cried out in pity, sympathy and remorse for the three small boys, the team of paranormal investigators were surprised and somewhat dismayed at how quickly they were forgotten. Bob lamented that in the wider world, empathy was a fickle thing. Especially if the pursuit of justice would take too much time, effort and money. Eventually, people stopped caring altogether and the press moved on to the next story to sell.

But that was when the dreams started.

November was well under way. The weather had been grim for the whole weekend. Cold, showery rain and blustery winds had drenched the city and stripped the last of the leaves from the trees. Now, black-brown rotting sludge, trampled underfoot and beneath the wheels of cars added an extra touch of grottiness to the overall, depressing vista. People were lamenting the end of the nice weather, the shorter days and the cold winds from the east. The conditions were however, normal for the time of year. But so was the annual tradition of moaning about them. In a few weeks, the Christmas decorations and lights would go up in the city centre and the public would once again have something to brighten their mood. Only a couple more weeks of grimness to endure. But it wasn't only the city centre that was suffering a bout of melancholy.

"Jesus, I'm bloody knackered." Frank mumbled. No one wanted to admit it but he did look like shit. Preparations for the season of joy started a heck of a lot earlier in the retail sector than most people realised. And Frank, being a manager, would be at the forefront of the planning to entice customers into the store and ensure sales met the forecast for shareholders. But that wasn't why he was tired.

"How come?" Sophie asked. Frank took a generous swig of his pint, set the glass back on the table, crossed his arms and let out a loud sigh.

"I keep having these sodding dreams about the kids at the Hall." He replied, the exasperation evident in his voice. "It's like, I could be dreaming about something, anything, like being on a beach or going to Disneyland or whatever."

"Since when have you ever wanted to go to Disneyland?" Sophie interrupted.

"Well, I don't." Frank said with a huff. "The point is that I'm having what anyone would call a 'normal' dream and then all of a sudden these three corpses turn up!"

"What? The three children? In your dream?" Steve asked.

"Yeah. All three. All bones and dead skin and no eyes and all that shit. I know they're from the dig because they all look like the ghost we saw out the window. All dressed in rags and everything."

"What happens in the dream when they turn up?" Wendy asked. Frank shook his head and chewed his bottom lip as though he was struggling to find the words.

"Then, it goes all bloody weird. Like dark and misty. And I can hear whispering but I can't make out the words. I can see them in the distance and it feels like they're trying to get closer. It feels like they're trying to call me closer. But I don't know. There's something feckin' freaky about them so I don't go any nearer. But I don't run away either. It's like I'm paralysed. Just standing there, looking at them. And then they all hold their arms up with their hands outstretched to me and I can, like, feel my own hand lifting up to reach out to them. And then I wake up."

"Sounds like the whole experience of the past few weeks has taken a toll on you." Bob mused. "Maybe you need a holiday. Clear your head. It's all been pretty hectic. And let's face it, discovering the bodies of three children on a ruined estate in the middle of Exmoor is bound to mess with your head."

"That's certainly true." Steve nodded. "We've all had a turbulent time recently. The investigation. The occurrences at the Hall. The discovery of the skeletons in the garden. The media attention and hype. Although it's been utterly fantastic on the one hand, it's also been a taxing time on the other. We're all tired. We've been put through our paces, both physically and mentally." He sat up straight in his seat and placed his hands on the table in front of him. "But it's done now. It's finished. We've collected the best evidence we've ever seen, made a discovery that's helped some poor souls to find peace and made the Exeter Society for the Paranormal famous. Even if only for a brief time."

"Yeah, you're right." Frank said with a sigh. "We've been living this one investigation for what feels like an age. I suppose because it's been at the forefront of our lives, it's been at the forefront of my dreams as well." He took another gulp of ale, satisfied both with the explanation that Steve had offered and the inevitability that, over time, the connection his mind had forged with the Hall would fade.

"How's Jackie?" Wendy asked. Since the last of the press interviews, no one had seen her.

"Strange." Bob replied thoughtfully. Then he chuckled. "I didn't mean to say that Jackie's strange!"

"Nah, you don't need to tell us that. We've known for years." Frank added. The group let out a round of sniggers.

"No, what I mean is..." Bob continued. "Well, I've been phoning her every couple of days and she's always seemed a bit, sort of distant on the phone."

"What do you mean 'distant'?" Sophie asked. It was evident to Dillon that Sophie cared a great deal for Jackie. After everything that Sophie had regaled him with based on Jackie's explanations of the Beyond, it didn't seem unreasonable that Sophie would regard Jackie as some kind of personal guru. Hearing that she wasn't her normal, albeit weird, self therefore caused a high level of concern in Sophie.

"Well," Bob sighed. "She's been out at her usual sites communing almost every day. That's a bit excessive, even for her." It was known by the group that Jackie would normally visit the Neolithic burial sites and stone circles near her home in Cornwall a couple of times a year. But recently, she had mentioned to Bob that she'd been out at those locations much more regularly. And not just in passing visits either. "Some days, she'd be there for four or five hours." Bob continued. "But she never told me why. She doesn't really say what she's doing there. Just that she has questions."

"What kind of questions?" Wendy asked abruptly. Dillon looked at her. She had an intense expression in her eyes. It seemed odd that she wanted to know what happened in Frank's dream, then how Jackie was and now the details of Jackie's communing with the old spirits with so much eagerness. Normally, Wendy was content to go with the flow and trust other people's decisions. It was unlike her to ask so many questions and Dillon got the impression that there was something playing on her mind.

"She didn't say." Bob replied with a shrug. "I get the feeling she didn't want to say. Not that she was trying to keep something secret or anything like that, but almost like it wasn't the right time for me to know. You get what I mean?" He looked round at the others. They seemed confused and concerned. Jackie wasn't usually so secretive and the increase in her supernatural activities was worrying. His gaze settled on Wendy. She was staring at the barely touched pint on the table in front of her and biting her lip.

"Wendy? Are you alright?" He asked. The others turned in their seats to see her and as she looked up, they could see the glistening lines of tears welling up in her eyes.

"Hey, hun? What's the matter?" Sophie asked as she reached out to wrap an arm around Wendy's shoulders.

"I don't know." She replied weakly. "I… I'm just scared I suppose."

"What's frightening you?" Sophie asked soothingly.

"Well," Wendy started. A tear rolled down her cheek and she sniffed. "It's just that… you know… We've freed those poor boy's spirits and that's great but… Well… Jackie's been really intense and I don't understand what's happening."

"There's nothing else happening, hun." Sophie leaned in and gave Wendy a hug.

"Yes there is." Wendy said. "It's like the ghosts of the Hall were trying to warn us of The Fallen and we ignored the dangers and went ahead and helped those boys. But what if we've angered The Fallen? What if Curwen-Oakes comes after us? What if Jackie's trying to understand more about everything because he's coming after us? What if the spirits of the boys are still here, getting into our dreams, to warn us that we're in danger?"

"We're not in danger, Wendy." Steve said reassuringly with a comforting smile.

"I don't know." Wendy sniffed again and wiped the tears from her cheeks. "I think we might be."

110

"How could you possibly know that?" Steve asked with a slow shake of his head and the same reassuring smile.

"Well, the dream that Frank has been having recently."

"They're just dreams, Wendy." Bob said calmly.

"But I've been having them too."

16

Sophie took Wendy home from the pub early. Despite everyone's best intentions and attempts, Wendy was still confused and frightened by what was happening. By ten o' clock, only the four men and the barman remained. The few other customers who had been in the pub earlier to escape the miserable weather outside had eventually decided that no time was going to be a good time to brave the elements to head home and that the sooner they got it over with, the better. Despite the lack of paying customers, the barman was happy to keep the lights on for the four regulars and the increasing number of pint glasses on the table in front of them was a pleasing, visual boost to his confidence that he was still making a profit.

"Not to put too fine a point on it but it's a bit fucked up, wouldn't you say?" Frank said. His speech was beginning to slur and now that the alcohol and circumstances had brought down his defences, Dillon caught a glimpse of the insecure melancholy that hid away in his core, masked by the jovial extrovert that he portrayed to the world.

"I know, man." Steve shook his head and reached out to pat Frank on the shoulder. He too was beginning to suffer the effects of having imbibed several pints and here again, Dillon could see his inner character emerging, a sort of aged Woodstock hippy who just wanted everyone to get along and everything to be cool.

"Any thoughts or suggestions about what's going on, then?" Bob asked. Although he had had the same number of drinks, or maybe more, as the other two, Bob still appeared to be sober. Frank and Steve rolled their eyes around to look at him.

"Well, Frank and Wendy's dreams only started recently, right?" Dillon said. He glanced over at Frank who gave a slow nod in response. Unlike Frank and Steve, Dillon had gone easy on the drinks. Because of his thin frame, he knew he couldn't drink too much, so he generally stuck to within his absolute limit of four pints over the course of an evening. Even that could be too much though and he seldom went beyond three. He could feel that the alcohol had slowed his reactions and numbed his feelings slightly but he still had full control of his speech and as his eyes moved around, he didn't feel as though his brain was struggling to keep up. "And there were no dreams before we found the skeletons?" Frank shook his head. "So, the dreams are linked in some way with having found those children's bodies."

"Ah, a logical approach. The mark of a true scientist." Bob said and rubbed his hands together. Dillon glanced round at Bob and for a moment felt as though he was in the presence of King Henry the Eighth. "I like this. Perhaps we can get to the bottom of what's going on through the application of the scientific method and logical reasoning." Frank and Steve both sat more upright in their seats and their eyes regained some of their former, sober sparkle. "So," Bob continued, folding his arms across his barrel-like chest. "We have determined that the dreams began *after* the discovery by the fountain. But... Do we know that Frank's dream is the same as Wendy's dream and that they have the same root cause?"

"Frank described his dream pretty graphically." Dillon said. "At least, enough for me to build up an image in my own mind. I'm sure that Wendy would have been able to do the same. If the dreams were too different, she would probably have not reacted in the same way. Therefore, I suppose we can assume that the dreams have sufficient similarities to conclude they are the same."

"Jesus Christ, Professor!" Frank laughed. "You're hurting my friggin' head! I'm going to need another drink before you lay any more of that kind of Mensa stuff on me!" Frank was loud enough that the barman could hear every word and as soon as Frank had uttered the words 'need another drink', he grinned and placed another glass under the pump.

"Okay." Bob said thoughtfully. "So the dreams are the same. They've both been dreaming about the boys coming back. Now we need to try and figure out why."

"You said they tried to reach out to you?" Steve said as he turned to face Frank. Frank nodded.

"Yup. Like they wanted something. They kind of held out their arms with their hands open. Like they were asking for something."

"Any thoughts about what they wanted?" Bob asked.

"Nope. Just that they wanted something from me."

"How did you *feel* at that point?" Steve asked. Dillon smirked at how Steve placed emphasis on the word 'feel', in a way not totally dissimilar to a New Age emotional therapist.

"Dunno, really." Frank replied. "It's like I said, I felt like I wanted to reach out my arm and take their hand but there was something really weird about the whole situation. It's like you're in a forest at night and you feel like there's a thousand pairs of eyes in the dark all watching you. It's that kind of feeling. Like, undirected fear.

113

Like a kind of unease at the situation but no clear reason why. You know what I'm trying to get at?" Frank looked up and smiled as the barman brought over another pint and placed it in front of him.

"Any more for any more, gentlemen?" He asked, looking round at Steve, Bob and Dillon. Both Steve and Dillon shook their heads but Bob nodded. Dillon didn't know whether to be surprised or not. Bob had six empty pint glasses in front of him that the barman stacked up and took away to make room for the seventh.

"Do you think it's that kind of feeling that's got Wendy so spooked?" Dillon asked.

"Maybe. Maybe." Frank nodded. "It's about that time that I wake up, so it's not a nice feeling and it kind of hangs around for a while. It's really difficult to get back to sleep afterward. You like, feel as though there's something in the room with you. Watching you. You know?"

"So." Bob said. "We've got matching nightmares that started around the same time and cause an unpleasant feeling of unease. Now then, you know what that sounds like to me?" He looked at the other three. Steve nodded as a broad smile spread over his face.

"Yeah… It's a message." He said.

"Exactly." Bob unfolded his arms and clapped his hands. "Now they're free from their tomb in the garden, those boys are trying to tell us something."

"Like the spirits in the Hall?" Frank added. "They were trying to tell us something, too."

"Yes. And what was it they were trying to say?" Bob asked, revelling in the positive direction this problem solving game was going in.

"They were trying to warn us of The Fallen. They were telling us to run. Both me and Frank actually heard them say that." Dillon replied.

"Precisely. Now then, let's put all these pieces together. Based on what Jackie said, we have a strong suspicion that Curwen-Oakes was trying to use Black Magic to open up the portal at the crossing of the Ley Lines. We believe that the purpose of these occult activities was to elicit information from the other side and he was using the bodies of the young boys at the school as vessels to communicate. We're pretty sure that the evil acts he carried out, the rituals of the Dark Arts, the torture and murders would've tainted his soul. He also committed suicide which may mean that his soul was trapped here. It wasn't his time to die so he may not have been able to cross over. We also know that over the past few hundred years, some of the spirits of people who have died in the Hall have remained because they have unfinished business. I refer once again to the ghost of the old soldier who Jackie met in the dormitory. Now, it may be that because the Hall is on such a powerful site with so much energy that these spirits could move from one plain to another quite easily. But they don't. And why? Because ever since Curwen-Oakes began his reign of terror, they've stayed to warn others about him. That's what the dreams are about. The boys are now free to add their voices to the chorus. Alexander Curwen-Oakes is The Fallen. He's got to be. And the worst thing about it is that he's still here."

"Well, that's all well and good, Boss." Frank said. "But what are we going to do about it?"

"Hmm…" Bob pursed his lips and frowned as he pondered the question. "Well, in my mind, there seems only one course of action to take."

"What's that then?" Frank asked, leaning forward out of curiosity.

"We've got to find Curwen-Oakes and confront him."

"Thanks for coming, Jackie." Bob said as he held open the passenger door of his car. The next morning after the revelation at the pub, Bob had phoned Jackie and told her everything; the shared dreams, the possibility that the boy's spirits were trying to warn the team about Curwen-Oakes and the idea to find where he was buried and conduct a ritual to help him cross over or, failing that, banish his spirit. Although she wasn't entirely sure of the idea, Jackie agreed that it couldn't hurt to find where Curwen-Oakes had been buried and carry out a ceremony. Bob spent the rest of the afternoon researching where the prisoners from Exeter prison would be interred and then he arranged to meet Jackie at Exeter train station on the Thursday morning.

"No problem." Jackie rasped as she folded down her pink umbrella and climbed in the car.

"So what do you think?" Bob asked as he slammed his door shut and took his glasses off to wipe the rain from the lenses.

"If we are right and the old Headmaster is The Fallen that we were warned about, then yes, this may be a way of dealing with him and sending him back to the other side." Jackie replied. She was staring out the windscreen and Bob put his glasses back on and looked at her. She seemed expressionless. Emotionless. Her comment was said without any feeling at all, as though she didn't really believe it herself. More disturbingly was the way she had said 'if we are right', which alarmed Bob because it cast doubt over the one and only hypothesis that they had. He decided it was better not to ask too many questions. Jackie would only put up with so much before she decided she'd had enough and that wasn't something anyone wanted to see. Or hear.

The station was located round the corner from Exeter prison and Bob drove past slowly, pointing it out as the place where Curwen-Oakes had taken his last breath before taking his own life. It was a large, red brick building with white stone blocks at the corners and around the barred windows. It still retained all its Victorian austerity from when it was built in 1850. They only had a glimpse of the main structure before they were driving past the intimidating outer walls, over thirty feet high. Bob continued to the Exeter Cemetery where he found that, following his suicide, Alexander Curwen-Oakes had been interred. The online burial records for the cemetery had been easy to navigate and thanks in part to Bob's tenacious research skills and the fact that Alexander Curwen-Oakes was quite an unusual name, it hadn't taken long to find the plot where he was buried.

"Here we are." Bob said as he steered the car into the cemetery. He parked close to the chapel where the World War One graves were arranged beneath a tall monument. Jackie got out and opened up her umbrella. She held it close to the top of her head so Bob could no longer see her face. He didn't realise that Jackie was using the umbrella not so much to hide her face but rather to block the sight of the hordes of wandering, lost souls who meandered endlessly around the cemetery. She knew she couldn't show any hint of being able to see or hear them. Although she was keen to help those in need, the sheer number of them in a graveyard would be simply overwhelming.

"So, we're looking for quadrant HD, in the lower corner of the site." Bob said as he consulted a printed map of the cemetery. He led the way along a tarmac path that glistened black in the drizzle. The misty rain added an even greater sombre feeling and as he walked, checking the map every few steps and looking around, he could feel the heaviness of the atmosphere. The skeletal trees no longer softened the vista as they would have done when they were in full leaf. Everything looked cold and still. The stones, streaked with rainwater faced him as silent monoliths, the names carved into their surfaces a reminder of the transience of life and that time will inevitably run out. Jackie followed close behind, keeping her eyes on the tarmac path in front of her. She could hear the voices, whispers, cries and sobs of the multitude that were gathered in that vast field of death and the sounds of misery tugged at her heart.

"I think it's down there." Bob halted and turned to his right. They had passed the Exeter Theatre Fire Memorial and the Garden of Remembrance that Bob had used as landmarks. Now they stood in the centre of a small square at the centre of a crossroads. Bob began to stride in the direction of the quadrant that he had highlighted on his map, eager to find the grave of Alexander Curwen-Oakes. He noticed that the graves in this area of the cemetery were much sparser in both their number and distribution. Looking forward in the direction he was headed, he saw that the stones became even more spread out with large areas of grass in between. It was the furthest corner of the cemetery from the entrance. More likely the plots were cheaper there, reserved for those who couldn't afford anywhere else or had died alone with no family to take care of the funeral. Perhaps they were also reserved for criminals or just people who were best forgotten. Like Alexander Curwen-Oakes.

"Shouldn't take long to find him." Bob said, waving his arm around at the few stones that occupied the near vicinity. He stuffed the map back into his pocket, wiped the water from his glasses and methodically began to check the name on each stone. Jackie waited, standing absolutely still, hidden beneath her umbrella.

"I've found him. Here he is!" Bob cried out after a few minutes. Jackie lifted the rim of her umbrella to see Bob standing around ten metres away next to a small, dark grey stone. He was smiling and pointing at it. Jackie walked over and stood looking down at the carved inscription.

"Doesn't say much, does it?" Bob said as they both read the name and the date. That was all there was; just the name Alexander Curwen-Oakes and the date he had died. No birthdate or even a comforting message such as 'Rest in Peace'. Just his name in life and the date he left it behind.

"It's got to be him." Bob mumbled. "There can't be that many people with a name like that who also happened to die at the same time, in the same place. It's got to be him."

"It is." Jackie said.

"Great." Bob said cheerfully, although he was picking up the fact that there was something not quite right with Jackie. She had lost all her humour and it dawned on him that ever since he had picked her up from the station, she hadn't stopped for a cigarette.

"What do we do now?" Bob asked, bending down to see Jackie beneath her umbrella.

"Nothing." Jackie replied. Bob stood up straight again and stared at the top of the umbrella, waiting for Jackie to continue. But she didn't. She just stood, staring down at the stone.

"Nothing?" Bob finally asked. "Why not?"

"Because he's not here." Jackie replied.

"I don't understand." Bob mumbled. He looked down at the stone. They were in the right place. It was the right name, the right date. It was him. There was no question about it. "Well, where is he, then?"

"He's not here in our realm." Jackie lifted the umbrella and turned to look up at Bob. "He's crossed over. He crossed over decades ago."

"But..." Bob stammered. "He can't have. He must still be here. All the spirits at the Hall said he was."

"Did they?" Jackie asked, squinting her eyes at him.

"Yeah. When we were there, they said The Fallen was coming. They all said it."

"Did they say his name?"

"Well...er..." Doubt crept into Bob's mind. He felt his stomach tense. He wracked his brain to remember everything that had happened at the Hall. Had the spirits mentioned Curwen-Oakes by name? No, they hadn't. HE had found the name of the old Headmaster. His team had put the pieces together, linking The Fallen with Curwen-Oakes. The association didn't come from the spirits in the Hall.

"You mean that Alexander Curwen-Oakes is not The Fallen?" He asked sheepishly.

"Despite his heinous crimes and depraved character, no." Jackie replied, not taking her eyes from him.

"So..." Bob started. "Who is The Fallen?" Jackie turned her head back to the stone and lowered the umbrella, hiding her from Bob's stare.

"Something much worse."

17

Sophie opened her eyes. She had been dreaming about being at a concert. The lights, the sound and the band were thrilling, exhilarating even. But not as thrilling as when the lead singer held out his hand and invited her up on stage to dance with him. As she danced, looking out across the sea of smiling faces in the audience all cheering her on, she heard the music crackle and spit from the huge speaker stacks either side of the stage. At first, she didn't pay any attention. The coloured lights and lasers still beamed through the air in the venue. The band and the audience were all jumping, smiling and shouting. But then she heard voices in between the crackling. Like distant voices in the static of long wave radio. Whispers. And the music broke up more and more frequently until eventually, all she could hear were the whispers through the speakers. The band and the crowd carried on regardless, but silent now. The guitarists posed, the drummer hit the skins and cymbals with overly exuberant abandon and the singer yelled into the microphone while punching the air with his fist in time to music that she could no longer hear. She didn't want to look out of place so she carried on dancing. But the whispering from the speakers grew louder. She couldn't make out the words but she recognised they were the whispers of a child. Something in her subconscious made a link with the boys at the Hall and she woke up.

Her bedroom was cold. That in itself wasn't unusual because, to save money, she always switched off the central heating before she went to bed. The boiler was on a timer so the heating would come on again at a quarter to seven in the morning, making the flat nice and toasty for when she got up for work. The fact that the heating hadn't come on and the room was cold hinted that it was still the middle of the night. She rolled over and glanced at the red digital display on her alarm clock. One fifty-eight. Although she wasn't particularly impressed at having woken up, she was happy that she still had plenty of time for a few more hours of good sleep before she needed to get up. If she had woken at around half past six, she would have been pissed off at having been cheated out of the last half an hour of sleep and with such a short time until the alarm sounded, she would have no hope of nodding off again. She licked her lips. They were dry. There was no way she could go back to sleep until she'd had a drink. She sat up in bed and reached out to the bedside table for the glass of water next to the alarm clock when she quickly pulled her arm back and tugged the duvet up under her chin. Her eyes fixed, unblinking at a silhouette standing in the shadow of its own dark presence a few feet from the end of her bed. The orange glow of the streetlights outside gently illuminated everything in the room; the furniture, the posters on her walls, her clothes thrown over the chair in the corner, but the silhouette was completely black. It was as though it consumed the light, reflecting nothing. Sophie felt her heart race. She slowly pulled her feet up toward her, bringing her knees up under her chin, further from the figure staring at her.

"Who are you? What do you want?" She cried, her voice cracking from fear. The figure stood still, silent and Sophie shifted herself back up against the headboard. From her slightly higher perspective, she could see that the figure was small and slight. It dawned on her that it was the silhouette of a child. A boy. Her mind clicked and the realisation that this was one of the spirits of the three boys from the Hall suddenly dawned on her. After all, Wendy and Frank had been having dreams about the victims buried in the grounds of the Hall. Was she still dreaming? Had she actually woken up or was this a dream like Wendy and Frank's? She lowered the duvet from under her chin and as she did so, the room filled with soft whispering. She recognised them as the sounds from the speakers at the concert. They were the same voices. But here, they were clearer. She still couldn't make out the words and she wondered if the whispering was being spoken in English but it was still too faint to tell. As the whispering continued, she felt her head start to swim. The fear slowly evaporated from her body and reality began to get fuzzy. She felt as though she was slightly drunk but she also felt happy and curious.

"You're one of the boys from Trevalling, aren't you?" She said. She leant forward slightly, lowering her face to the same height as she imagined where the eyes of the boy would be. That is, if she could see them. The boy remained still and didn't answer but the disembodied whispers continued to swirl around her.

"What's your name, hun?" She asked. There was no reply. She blinked rapidly to try and straighten her vision. "Don't be afraid. I won't hurt you. I want to help. Tell me how I can help you." Still there was no response and the whispering now felt as though it had impregnated her skull, seeping through the pores of her cranium. Sophie crawled out from under the bed covers and made her way down to the end of the bed so she was only a few feet from the dark form and looking directly into its face. She could smell damp earth and the sickly smell of decaying flesh.

"Have you come to warn me about The Fallen?" As soon as she asked that question, the whispering stopped. She froze. The figure slowly tilted its head to one side and a quiet, rasping, gurgling voice emanated from it.

Come with us.

Sophie watched as the boy turned and left the bedroom. She clambered off the bed, focussing on keeping her balance and went to the doorway. She saw the black shape of the boy walk along the hallway toward the front door. Just before the door, it stopped and turned. Although she couldn't make out any features, she knew it was looking back at her.

Come with us.

Sophie gulped. Her stomach was turning somersaults and her mind was spinning. She reached out for the doorframe for balance and although she knew she was holding on to it, she couldn't feel it. *'Am I dreaming?'* She thought as she tottered down the hallway. *'This can't be real. It doesn't feel real. I must be dreaming.'* She stopped as she saw the dark figure turn to face the front door and then walk straight through it as though it wasn't there. Sophie sped up along the hallway, banging into the walls on either side as she went. The hallway seemed to elongate and then shorten ahead of her, oscillating in time with her deep breathing. She reached the door and leant against it as she gasped for breath. It took three attempts for her to grab the handle and open the door. She stepped out onto the landing shared with the flat opposite and saw the boy descending the stairs. Grabbing hold of the bannister in front of her, she quickly made her way to the top of the staircase in time to see the boy disappear through the front door of the building. Slowly and carefully she navigated the stairs, one step at a time and opened the door. She didn't notice the freezing cold of the still, night air and nor did she notice the eerie silence that dominated the streets at that time of night. She glanced around, as the street bathed in the orange light of the streetlamps swam before her eyes. She spotted the boy. He was just turning the corner at the end of the road, heading in the direction of the river. She half tottered, half fell out of the doorway and tried as best she could to jog in a straight line after him. Reaching the corner, she saw the silhouette making its way toward the footbridge that crossed the river to the parkland on the other side. She stumbled after him, unaware that she was shivering all over and her hands had gone numb. White clouds of breath rose up in front of her face, disrupting her vision even further. It was like looking through a swirling, tumbling mist. She reached the steps of the footbridge and glanced up. The boy was already in the centre of the bridge, looking back at her.

Come with us.

Sophie clambered up the steps on all fours, swaying gently to either side until she reached the top. She looked across the bridge to the centre but the boy was gone. She stood looking around, breathing deeply but unaware of the pain in her throat caused by the stinging cold air.

"Where are you?" She called out. Her voice cracked and was filled with pity. "I want to help you. Don't go. Tell me what to do."

Come with us.

Sophie staggered toward the centre of the bridge where she had last seen the boy. She leant against the metal railing and as she did so, she looked down at the river. The surface of the water was obscured by a thin, undulating white fog and in the centre, right below her, the boy was standing, looking up at her.

"How did you get down there?" She asked as she leant over the railing. "Are you standing on ice?"

Come with us.

"What for? Where? Please tell me what you want me to do." Sophie called down. The boy held up an arm and reached out his hand to her. She felt a rush of warmth flood through her body. At last, in that moment, she felt that she understood everything that Jackie had told her. It wasn't just that she understood the words that Jackie had said. She could *feel* the truth. Somehow, the spirit below her was infusing her with the truth. The inevitability of death. It was nothing to be feared. It was just a natural progression to a previous state of existence. Life and being alive was the aberration. Death was the normal state. The ethereal existence before birth and after death was the proper way of things.

Her vision began to fill with colours that had no defined origin. At first, the glowing lights softly appeared in her peripheral vision. Then, they encroached further, filling her surroundings with beauty. She looked around at the dark sky as a kaleidoscope of colour flashed and glided before her eyes. A smile spread over her lips and a tear fell down her cheek. It was beautiful. It was perfect. She looked down at the boy in the mist and saw that he had been joined by the other two. All three stood in a row looking up at her and now she could see their features clearly. Their skin was smooth and plump, their clothes neat and tidy. Their hair was perfectly combed and their eyes sparkled. All three were smiling at her. The boy in the middle, the one she had followed, still had his arm raised and his hand outstretched to her and as she watched, the three started to slowly sink down into the mist.

"Wait!" She cried out. "Wait. Don't go!" She clambered up onto the railing and swung her legs over. In one decisive movement, she pushed off with her hands and fell. A split second later and the world disappeared. She was surrounded by freezing, black water but she could neither feel the cold nor see the darkness. She felt warm from an inner glow and she was surrounded by bright colours. It was utterly beautiful. She wondered if this was what being back in the womb was like. The three boys appeared in front of her, seeming to hover in the swirling colours. They were smiling and their eyes reflected the various bright hues. Two of them held out their hands and Sophie reached out, placing her hands in theirs. She felt them close their hands around hers. And then she felt their grip tighten. As their clasp bordered on painful, she looked down at the hands holding her and, to her horror, saw they had lost most of their flesh and colour. Now, she was gripped by skeletal fingers with wasted tissues hanging from membranous sinews. She looked back up at the faces of the two boys and she was filled with panic. The colours in the water faded to a cold, dirty grey and then she felt the stabbing pain of the cold all over her body. The faces that grimaced at her were the decaying visages of the corpses at the Hall. Black teeth grinned at her and eyeless sockets watched with morbid curiosity as Sophie struggled in vain to escape. And then she felt a burning sensation arise in her chest. She needed to breathe. The feeling intensified, like a fire burning her inside. She tried to kick upward to escape the vice-like grip that held her tight and the cadaverous forms responded by pulling her down further. She felt the third boy grab her ankles and join his dead brethren in bringing her deeper and deeper down into the murky depths. Sophie's lungs felt as though they were about to implode and when she could hold on no longer, she opened her mouth and took a huge breath. The disgusting taste of the cold river water filled her mouth. Earthy, rancid, toxic. But it was nothing compared to the pain of the water rushing down her throat and filling her lungs. She gulped more and more as her body instinctively fought for air. More water rushed in and as her brain was starved of life-sustaining oxygen, her vision began to tunnel. As everything went black and all sensation ceased, Sophie stopped struggling.

The three spectres continued to hold on to Sophie's lifeless body. They stared with an emotionless gaze into her wide, dead eyes. They were intrigued. Fascinated. They couldn't quite understand. Where had the light in Sophie's eyes gone? Where did she go? It was a strange thing for them indeed. They had never seen death before. It was something that they had not experienced. Something that seemed alien to them. Something that they knew they had to investigate further. To see more. To know more.

Finally sensing that Sophie was no longer with them and that all they were holding onto was the fleshy vessel that Sophie once occupied, they let her hands and wrists go. They watched as Sophie's body sank to the bottom of the river and lay face down in the mud. And then they faded away.

18

By mid-Monday morning, they had all heard the news. Wendy was the first to find out. She had tried repeatedly calling Sophie on her mobile when she hadn't arrived for work on the Friday morning. Reporting that something strange was going on to her line manager, he volunteered to drive out to Sophie's flat to check she was okay. He got no response at her front door so he then tried her neighbour. A young woman answered and told him that Sophie had gone out. When the neighbour had left for work in the morning, she had noticed how cold the landing was and then saw that the door to Sophie's flat was wide open. After knocking and calling out, the neighbour entered to find the flat empty. She was reluctant to close the flat door fully in case Sophie didn't have her keys but remembering that she had been entrusted with a spare, she closed it anyway. She was more puzzled and concerned that the front door downstairs had also been left open. Sophie never left the front door open. She was always careful when entering the building to check around her that no weirdos had been following and would bundle her into the small hallway to rob or rape her. And when she left, she always tugged the door three times to make sure it was firmly shut. Sophie's manager recognised that something bad may have happened to Sophie so he phoned the police to file a missing person's report.

When Sophie didn't turn up all day Friday and Saturday, the police began a more thorough search and issued a photo of her on social media, asking for anyone who had seen her to come forward. Saturday came and went and still there was no sign of her. But then the police received the phone-call they had been dreading.

Two middle-aged men out fishing on the Sunday morning had spotted something in the river. An indistinguishable mass had washed up against the opposite bank of a shallow bend in the river. When they recognised that the shape had shoulders and hair, they immediately called the police. Sophie's body was recovered just over a kilometre from where she had drowned.

The papers the next morning reported the gruesome discovery on the front page. The coroner had estimated the time of death at some point between ten o'clock in the evening the previous Thursday and four o'clock in the morning on the Friday. Although Sophie had been in the water for almost three days, the cold had delayed the process of decay. Her skin was blanched almost pearl white but her body was still in such a good condition that a full post-mortem examination concluded that there were no signs on the body of an attack and that the cause of death was drowning. Based on the coroner's evidence and that Sophie left her flat alone, in nothing more than her pyjamas and in the middle of the night, leaving all the doors open, the police concluded that she had committed suicide by jumping off one of the bridges further upstream. The shock of the cold water would have paralysed her body and, gasping for air but inhaling only water, she would have drowned quickly.

Wendy saw the front page of the paper when she popped into her local convenience store for her morning coffee on the way to work. It was the photo of Sophie that the police had issued as part of their missing person campaign that first caught her eye but the headline cut through her like a knife; 'Missing woman found in River Exe'. She fainted there and then and when she came to, one of the shop assistants helped her to get home. No sooner had she sat down on her sofa, shaking all over, when her line manager called to tell her that he'd seen the news in the paper and that she should stay home that day. Hearing it from someone else made it all the more real and after hanging up the phone, Wendy sat and cried for the rest of the day.

Bob also saw the headline on the front page. He immediately called Steve, who then called Frank. Then he phoned Wendy and Dillon.

"Hello?" Dillon answered his mobile with an air of suspicion in his voice. No one ever called his personal mobile. Not during the day anyway. His parents only called him from the south of France once a month to check he was alright. And they only ever called him during the evening. Never while he was at work. Dillon suspected it might have been a cold caller and he was surprised to hear Bob's voice on the other end of the line.

"Hi Dillon." Bob said flatly. Dillon immediately sensed from the tone of Bob's voice that something was wrong.

"What's up?"

"They've found Sophie." At hearing those words, Dillon froze. It was clear from the sadness in Bob's tone that she had not been found alive and well. Wendy had been worried about Sophie on Friday and although the police had issued a missing person case the following morning, everyone was confident that she would turn up unharmed. They speculated that she had just taken off early on Friday morning to go and see her parents in Saltash, near Plymouth. They thought perhaps there was a family emergency that she needed to attend to. But they all agreed it was strange that she hadn't called or told anyone. They were all in denial at the merest hint of a prospect that something bad may have happened to her and all through Saturday and Sunday, they clung on to hope.

"Dead?" Dillon mumbled in disbelief.

"Yes. I'm afraid so." Bob sighed. "Her body was found downstream in the river yesterday morning. It's in the local paper. You haven't seen it?"

"No. No… I don't read the newspapers." Dillon replied as he held the phone between his ear and shoulder and leant forward to type the web address of The Exeter Daily into his browser. He scrolled down past the banner at the top of the screen and stopped abruptly when Sophie's photo appeared. It was the top story in the column and he clicked on the headline next to it. He read the short article quickly while Bob stayed silent on the phone.

"Oh my God." Dillon whispered. He felt an ache in the pit of his stomach as though he'd just been punched and his fingers felt numb.

"I know. It's tragic news. Not what any of us expected to hear." Bob said quietly.

"How's Wendy?" Dillon asked as his mind clicked back from shock to reality.

"Well, as you can imagine, she's utterly devastated." Bob said. "I spoke to her just before calling you. She's not in work today. But she's in a dreadful state. I told her I'd go round to see her after I'd spoken with you. I'll take her out to a café or something. Get her out of her house. Try and just, you know, help her through it."

"Jesus." Dillon mumbled.

"Yeah, I know. Steve just can't believe it. I haven't spoken to Frank yet. Steve was going to give him a ring."

"She was in the river?" Dillon muttered, trying to come to understand what the hell had happened.

"That's where they found her." Bob sighed again. "I suppose that, for what it's worth, it's a blessing that the police found no evidence of foul play and aren't looking for anyone else in connection with her death."

"Suicide?" Dillon asked in disbelief.

"Seems that way, yeah." Bob replied. "But it's weird if you ask me. No note or messages. No texts to say goodbye and definitely no hint in the last few weeks or months even, that she was even considering this. It's just totally out of the blue."

"Yeah." Dillon said flatly. As he pondered Bob's words, something that Sophie had said at the hall shot through his mind; *"I don't know about you, but after everything Jackie's told us, I almost can't wait to fucking die."*

"I think it's important that we still meet up tomorrow evening. As per usual. We need to get together and come to terms with Sophie's loss as a group, a team. And we need to show support for each other. To help us through this. Show that we're there for each other. Especially Wendy. She and Sophie were very close. Very close. She's taken it really badly. I mean, really badly. We need to be there for her."

"Yeah. I agree." Dillon said. Although he knew that Wendy would be devastated by the loss of her best friend, he felt a need, a compulsion to see her. He felt like he wanted to be there for her. To comfort her. To provide the shoulder for her to cry on. He wanted to hold her and keep her warm and safe and tell her everything was going to be okay.

"Okay." Bob said. "Well, take it easy, mate. Do what you need to and I'll see you tomorrow night."

"Yeah. And thanks for letting me know, Bob."

"No problem. I just wish I had been calling with better news."

19

"I still can't believe it." Frank said, slowly shaking his head from side to side. The five friends all sat around their usual table in the Waggon and Horses, half-heartedly sipping at their pints. The barman had offered their first drink on the house in commiseration. He didn't say much other than that Sophie was 'a lovely lass' and she would be very sorely missed. He knew not to intrude too much on the group's grief. Bob, Steve and Frank kept hesitating for minutes on end, staring into space or at the table as though they were trying to come up with a plan to fix everything and bring Sophie back. Then they would shake their heads and take a sip of ale. Wendy sat hunched in her seat looking downcast. She looked gaunt, as though she had lost the will to live. Her eyes, still bloodshot from all the crying, peered out over dark circles and sunken cheeks. It was clear that she had been neither eating nor sleeping since she heard the news. Her hair was unwashed and she had neglected to put on any make-up. Although the make-up that she did wear was very subtle, the absence of it made her skin and her lips appear paler as though all the blood had drained from her face.

"I still can't understand why she didn't say anything." Wendy said. Her voice was weak, almost a whisper and she didn't lift her eyes from the glass that stood on the table in front of her.

"I mean, she was fine on Thursday. She didn't say anything. She was bitching about one customer who was giving her a hard time and said that she had to sort out a load of paperwork on Friday. So she clearly wasn't planning this."

"Sadly, we'll never know what happened." Bob said. "I don't believe anyone was to blame. It was no-one's fault. It was a decision, possibly on the spur of the moment, that she made completely by herself."

"But why?" Frank responded. "She was such a strong character. She had everything going for her and everything to look forward to. I mean, Christ almighty, what possible reason did she have to... you know." He looked over at Wendy. He was mindful to avoid any mention of the words 'kill herself' or 'commit suicide'.

"We don't know." Steve replied softly. "And it won't do us any good to sit here trying to work it out or understand what was going through her mind. We need to come to terms with what has happened and accept that Sophie is no longer with us. We shouldn't speculate or blame ourselves in any way over this tragic incident. It will drive us insane. That's not what she would have wanted. She loved us all. In her own way. We were her family and we knew her best. We need to make sure we remember Sophie for all the good times we had with her. The fun, the laughter, the excitement, the jokes and jibes. That's what we need to cling on to."

The rest of the group nodded. Steve was right. There was no good to be had in dwelling on Sophie's death. It was best to remember her in life. Frank stood and went to the bar. He returned a few minutes later with a circular plastic tray and five shot glasses filled to the rims with a viscous black liquid.

"Here we go then." He said as he placed a glass in front of the others and one for himself. He sat down and placed the tray on the floor beside him.

"What is it?" Dillon asked.

"Black Sambuca." Frank answered with a smile. "I thought it would be a fitting toast for a Goth." He lifted the glass before him high into the air and paused as the others did the same. He took a deep breath, straightened his back and let out a long sigh, focussing his mind on the moment.

"To Sophie." He said firmly.

"To Sophie." The others repeated in chorus and together they drained the contents of the glasses. At that moment, the pub door opened and Jackie walked in.

"Well, hello." Frank said cheerfully as though the black Sambuca had had an immediate effect on his mood. "I can't remember the last time you joined us for a drink."

"It's been a while." Jackie rasped. She headed straight for Wendy, leant over and gave her a big hug. Wendy buried her face into Jackie's shoulder and held her tight. Dillon was close enough to hear Jackie whisper 'I'm sorry, love. But she's in a better place now.' Wendy pulled away and looked up into Jackie's face. Jackie gave a broad smile and the look in her eyes seemed to give Wendy immediate comfort. It was a look of knowing. 'Trust me, love' she said as her smile broadened further.

"What are you drinking, Jackie?" Frank asked as he stood to pull over a chair from a nearby table.

"Glass of white wine, my dear." She replied, taking off her coat and hanging it on the back of the chair. "Make it a large one." Frank winked and went to place the order at the bar.

"Nice to see you, Jackie." Steve said.

"Yeah. It's good to be here with you all. Shame it ain't under better circumstances."

"Nevertheless, you are very welcome." Steve added.

"Truth is," Jackie started as Frank returned with her wine, "Bob called me yesterday afternoon and told me what happened." She reached out and held Wendy's hand. "I spent the whole night thinking about everything and decided it best to talk it over with you. I know you all meet here every Tuesday evening so I decided I'd get the train and join you."

"What was it you were thinking about?" Bob asked.

"Well, since we found those three boys in the grounds of the old school, I've been visiting with the old spirits." She paused to take a sip of wine. She swallowed a mouthful and winked at Frank.

"Yes, you did say you'd been going up to the old stone circles quite regularly. But you never said why." Bob confirmed.

"That's because I didn't really know why." Jackie replied. The others watched her closely. She had a way of speaking and a manner that commanded attention. No one was in any doubt that Jackie knew more than the rest of them put together. She had, after all, acquired her insights and knowledge from a higher source.

"So, were you looking for something?" Steve asked.

"Yes. Answers. But I didn't want to say anything until I was sure I was asking the right questions. I'm pretty sure now that I know what's going on. But I was hoping for more. In light of recent events though, I think it's best to tell you all I've learned."

"You have our full attention." Bob said.

"Do you all remember when we were in the chapel in the house and talking with the children the first time?" She paused to look round at the others. They all nodded. "And do you remember all the children ran away just before we heard three loud bangs?" Again, the others nodded. "It played on my mind for days afterward. What was it that had arrived and scared off the others? When we thought that The Fallen was more than likely the vengeful, twisted spirit of Alexander Curwen-Oakes, we presumed it was he who had arrived and frightened the children. We pieced together the few pieces of the puzzle we had and concluded that he was using the young schoolchildren as vessels to contact the other side and elicit information from the dead. We found out that some of the children had died during the ritual. They just weren't strong enough to survive the ordeal. And then we discovered that their old Headmaster had buried them somewhere in the grounds. We were successful in finding the remains of three of them. And that reminded me of the three bangs in the hall. Three bangs, three victims. Was it a coincidence? And if it wasn't, then why were all the other children's spirits scared of these three?" She paused, almost for dramatic effect and took another sip of wine.

"Now, do you remember when we opened up the grave of the three boys?" The others nodded, but now they were all wide-eyed in fascination. "And when the slab was lifted, do you remember the cold presence that rose up and enveloped us all? We believed that we had found Curwen-Oakes' victims and that we'd freed their spirits which had been trapped in the earth since they were buried."

"But you don't believe that?" Frank asked. Jackie frowned and sighed.

"There was definitely something trapped in that grave." She said. "It was after the discovery that your dreams started, yes?" She looked at both Frank and Wendy. They nodded.

"I've been having them too." Steve said. Everyone looked at him. "It's not just a one-off either that may have been subconsciously inspired by Frank's description of his dreams. I've had the same dream almost every night for the past week and a bit. Every time, I see those boys and I hear whispering. But recently, in the last couple of days, the whispers have been louder and the boys have been a bit closer. I've heard them laughing as well." He stopped and looked at the others. Bob reached out and patted him on the shoulder.

"The thing that confused me," Jackie continued after swallowing another mouthful of wine, "was that, if the spirits were freed from the grave when we opened it up, why were you dreaming about them at all? Surely they should have crossed over and moved on? They were hanging around for some reason. And we believed that they, like the other spirits in the hall, were trying to warn us of The Fallen – of Alexander Curwen-Oakes. But there's one huge problem with that. Curwen-Oakes has crossed over. He's not here. Bob and I went to visit his grave last Thursday and I couldn't sense him at all. He's not here."

"But…" Wendy stuttered. "If we thought that the spirit of Curwen-Oakes was The Fallen, and he's crossed over, then who is The Fallen?"

Jackie sighed. She placed her hands in her lap and interlocked her fingers. She tilted her head back and looked up at the ceiling.

"It's not *who*, it's *what*." She said. The others watched her, frozen in a moment of confusion, waiting for some explanation. She frowned and lowered her head, looking from one bewildered face to the next.

"I had my suspicions that something wasn't quite right. But I didn't know what or why. There was something I sensed, something I felt that I just couldn't explain. It wasn't like the feeling from other spirits who I normally communicate with. In my time, I've felt all manner of different emotions from a whole range of different apparitions. But nothing like this. And that alone made me very nervous. That's why I visited with the old ghosts of the circles. To ask them questions. To find out what they knew. To get some answers. And I'm afraid it's not good. You see, we were right that Alexander Curwen-Oakes was indeed using rituals based on necromancy, harnessing the power where the Ley Lines crossed under the cellar. He used the boys as vessels that spirits from the Beyond could use to return through the portal and occupy. Then, using the children's own voices, he could make the spirits speak and answer his questions. But the whole thing is very hit-and-miss. I'm not saying that Curwen-Oakes was an amateur. He really knew his stuff. The rituals he was employing were top level, super difficult and dangerous Black Magic. But inevitably, it's just like using a Ouija board. You can open the gate, but you can't control who's going to walk through."

"So, who did come through?" Wendy asked.

"The first thing you need to understand is the nature of the other realms. We are only familiar with the one we are in right now; the realm of the physical and the living. We are souls trapped in bodies for the duration of our lifetime. But when the body dies, the spirit is released and can cross the dimensional barrier to the Beyond. Ancient oracles and magicians only saw glimpses of it. They called it the 'Afterlife'. But that's a massive understatement. They thought there was only one realm. But the number is infinite. The dimension that we leave to enter this realm of the physical when we're born is the same as the one to which we will return when we die. It's the closest to us. It's relatively easy for spirits to slip into this dimension and occupy a child before it's born. It's about the only thing the Catholics have got right. What they call The Quickening is the moment that the spirit enters the developing baby. From that point, it's trapped until death where it will cross back over to where it came from. For a long time, people didn't make the link between the realms where spirits came from and where they eventually go to. But it's the same place. It's just that, because people live a life and have a personality and a 'soul', explaining where that goes after death was more important than understanding where it came from in the first place. That's why the realm closest to us is called the Land of the Dead in so many ancient

133

texts. But there are others. And once a spirit has crossed over to the Land of the Dead, there's nothing stopping it, unlike here in the physical realm, from slipping from one realm to another."

"What are the other realms like?" Steve asked. Jackie's descriptions were speaking directly to his creative mind.

"Unlike this one, others are timeless, endless manifestations of beauty. Not just visually but the beauty flows through the spirit, nourishing it. All these realms and dimensions have been in existence since before the birth of our Universe. Only the one we're in now is tied to the origin of the Universe. The Big Bang as the scientists call it. That was the origin of this dimension. Other dimensions and realms can appear and disappear, morphing or growing out of those that already exist and then fading back into them again. Some of them are quite new and others are old. But there are some that are the oldest of all. And when Alexander Curwen-Oakes was practising his rituals, he accidentally opened a portal to one of those."

"Why's that a bad thing?" Frank asked nervously.

"The Elder realms are dark. But not just in the sense of the absence of light. They are the manifestation of emptiness. They are the Void. No spirit that has ever occupied any other realm will venture into those. Especially the spirits that have experienced life. The blackness permeates everything, infecting with chaos and insanity. There are entities there though. I won't call them spirits or souls because that would imply some degree of familiarity or even humanity. It would be more accurate to simply call them 'entities' or 'Fallen Ones'."

"Fallen Ones?" Bob interrupted. "You mean, like The Fallen?"

"Yes." Jackie answered. "They do break through every once in a while. Historical records are peppered with references to them. Ancient cultures and modern day religions call them Demons."

There was an audible gasp from the group sat around the table. Their eyes widened and their mouths dropped open. No one knew what to say. Jackie paused to let the information sink in. It was not an easy thing to accept.

"You mean..." Steve stammered. "If they're demonic, then the realm they're from is Hell?"

"That's only a name that ancient people gave it." Jackie shrugged. "The truth is, it has no name because it has no language. It is the most primeval of dimensions where everything we know and understand about emotions, intelligence, morality, everything that makes us human, just fades into oblivion."

"Shit." Frank muttered and raised his pint glass to his lips. He swallowed three large mouthfuls, placed his glass back on the table, crossed his arms over his chest and sat, shaking his head.

"When Curwen-Oakes conducted his rituals, he made a disastrous mistake. He allowed some of these entities to cross from their black realm into ours. But they are uncontrollable. They have no idea what we're like or how we work. They have no idea about the cycle of life and death. They don't understand the other realms full of light and warmth. Theirs is a place of perpetual darkness, beyond time and space. To our understanding, it is a place of horror, terror, suffering and agony. To call it Hell would not even come close. But to them, it's normal. They don't have feelings like we do. They cannot feel happiness, sadness, empathy or remorse. These are alien concepts to them. They don't understand pain. They don't understand death. At some point, Curwen-Oakes must have realised his error and conducted another ritual. He would have used a binding curse to trap the entities he summoned within the bodies of the child victims and then bury them in the grounds where they would lay undisturbed forever. But when we found them, although our intentions were good, we broke the seal of the grave and, more importantly, broke the binding curse."

"So we've got demons after us?" Frank asked, the pitch of his voice high with incredulity.

"That's only what we call them. I'm afraid that in reality, they're much worse than any portrayal of demons in any text or painting."

"So why are we having these dreams about them?" Steve asked.

"When we broke open the grave, we were the first things they encountered. The vessels they had inhabited and been trapped in were gone. We had something that they had been missing for the past several decades. We have life. And they were drawn to it. Like moths to a flame. They are curious. They want to investigate us. They want to know what we are. But the very heart of the problem is the fact that they don't understand. What is normal to them is dangerous for us. Perhaps even fatal."

"Wait a minute." Wendy suddenly said. "Do you think they had anything to do with Sophie's death?" Jackie looked at her, took hold of her hand and closed her eyes for a few seconds.

"I don't know." She answered softly. "But I certainly wouldn't rule it out."

Jackie's revelation sparked an hour of debate within the group. The members of the team were confused, frightened and they needed answers. They needed to know how to stop The Fallen from harming anyone else. It wasn't clear that they may have been involved in Sophie's apparent suicide, but it was too much of a risk to ignore even the slightest possibility.

"So what can we do about it, then?" Frank asked. For the last five minutes of the conversation, the group had determined that there was indeed a significant threat posed by The Fallen. They concluded that the dreams were the method by which The Fallen were seeking them out. Jackie had hinted that in the dream-state, the soul of the dreamer could undergo a kind of astral projection. It was at this point that the spirit would be exposed, vulnerable and attract the attention of The Fallen who were looking for them.

"I mean, it's not like we can stop dreaming, is it? Sooner or later they'll find us. And if we're right, and they did have something to do with Sophie, then, I mean… you know… we're fucked!"

"Could we call a priest or an exorcist?" Dillon asked. Jackie pursed her lips as though someone had just stabbed her with a needle.

"No, my dear. They offer nothing. Never have, never will. Their understanding of the Beyond is based on the make-believe of a primitive culture. They are under the toxic delusion that their god will protect them. But let me tell you something. There are no such things as gods. Never have been. Never will be. The people who claim to be possessed are just wackos who've taken their belief in their god and the devil a little bit too far. And along comes one of these charlatans who chucks some water on them and spouts a load of shit in Latin and triumphantly says they've exorcised the demon. Well, of course they have. For the simple reason that there wasn't one in the first place. The priests are just as deluded as the wackos with made up demons inside them. You've never heard of an atheist being possessed by a devil, have you? All those records of possessions and exorcisms are just lies and bullshit."

"How can you be so sure?" Dillon asked nervously, shocked at Jackie's sharp response.

"Because if someone is possessed by one of the things we're dealing with, only one thing's going to happen."

"What's that?" Dillon muttered.

"They die."

"Well, we can't stop the dreams and we can't allow anyone to die." Bob said. "But I think we're all agreed that sooner or later, they'll find us. So we need a plan of what we *can* do."

"I was thinking." Wendy began. "We released them from the grave when we opened it. But they'd been trapped there for decades. What was it you said was keeping them there?"

"Good question." Steve said.

"I believe that Curwen-Oakes must have used a binding curse of some kind. I have a few in my books at home but I'll need to consult the old spirits again to understand which may be the most effective against these entities." Jackie replied thoughtfully.

"Yeah, but we can't re-bury the boys after trapping The Fallen in them again, can we? The police have got the bodies." Frank added.

"True." Jackie replied with a nod. "But the boys were just the vessels. The entities were also trapped in the grave, not just the bodies. It's possible we could bind The Fallen to a place or object rather than a body."

"How do we do that?" Bob asked.

"It's like using magic to erect barriers. Think of each of the realms of the Beyond having borders. It's possible to slip over those borders where realms are close together or where there are regions of high energy. But otherwise, the borders limit those dimensions, to an extent, and differentiate them from each other."

"I thought the dimensions were endless?" Wendy asked.

"They are, if you're in them." Jackie smiled. She held up her right hand and raised her little finger. "The borders that contain a dimension could contain the same area as my little fingernail. But once you're inside it, there is no time or space. It is, in effect, endless. Just think about the Universe that we occupy. Scientists say it's been expanding and growing since the Big Bang. True. But expanding and growing into what? Well that's an irrelevant question because at the very edge of the Universe is the border that contains it. It's not fixed. It's fluid. It can expand and contract. What's beyond it? The other realms, each with their own border to cross."

"Shit, man…" Frank mumbled, rubbing his eyes with the heels of his palms. "You're doing my head in."

"Sorry, love." Jackie laughed, a deep throaty cackle. "The point is that we can create artificial borders with a binding curse and once bound inside, The Fallen will be trapped in an infinite dimension of our making."

"But where are we going to create this new, artificial dimension?" Asked Steve.

"It will require energy to generate and maintain it." Jackie mused. The group sat in silence, thinking for a few seconds.

"What about back at Trevalling Hall?" Dillon suggested. The others looked at him. He felt his cheeks flush. "Well, it's isolated. Because it's a building, it's a clearly defined space and there's enough energy with the Ley Lines crossing right underneath it to maintain the binding curse forever."

"That." Said Jackie with a broad smile. "Is a bloody good idea."

"Just one thing before we go back." Wendy said. "Can we wait until after Sophie's funeral? It just wouldn't feel right otherwise."

"Of course." Bob smiled. "We'll do it in her memory."

20

It was a surprisingly bright, sunny day for early December. After the dismal weather of November, the warmth of the sun made a welcome change. But the tell-tale signs that winter was fast approaching were never too far away. White clouds of breath rising up from mouths half-tucked into scarves that were in turn, tucked into the collars of heavy overcoats were testament to the chill in the air that nipped at exposed cheeks and fingers. The bare boughs of trees in the grounds of the crematorium seemed to point more vertically than when laden with leaves, perhaps to prepare for the weight of snow in the months ahead, or just trying to reach higher to the warm light that seemed to diminish with each passing day.

The crowd that gathered outside the small chapel at the Weston Mill Crematorium waited patiently and in silence as the hearse came into view along the road, followed by an entourage of shiny black cars. As the procession drew closer, everyone could see the pure, brilliant white flowers that adorned each side of the coffin and had been carefully arranged into a name: Sophie. On top of the coffin were more flowers, a long spray of white roses, lilies and carnations amidst verdant branches of ferns and shrubs.

Dillon looked around. The crowd were mostly young. Probably Sophie's work colleagues. Others, more mature in their years, were undoubtedly family and close family friends. Those who were Sophie's acquaintances from the Goth world and music scene were easy to spot because even though everyone had dressed in black, this group went one step further with frilly shirts, black top hats and black canes with silver tops. They added a surreal comic book edge to the appearance of the crowd which in a strange way, fitted the occasion perfectly.

Sophie's parents emerged from the first car that pulled up behind the hearse. Sophie's mother had a black veil drawn over her face and she was holding a handkerchief to her mouth underneath it. The thin black netting couldn't hide her grief well enough. Her husband, holding her arm and leading her slowly to the chapel door tried desperately to maintain his composure but it was obvious he was in pain. Their only daughter had been taken from them. And at such a young age. It was the kind of pain that one wouldn't wish on their worst enemy. And the kind of pain that would last a lifetime.

The crowd entered the chapel after the family and took their seats. Playing softly in the background was a song with no words but had keyboards, guitars and strings that floated over the heads of the congregation. The melody and harmonies almost seemed to make the chapel feel bigger. It pushed against the walls, filling the space with emotion, and the chapel felt more like a cathedral. Somewhere in the building, someone faded the music and a classical piece from Mozart's Requiem took over. As the music focussed minds on the solemn inevitability of death, the pall-bearers entered, carrying Sophie's coffin. The white floral spray was still on top and it seemed to shine, reflecting the sunlight that poured in through the tall chapel windows.

Once the coffin had been placed to one side at the front, the vicar from Sophie's local church in Saltash, just across the river Tamar, stood to address Sophie's family and friends. After a prayer of welcome, he spoke of Sophie's childhood, her successes and achievements, her friendly nature and sense of humour. Some stories with which he regaled the congregation had obviously been supplied by people in the room and in between the few chuckles at some of the more amusing tales, there were audible sniffs as people fought to hold back the tears. Memories that now and forever would be the only lasting reminder of Sophie's existence. After a moment of reflection, accompanied by a simple classical piece for a string quartet, the vicar read a passage from the Bible and led the congregation in a prayer before issuing the Committal.

After the curtains closed around Sophie's coffin and people were invited to gather in the garden of remembrance, the vicar led Sophie's mother and father outside, followed slowly by everyone else.

"Too short." Bob muttered to Dillon. Dillon looked round at him. They were still sitting in their seats, waiting patiently to exit the chapel. Nobody seemed to be in a rush.

"What do you mean?" Dillon asked. Bob turned his head.

"The service. Too short. A whole life condensed into what, half an hour? Forty-five minutes? It just doesn't seem to do the whole thing enough justice."

"This was not for Sophie." Jackie whispered from behind them as she leant forward in her seat. Bob and Dillon turned to face her. "She's long gone. She's in a better place. This whole thing is purely for those of us left behind. Call it closure if you want. But I think of it more as a reminder to the rest of us that we're still trapped here. She's free now. The most depressing thing about funerals is knowing that we've still got umpteen more years left to endure before we're free."

"I never thought of it like that." Dillon mused.

"That's because you didn't know what comes after. Now you know. Now you know that death is not the end. It's a new beginning." Jackie smiled.

"True. True." Bob nodded.

"Good." Jackie said. "Now, I'm off for a fag. I'll catch up with you outside."

"The flowers are pretty, aren't they?" Wendy asked as Bob and Dillon joined her, Steve and Frank in the Garden of Remembrance. The staff of the funeral directors had laid out all the floral tributes with their accompanying cards inscribed with heartfelt, sentimental messages. The crowd slowly filed past them, pausing to read and reflect on them all.

"Yes. They are." Dillon replied softly.

"Sophie would've hated them." She grinned. Dillon was surprised at how well Wendy seemed to have coped with the funeral. He thought she would have been inconsolable. But the colour had returned to her cheeks and she appeared to be in a positive mood. Perhaps Jackie was right. Perhaps the only real function of a funeral service was to offer closure to those left behind. Perhaps by attending the service, Wendy felt that she had said her goodbyes to her best friend. Maybe, after the week and a half since they had last met in the Waggon and Horses, Wendy had come to terms with Sophie's loss. Maybe now, she could think about moving on.

"Didn't she like roses?" Dillon asked.

"Well, yes." Wendy said. "But only if they were painted black." She smiled again but as her cheeks rose, Dillon could see the line of tears in her eyes.

"Let's take this weekend to fully deal with this tragic event." Bob said. "We'll meet up next Tuesday as per usual and start planning how we're going to put an end to all this."

"Yeah." Nodded Frank. He was staring at the card attached to the largest bouquet of flowers. It was the card written by Sophie's parents. He read the last couple of lines to himself 'Losing you will leave a hole that nothing will ever fill. We will love you forever. Gone but not forgotten, our darling daughter.'

"We've got to stop those bastards." He added although he found it difficult to speak. The emotion that welled up inside him from reading the card constricted his throat.

"We will." Jackie said as she approached. The smell of cigarette smoke was strong and seemed to follow her around. "I'll go back to consult the old spirits on Saturday to see if they can tell me which binding curse will be the most effective. There are a couple I know of but I need some ingredients first."

"Ingredients?" Dillon asked.

"Yeah. But nothing too difficult to get hold of. A few things I've already got in stock but others need to be fresh. Things that you can get in the supermarket or a garden centre. Stuff like fresh Sage for example. That's powerful stuff and it's got to be really fresh. Gives off more smoke when it's still green."

"Send me an email with all the binding curses and their respective lists of ingredients and I'll go shopping on Saturday. We'll pay for it all out of the ESP coffers." Bob said. Jackie gave him a grin.

"Okay. Thanks for that. I'll send you the complete rituals and spells and the shopping lists for each one later this evening when I get home. I'll know by Sunday morning which one to use but if you've got the stuff ready in advance, then we'll be good to go."

"So," started Steve. "Assuming that we get most of the things necessary for the ritual this weekend, we could perform it next weekend?"

"That's what I'm thinking." Bob nodded.

"Which would mean our planning meeting on Tuesday will be more like a council of war?" Frank smiled.

"I can't think of a better way of putting it." Bob mumbled as he watched Sophie's parents leaning forward together to read the condolence cards.

21

Jackie sat on a collapsible camping chair, huddled under a blanket. Her feet were cold inside her wellington boots and she had to keep lifting the soles off the sodden, boggy ground to prevent them slowly sinking into the mire. At this time of year, Bodmin moor was a bleak, grey place. The saturated, marshy ground squelched underfoot and seemed to drain the colour of the grass and sedges down into the black earth. The sky, laden with grey clouds that scudded overhead felt so low that if you raised your hand, you could almost touch it. Around her, the twelve grey monoliths of the Bronze Age Trippet stone circle stood facing her with blank, timeless expressions. Despite the nineteenth century boundary marker stone erected in the centre which she was using as a windbreak, this was one of the oldest circles near her home and a site of considerable energy. Here, she could commune with the spirits who had occupied bodies and lived in the physical realm several thousands of years ago. They'd had all that time, since the deaths of their bodies to cross over and explore the myriad dimensions of The Beyond. The knowledge they could impart was some of the most valuable and also the rarest. It was because of this wisdom that Jackie had decided to consult them. They would know about the darker realms. They would have a better understanding of the nature of the beings that dwelled there. And most importantly, they would know how to control or fight them. They knew Jackie and they would be willing to give her the answers that she was seeking. But although Jackie had been waiting for them to arrive for almost three hours already, there was no sign of them.

Jackie shivered and pulled the collar of her coat further up around her ears. She adjusted the blanket over her legs and shuffled her feet in her boots. Huddling down further so her nose was tucked into her scarf, she glanced around the circle for any sign of one of the elder spirits. There was nothing. Just as she was about to reach into her coat pocket for her packet of cigarettes, the wind dropped to a mere breath and beneath it, she heard a noise.

A low hum seemed to surround her. The sound, more felt than heard rose up from the ground within the circle and vibrated the air. It was like stepping into a steam room. The sound made the air feel thick and heavy. Jackie knew that this was a surge of energy from deep within the ground. The same energy that the Bronze Age architects of the circle had felt and worshipped. But in all the years that she had consulted the elder spirits, she had never experienced anything like this. She looked around the circle. The stones remained unyielding. She felt as though it was getting dark but she could see that, beyond the circle, the moors were lit by rays of sunlight that streaked down in between the clouds. She looked around her again and noticed her breath was forming larger clouds in front of her face. The air grew colder and she knew this heralded a visitation. She stood so that she might see behind the central stone. As she took a step forward, she felt a crunch underfoot. Looking down she saw the thin grass was covered with a thick layer of frost. All the grass in the circle was coated with spiky ice crystals, but not the grass beyond. She placed a hand on the central stone to steady herself as the humming began to penetrate her mind. Dropping the blanket onto the chair, she walked around the stone, still holding on for balance. As she came back round to the chair again, she stopped abruptly and stared at the spectral form of a young boy standing a few metres in front of her. He was unlike the spirits of the other boys who she first met in the old house. This one was the walking embodiment of decay. Withered, torn, grey flesh hung loosely from the skeletal form that was barely covered by the ripped and dirty rags of the clothes it had been buried in. The skin and tissue were missing from the lower jaw and scalp and the jawbone was held in place only by a few sinewy threads. Where the nose had once been, there was now a triangular hole and either side were the abyssal black orbits where innocent eyes once looked upon the world.

"You're one of them, aren't you?" Jackie said. She tried to remain calm and steadfast, not letting any hint of fear show through. Nevertheless, there was something terrifying about this phantom. But it wasn't the appearance of it. Jackie had seen many bodies and spirits in a similar or worse state. It was the aura, the presence, the effect that this entity had on its surroundings. It felt like death.

"You're one of the three who we found at the old school, aren't you?" Jackie asked again. The figure stood motionless, neither responding nor shifting its empty, black gaze from her.

"Why are you here? What do you want?" Jackie raised her voice in an authoritative manner to command an answer. But the spectre stood motionless and continued to stare.

"Tell me your name." Jackie demanded. The figure cocked its head to one side like a dog trying to understand a command from its human master. The low, rasping, sickening voice that Jackie heard seemed to form within her head. The mouth of the spirit, filled with blackened teeth, didn't move.

"Name? What is name?"

"Your name. What are you called?" Jackie explained. There was a pause and the figure straightened its head again. If it had any flesh around its mouth, Jackie would have sworn that it grinned.

"We have no name."

"You must be called something?" Jackie asked, her voice beginning to crack. She knew that every spirit had a name. Even the demonic entities of the nether-realms had names. For this thing to not have a name could only mean one of two things; either it was very, very old, pre-dating the origin of the other realms and dimensions, or it was from such a dark place that any concept of existence itself was questionable.

"If you have no name, then what are you?" Asked Jackie. The figure took a shaky step forward, tottering on its skeletal legs. It glanced to Jackie's left and right and as she quickly followed to see what it was looking at, she found herself flanked by the other two phantoms. They were in a similar state of decomposition to the first and their blank, piercing stare seemed to burrow into her soul. The humming grew louder in her skull, filling her brain with white noise. She felt her head start to swim and she clamped her hands to her temples to try and blot out the hideous sound. The three figures stepped closer and the first held its arms out to its sides.

"We are Oblivion."

Jackie fell to her knees. She felt the crunch of ice cold crystals of frost through her leggings. She looked up at the three hideous apparitions who now loomed over her.

"Please." She begged. "What do you want?"

"Want? What is want?"

"What are you going to do with me?" Jackie sobbed.

"Come with us."

The two figures flanking her reached out and placed a bony hand on each of her shoulders. Her head flopped forward. It became difficult to remain upright. All the energy in her body was being drained away. Through her tear-filled eyes, she saw the ground beneath her grow dark and then, as the grasses and mosses shimmered out of existence, the earth became transparent. She looked up and saw, beyond her three captors, an undulating curtain that encircled the stones. It reached up as far as she could see, separating the world beyond from the portal that was opening up within the circle.

"Please…" Jackie begged, her voice weak.

"Come with us."

As the ground beneath her knees vanished, she felt herself fall. Beneath where the surface of the moor had been, she fell into total emptiness. The darkness that surrounded her was absolute and the silence deafening. As she plummeted, she looked up above her and saw the bright hole of the portal becoming ever more distant until it was nothing more than a pin-prick of light, like a solitary star in the void of space. And then, as she descended further, even that disappeared. By that point, Jackie couldn't tell if she was falling anymore. The sensation of gravity had diminished. She was in a blackness so pure, so suffocating that she may as well have been blind. And then, from out of the darkness, she heard distant screams.

She had been noticed. Her presence had been felt. She had disrupted the perfect dark. And now, the creatures and things that inhabited this realm were coming to investigate. She felt fear grip her. She turned and tumbled as she floated in the perpetual ink-black void. She couldn't feel her heart beating and nor was she breathing. Was she dead? Is this what it was like? To be conscious but frozen? All earthly and bodily functions halted? Was this her eternity? She scanned the blackness for any sign of movement, any hint that something else was there but she only saw absence. What she felt however was something altogether more horrific. From every side, above and below her, she could sense the presence of dozens, perhaps hundreds or thousands of beings. She could feel them watching. Their gaze penetrated her, trying to understand what she was. But the overall impression that she could feel was that these entities were emotionless, devoid of empathy, warmth, rationality, logic. They were the chaos that ruled the darkness before the concept of light. These were the spectres of abomination. The shadows of oblivion. No other spirit came close to their level of horror. The seekers of ruin and desolation. The destroyers of light. The tormentors of the wretched. Relentless, unforgiving, vengeful. Even the dark spirits of the occult would shy away in terror from them. And now they had Jackie. They had a new plaything. Something that could hear their every whisper, could feel their every cut and more fascinating still, something that could bleed.

"Don't hurt me." Jackie mouthed the words but no sound emerged. She felt a solitary tear roll from her eye, down her cheek to her chin. And then it dropped into the void. There was a tense pause as every nightmarish form watched the teardrop fall. And then they came for her.

"I've got some bad news." Bob said once everyone had their drinks.

"What's up?" Frank asked nervously. He and the others picked up on the tone of Bob's voice and it chilled them to the bone.

"I got a phone call on Sunday afternoon from Jackie's daughter." He started.

"I didn't know she had a daughter." Wendy exclaimed.

"They weren't very close." Steve said. "They had a very rocky relationship and when she was a teenager, Cassie, that's her name by the way, got in with a Christian Fellowship group at her school. She came to blows with Jackie over her gift. Cassie said that Jackie was in league with Satan and even tried to have her committed as a mental patient. This went on for years and she even reported Jackie to Social Services. The authorities took Cassie's side. I have to admit that Jackie didn't really help herself because she argued every step of the way that she could see and speak to ghosts. It was determined that Jackie wasn't in a fit mental state to take care of Cassie so she was taken into care."

"Jesus." Frank shook his head in disbelief.

"So that's why Jackie had such an issue with religion." Dillon mused. Bob looked at him with a perplexed expression. "Well, I mean that when I suggested using a priest or exorcist, she almost tore my head off."

"True." Steve said. "There's no doubt that she blames the church for coming between her and her daughter. Plus she knows for a fact that everything that they preach in church is just made up."

"So, why did Cassie call you?" Wendy asked Bob.

"She called because Jackie was taken into hospital on Saturday afternoon and they contacted her as the next of kin. Cassie doesn't want anything to do with her mother so she contacted me."

"Is she alright? What happened?" Frank asked.

"No. And, I don't know." Bob replied thoughtfully. "As far as I can gather, there was a guy driving past the Trippet Stone Circle on his way from Churchtown to the A30. He could see the stone circle but he also noticed something else, like someone had dumped some rubbish in the middle. He pulled over into a layby and went to investigate. He found a camping chair, blanket and Jackie huddled up on the floor."

"How do you know all this?" Wendy asked.

"I went to the hospital yesterday evening to visit. I spoke to one of the doctors. He told me how she was found. But he couldn't tell me what had happened."

"Why not? Did Jackie not say anything?" Asked Frank.

"No, she couldn't. I saw her in the ward that she's been moved to for observation and they've got her on life support, even though she's conscious. Her eyes were open but her pupils were like dinner plates. The doctor said that she was totally unresponsive to any external stimuli at all. He said there was no brain activity at all. No consciousness. Nothing. It's like she's in a coma but awake. I asked if she would recover and he said that he had never seen anything like it before. Her brain had just switched off. He doesn't think she'll ever come back."

"And she was found like that in the middle of a stone circle?" Steve asked.

"Yeah."

"She must have gone to consult the spirits to ask about the binding curses." Steve mused.

"I think you're right. But whatever happened while she was there, we'll never know."

Jackie had been returned a mere fraction of a second after she had fallen into the abyss. If anyone had been walking by at the time, they wouldn't have even noticed her blink out of existence and then come back again. But in the eternal void, where time and space have no meaning, she spent the equivalent of sixty-eight years. For every second of that time in that nightmarish place, she was subjected to constant howling and screaming that pierced the fabric of her mind. The creatures of oblivion clawed at her, slicing and cutting, tasting the blood that dripped from the wounds. They took it in turns to possess her body, just to experience what fear and pain felt like. And then they found a new sensation that emerged from within; the feeling of wanting to die. This was something new and alien to them. They did not know death. They had never experienced the fearful longing for release. And they were captivated by it. Now they had a new experiment to trial. A new game to play. They sliced at Jackie's throat and plunged their spectral hands into her chest to remove the warmth from her heart. And each time she died, one of them would inhabit her body, just to feel the sensation of death. And then they would bring her back to start all over again. Jackie died over a million times and each time she was brought back, she was subjected to the horror and torture of the wraiths anew. Eventually, her mind gave up. Maybe because the experiences that she was subject to were beyond comprehension. Maybe it was a protective measure; you can't be hurt if you can't feel the pain any longer. Once her brain switched off and died for the final time, the phantoms grew weary of their explorations. To purge their realm of her physical being, they took her back to the stone circle and left her back in her own dimension. Then, the portal was closed and the emptiness was restored to its prior state of pure darkness.

"So, what do we do now?" Frank asked. Even after much debate and hypothesising, the team couldn't determine if Jackie's 'episode' had any connection to The Fallen or Sophie's death. But it wasn't something they were going to risk. They still needed to deal with the spectres that were now haunting them.

"Without Jackie, we can't do the binding curse this weekend." Steve said, looking at Bob.

"Well." Bob began. He fished in his pocket and pulled out a couple of sheets of folded paper. He unfolded them and laid them on the table in front of him. Each sheet had a column of text that ran down the centre. They looked like songs with short lines and identifiable verses.

"What are they?" Asked Wendy.

"These are the four binding curses that Jackie emailed me on Friday evening. She also sent me a shopping list of the ingredients required for each curse. So on Saturday morning, I bought pretty much everything that she needed. Except for the fresh stuff of course. Realistically speaking, we have everything here to conduct the ritual and cast the binding curse ourselves."

"But which one?" Frank asked.

"Well, in the body of the email, Jackie did say that she thought the first one would be the best and most likely to work. She said that it would hold the spirits that it targeted within the walls of the old manor. Once it had been cast, no matter what, those spirits should be trapped there indefinitely."

"Whilst I agree with the concept," Steve started thoughtfully, "Without Jackie's expertise and experience, what chance do we have?"

"You and I have seen her perform rituals like this a hundred times over the years." Bob said. "And besides, it's not like she went on any courses or was taught how to do these things. We've just got to follow the instructions and say the right words at the right time."

"Sounds risky." Frank murmured. "What if we fuck it up?"

"Well," Bob sighed. "That's a risk we'll have to take. But at least having a go and trying to get rid of these things is better than doing nothing." The others pondered their options in silence for a few moments. Ultimately, Bob was right. They couldn't just sit back and do nothing. If The Fallen were responsible for Sophie's death and if they were somehow involved in what happened to Jackie, then who knows what they would do next. Who they would come after. Who they would kill. It didn't bear thinking about. They needed to be confronted. They needed to be dealt with. They needed to be banished or bound. Every member of the group felt a responsibility for what was happening. They were all there when the bodies of the boys were discovered and The Fallen were released. They had a duty to put it right. To end it. But deep down they all knew, with an accompanying feeling of dread, that they were alone. Just the five of them. Against the darkest forces in existence.

22

Bob, Steve and Frank planned to meet up and get to Trevallyn House just after eleven o'clock on the Saturday morning. It was a dreary day, much like the last time they had been at the hall. Although it hadn't rained all morning, the rain that had fallen overnight had saturated everything. The site that awaited their arrival and the surrounding moors were bathed in melancholy. With an accompanying biting chill in the air, the grey rain-streaked old ruin appeared even more threatening than it had on their previous visits. Particularly as now, in the backs of their minds, the three knew what was waiting for them.

"When are Wendy and Dillon going to get here?" Frank asked as Bob navigated the potholes in the old driveway.

"Not sure." He replied. "Car trouble. Wendy called me earlier and said they'll be here as soon as possible."

"Should we wait for them?" Steve asked.

"I'm not sure that's a good idea." Bob replied. "I have a funny feeling that our presence here won't be welcomed, so hanging around waiting for Wendy and Dillon to arrive might not be the best plan."

"Yeah." Added Frank. "And it'd be good to get this over and done with before lunch. If this all goes according to plan, the first round's on me."

"Good man." Steve said with a smile. "That's the spirit."

"Spirit? Where?" Frank joked. The three laughed and then abruptly fell silent as they turned the last bend of the driveway, emerging from the treeline and saw the manor looming ahead of them.

"Is it just me or does it look bigger and darker than before?" Frank asked.

"It's just our imagination." Steve replied uncertainly. "It's a dark day and we're all a bit nervous of what we're going to find here."

"If you say so." Frank said, leaning forward between the two font seats and eyeing up the derelict building with nervous suspicion.

Bob pulled the car up right in front of the steps. The three men climbed out and stood for a few moments, looking up at the foreboding edifice.

"You hear that?" Steve whispered.

"Yeah." Frank replied.

"It's the same kind of sound we heard in the cellar." Said Bob. "It's like, I can almost hear a low humming and the air feels charged, like with electricity."

"Do you think the portal's already open in the cellar?" Steve asked.

"Not sure." Bob frowned and bit his lower lip. "There's something about this that feels different. It's like it feels darker, more...more... what's the word?"

"Malevolent." Steve looked up at the empty black windows. The sense of being watched by unseen, evil eyes was overpowering.

"Yeah. That's it. Malevolent." Bob said, following Steve's gaze up to the windows of the first floor. "Something doesn't want us here. That's for sure."

"You think it's them? The Fallen?" Frank couldn't hide the nervousness in his voice. He had convinced himself that they had the element of surprise. But now? Now he felt as though they were expected.

"I don't know." Bob replied. "What we do know is that there are lots of spirits here, all gathered in this place near the portal. It could be anything." Despite his best efforts to maintain a sense of calm amongst the three of them by playing down any fanciful assumptions, he didn't really believe his own words.

"Come on." Steve said, walking to the back of the car and opening the boot. "Let's get on. The longer we stand around here, the more time we give them to prepare themselves."

"Do you think they know why we're here?" Frank asked as he joined Steve at the back of the car.

"Not a clue." Steve replied with a shrug. "But I don't really want to take the risk."

The three shared between them torches, matches and a carrier bag each filled with the ingredients that Jackie had specified for the different variations of the binding curse. They had decided against camcorders, voice recorders or any other equipment that they would usually arm themselves with for the purpose of a paranormal investigation. They had a job to do. They didn't have time to dither with trying to capture footage of the multitude of ghosts in the building. They had enough of that already. They needed to be focussed, professional, quick and ruthless in the execution of the binding curse. Any delay could potentially hand over the power to The Fallen and that was something they really didn't want to do.

"Okay. Let's go." Bob said firmly. He switched on his torch, pointed it at the doorway and the beam cut into the darkness where it was subsequently consumed. He marched up the steps with the carrier bag rustling by his side and entered the ruin. Frank and Steve followed, their torch beams scything through the inky blackness, illuminating every corner and crevice to make the hidden visible.

"Where shall we start?" Steve asked.

"Chapel first. That's where it all began." Bob answered. He already had a plan in his mind of how this was going to play out. Carry out the ritual in the chapel, then the dormitories upstairs, then the classrooms downstairs and then finally in the cellar. His logic was to cut off any exits or escape routes, one room at a time, driving the Fallen closer to the portal. Once trapped, they could be bound to the cellar forever. The energy of the ley lines and the portal would help to strengthen the power of the binding curse, ensuring that The Fallen would never hurt anyone ever again.

"Right. Let's get started." Bob said as the three entered the old chapel. His voice echoed in the emptiness, bouncing off the walls and slowly dissipating into silence. He made his way to the centre of the room, scanning in wide arcs with his torch as he went. Once in the middle, he dropped the carrier bag, knelt next to it, opened it up and began removing the contents. The bag rustled each time he reached in to remove a jar, bottle or sprig of herbs. The noise made Steve feel uneasy and he looked around the room, aware that the sound could attract unwanted attention.

"Quiet." Steve said suddenly. There was an urgency in his voice that made Bob freeze immediately. The three listened, slowly waving their torch beams around the room.

"What?" Bob whispered after a few moments. He slowly rose to his feet and stood next to Steve. "What did you hear?"

"It's what I can't hear that's worrying me." Steve whispered in reply.

"What do you mean?" Frank asked.

"The humming has stopped. And, well, this place was virtually alive last time we were here. But listen now. It's totally dead." He paused and held his breath. Frank and Bob strained their ears to listen into the blackness. Steve was right. There wasn't so much as a creak of a floorboard or a breath of a draught through a crack in the wall somewhere. The whole building was a temple of utter silence.

"That's good, isn't it?" Frank said, looking between Bob and Steve for some hint that the quiet was a positive thing.

"I don't think so." Steve murmured. "You remember how Jackie said this place was full of spirits? Well, where are they now? The only thing I can think of is that they've all scarpered or are all hiding. Either way, why would they do that?"

"The Fallen." Bob growled.

"Exactly. Remember when Jackie was talking with the spirits of some of the children? Then they all disappeared just as The Fallen made their presence known?" Steve's voice was tinged with fear.

"Yeah." What Steve was getting at began to dawn on Bob. "So if there are no other spirits around, then…" He trailed off.

"The Fallen are already here." Steve said.

"Shit." Frank muttered and he began systematically waving his torch around the room, looking for any sign of movement, any hint that they weren't alone. As they realised they were potentially compromised and totally unprepared, the three men began to feel the icy grip of panic. Their hearts started to race and their breathing rate accelerated, drawing the damp, mildew laden air deep into their lungs.

"Come on. We've got to get a move on. Frank, keep a lookout." Bob said urgently as he knelt down again by the carrier bag and finished removing the contents. He laid out the jars and herbs in the order that they would be used according to Jackie's instructions. He held up a bunch of fresh sage branches, tied with a purple ribbon and gave it to Steve before he stood up next to him. Reaching into his coat pocket, he pulled out a box of matches.

"Hey, guys." Frank said. "My head's starting to hurt." He raised his free hand to his left temple and rubbed furiously at the skin to try and dislodge the throbbing sensation that ran behind his eyes.

"Mine too." Steve said. "Stick with it. Don't stop." He held the bunch of sage close to Bob as Bob removed three matches, closed the matchbox and struck all three together. They didn't light. He tried again, rotating the matches to try another. Again they didn't light.

"Fellas. Something weird is happening here." Frank said, his voice trembling. His unwavering stare was fixed upon the end of the room where a creeping black mist was starting to obscure the wall. It seemed to seep from the rotting plaster and slide over the vertical surface. It crept downward, over the dusty floor and around the corners like black water. Almost but not entirely transparent, it hid the details of the old building behind it and swallowed any light from Frank's torch that fell upon it.

"God, my head's on fire." Said Steve.

"Mine too." Bob replied through gritted teeth. He tried to strike the matches again. "Come on, you son of a bitch!" He cried out.

"Guys, I'm feeling fucking awful here." Frank said, his voice quavering. Steve looked round just as Frank tottered to one side and fell over. He scrambled to his knees and resumed pointing his torch at the encroaching darkness. "My eyesight's going! I've got tunnel vision and the whole goddamn room is spinning!"

"Me too." Steve replied. He tried desperately to stay standing upright but he could feel his body swaying. Looking down by his feet, he saw a thin, black tide rise up from the ground and wash over the floor. His stomach turned and his head swam.

"Come on, you bastard!" Bob cried out as he struck the matches again and again. Suddenly, the matches burst into flame. Bob cried out as the bright blue fire shot up from the sticks. He dropped the matches and as they fell into the mist, the blue flame was extinguished.

"Shit!" He yelled. He looked round at Frank and Steve, his eyes wide with panic as he tried to see through the dark fog that was now gradually filling the room. Steve was swaying, falling from one foot to the other as though he were trying to stand still on the deck of a ship in a storm. Frank was kneeling on what Bob presumed was the ground, but he couldn't see Frank's knees because they were hidden by the blackness that lapped against his legs. "We're not going to do this. We've got to get out of here. Leave the stuff. Let's go!" Bob half ran, half fell forward in the direction of the doorway and promptly stopped as he saw the ink- black fog that filled the end of the room.

"Bob!" Frank yelled suddenly. "Where'd you go? I can't see you!" Bob wheeled round, trying not to fall over and looked back at Frank. He was desperately struggling to get to his feet and waving his torch around, looking for Bob.

"I'm right here, Frank!" Bob yelled back. "Come on, let's get out of here!"

"Bob! Bob!" Frank cried out. "Where the fuck did you go? Bob!"

"Frank, I'm here. Walk forward to me!" Bob took a few steps back toward where Frank was now standing, turning one way and then the other, his torch held out in front of him. Bob was within a few metres of his friend, close enough that he could almost reach out and take hold of the outstretched torch when Frank suddenly vanished.

"Shit! Frank? Frank!" Bob hollered. He spun round, looking for Frank and kicking at the black mist that was rising up his legs. There was no sign of him. He had disappeared completely. There wasn't even the slightest glow of his torch-light. He'd gone.

"Steve! Do you see where Frank went?" Bob asked. There was no answer and Bob turned to where he had last seen Steve. But, like Frank, Steve was nowhere to be seen.

"Bob! Steve!" Frank yelled. He was too afraid to move from where he was standing but he found himself completely alone in the old chapel. The dark fog now covered every wall, the floor and the ceiling. The structure of the building, now barely visible through the inky vapour seemed to oscillate in and out of reality. It rippled as if seen underwater, fading into nothingness and then slowly coming back into focus. He stepped forward in the direction where he saw Bob blink out of existence. He was shaking all over and he held the torch now with both hands, brandishing it as though it were the last vestige of hope and salvation that he had. As he slowly moved through the mist, it washed up in tall curtains and soon began to fill the room completely.

"Bob! Steve!" He yelled. He was shouting so loud it was hurting his throat. "Where are you?"

He spun around as he heard a disembodied sigh behind him. In the dark clouds that now surrounded him, he could see shapeless forms gliding and encircling him. His head throbbed with pain and his vision swam. He heard voices speaking to him from the darkness. The sound chilled him to the bone. Wordless, breathy, echoing whispers that conjured up images in his mind of the fearsome creatures that were speaking. They came from all around him and he stumbled forward as the urge to escape suddenly overtook him. He ran forward in the direction of where he believed the doorway to be and, still holding his torch in front of him like a sword, sprinted out of the room.

"Frank! Steve!" Bob shouted. He had made his way back to the centre of the chapel and found the carrier bag of ingredients. The fresh, green, fragrant herbs that he had bought were now decayed and oozed black slime. The mist rose up around him and he ran through it, one way to where Frank had been kneeling and then the other to where he had last seen Steve. He found neither and terror gripped him tight.

"Who's there?" He cried out as he heard a voice behind him. "Steve? Frank? Is that you?" He waved the torch around, desperately looking for his friends. "Follow the light of my torch if you can!" A cold shiver ran through his body as he felt something rest on his shoulder. He swung around, almost losing his balance and froze solid as he stared into the face of a thing so hideous, so indescribable that for a second, all words and rational thought escaped him. It was a vision of pure abomination; a wretched, blasphemous nightmare that defiled the very fabric of reality. Its eyeless gaze pierced his soul and drank deep of his fear and horror. As a wasted, three-digit claw slowly reached out for him, Bob screamed, turned and ran. He made it to the end of the chapel and by a miracle ran straight through the doorway, his screams mingling with the rasping whisperings of the beings in the chapel.

"Bob? Frank?" Steve whispered as he slowly turned on the spot. He was too afraid to raise his voice and, trying to make himself as inconspicuous as possible, he cupped his hand over the end of his torch to mute the bright light that he was sure would lead the creatures toward him. He had only taken his eyes off his two friends for a moment as he rubbed his temples to alleviate the headache that filled his skull, but when he looked again, they were both gone. He tip-toed forward to where Bob had vanished, being careful not to disrupt the black fog too much. He was aware of the fact that he was not alone, but it wasn't Bob or Frank who were with him. Voices and sighs reverberated in the dark clouds that billowed through the room and every so often, he would see long, thin blurred shapes swim through the mist in front of him. They seemed to defy gravity, gliding upwards and disappearing into the blackness, their multitude of strange, tentacle-like appendages trailing behind them and clawed limbs outstretched, feeling ahead. When he saw them, he stopped and closed his hand tightly over the torch. He held his breath and tried to stand perfectly still but he still felt as though he was swaying from one side to the next. His vision seemed to come and go, gradually switching from tunnel vision to blurred focus and back again. Only when he was sure the creatures had passed did he start to move forward again. Slowly but surely, he made it to the doorway of the chapel but his heart sank as he found the corridor outside filled with the same black fog and the same murmurs of the horrors that were searching for him.

"Frank? Bob?" He whispered, looking along the corridor, one way and then the next. With his head in so much pain, his eyesight compromised and the darkness that was consuming the old building, he felt unsure of his bearings. He couldn't remember where the corridor led. Which way would be the quickest to escape? He looked to his left and saw only darkness. But when he looked to his right, he cried out in shock. A few metres away was the figure of a boy. Steve recognised him as one of the three they had found in the shallow grave outside. The flesh was grey and rotten with rips and tears that exposed the decaying tissues and bones beneath. The face was of pure gangrenous putrefaction; the eyes were completely absent and the empty sockets wept black slime from where the nose should have been to the upper jaw, where the drips fell in the absence of a mandible onto the dirty, torn shirt that clung to the withered chest beneath. The figure raised its only arm and held out a skeletal hand. A voice, gurgling, rasping and barely human filled Steve's head.

Come with us.

Steve let out a startled cry, turned and ran along the corridor to his left. He didn't look back and he carried on until he felt that he had entered another space. Another room? But which one? Something in his mind told him that the front of the building and his escape lay to the right, so he turned and fell down a steep set of steps, hitting his head on the rotten wooden door at the bottom.

Frank stood outside the chapel and gazed to his left and right. He couldn't make out any features of the building and he felt completely lost. He could only see black clouds that filled the space like thick, acrid smoke. From his right, he thought he heard a cry. Not like the whispers that he had heard in the chapel behind him. A human cry. He strained his eyes to see and for a second, thought he saw a flicker of light. Was it a torch?

"Bob! Steve! I'm coming!" He shouted hoarsely and started to run towards where he thought he had seen the light. He came to an abrupt halt as he reached the bottom of a wide staircase. Although he couldn't see more than a few steps up, he recognised where he was. It was the main staircase that led up to the dormitories. The dark fog crept downward, washing over his feet and the black mist that filled the stairwell obscured any sign of the light he was sure he'd seen. He tentatively stepped up onto the first stair and craned his neck forward, looking up to try to see the floor above. Was it his imagination or did it seem brighter up there? Less dark?

Perhaps he could escape somehow from the first floor? Maybe find his way to one of the windows at the front of the building and call out for help. Yes, Bob and Steve must have got out by now. He could call out to them. They could tell him how to escape. He began to climb the stairs quickly. He was careful to only take one step at a time rather than run up two at a time, because he couldn't see where he was putting his feet. One slip and he would fall backward to the bottom. Back into the dark.

"Bob? Steve?" He called out as he reached the top. The upper floor was just as dark as downstairs but here, the blackness was different. It felt as though it was raining darkness and clouds of black ash swirled through the upper floor, obscuring everything from view. Frank knew he was facing the front of the building so he slowly crept forward, holding his torch with one hand and feeling into the dark with the other. After a few, tottering steps his hand hit a wall. He felt along it and soon found a corner. He felt a warmth of success and hope fill him and he started to follow the wall that led to the front of the building. Soon he found stonework in front of him and he realised that this was the front of the building. He placed the torch in his pocket and used both hands to feel along the wall until he found the first window frame. A sigh of relief escaped his lips and he moved further to the side so he would be facing the window. He placed his hands on the ledge and leant forward, expecting his head to emerge from the black ash-laden fog and into the light of the real world. But his heart sank and the smile fell from his face as he saw darkness that stretched on for eternity. The world had gone. It had vanished just like Bob and Steve. He was staring into a realm of nothingness. But he wasn't alone. Something made him step away from the window. A primeval instinct that he was being watched. The feeling like prey being watched by a predator. He turned and saw the decomposed form of a boy standing a few metres from him. He shrieked in fear and stumbled backward. The torch fell from his pocket and the beam only just illuminated the cadaverous wretch standing in front of him. The empty sockets stared straight at him and the creature raised an arm, holding out a withered, bony hand.

Come with us.

Frank screamed and staggered backwards. He reached out on either side for a means of escape but his hands hit the walls of the passageway. He realised now that he was in the corridor that linked the staff offices where Dillon had carried out his first vigil. But what was at the end of this corridor? He couldn't remember.

Perhaps a way to escape? He turned his head and looked behind him but he could only see blackness. A cry left his mouth as he turned his head back and found that the hideous form of the boy was now even closer to him, its hand still outstretched, reaching for him. Frank staggered backwards along the passageway, his hands groping along the walls on either side until he felt a crack in the floor behind him. His heel slid over the edge and he stepped backwards with his other foot to find the floor again but it found nothing. His hands scraped along the wall as he looked over his shoulder and screamed. He was falling over the edge of the first floor into the abyss of the ground floor beneath. He hadn't realised it, but he had reached the end of the building that was still intact and what now lay behind him were the ruins and rubble of the wing that had collapsed. He scrambled to find a hold on the walls but there was nothing to grab on to. As he felt himself fall backwards, he turned his body in a desperate attempt to see what he was falling into. The darkness rose up to meet him and in the last split second before he hit the ground, the blackness disappeared as if the mist had been blown away by a strong wind. He saw the remains of what had been a washroom or shower block and his eyes focussed on a rusted pipe sticking up out of the ground. He didn't have time to scream again. He felt the pipe tear into his chest as the corroded metal pierced his ribcage, skewering his heart in the process and emerged, bloody and glistening from his back. As the final seconds of life left his body, Frank slumped and became still. The spectre of the boy stepped forward from the shadows, glided through the rubble and slid his bony fingers along the bloody pipe. He raised the dripping red liquid to his mouth and wiped it on his black, rotted tongue.

Steve sat upright at the bottom of the stairs. His ankle was burning with white hot pain and his back felt as though he'd been hit by a bus. He groaned and raised his torch to see where he was. As the light illuminated the old planks of the door, he quickly realised that he had fallen down the steps of the old cellar. The torch flickered. It had obviously been damaged during the fall. He hit it against the palm of his hand and it went out, came back on and then went out again.

"Don't do this to me, you bastard thing." He hissed, hitting the torch again but he froze and hid the flickering light with his hand as he heard a noise at the top of the staircase in the room above him. He looked up just in time to see a dark, wraith-like form glide through the black mist above him. It sighed as it passed overhead and once it had gone, Steve instinctively pushed open the door of the cellar and dragged himself through to hide. He slid down the step on the other side, wincing with the pain from his ankle and fell onto the dusty ground. Reaching back up behind him, he gently closed the door. He scanned the small room with the torch that flickered on and off. There was no sign of the black fog and no sign of the portal either. The room seemed completely normal. He breathed a quiet sigh of relief and decided that he could hide there in the cellar until normality had been restored in the house above him, however long that may be. He could also attend to his badly sprained ankle and maybe fashion some kind of supportive brace from his belt. As he leant forward to remove his belt, he heard a faint sound from the other side of the cellar. He stopped immediately and picked up the torch from the floor in front of him. He turned it to scan the room and saw the wall at the far end was bleeding. A viscous black slime was running from the cracks between the stones and forming puddles on the floor. From the puddles, a wispy black vapour rose up in undulating columns. Steve felt his heart race and he turned to open the door, eager to escape whatever was happening. He pushed and pulled at the door but it wouldn't budge. It was as though it was locked. But that was impossible. He had come in through that very door only moments earlier. He tugged and pushed harder but the door remained firm. Pulling himself to his knees and crying out as lightning bolts of pain from his ankle shot up his leg, he barged the door with his shoulder. It didn't move. He barged again, harder and harder until he hit it so hard that he fell back into the room. Sprawling on the floor, Steve grabbed the flickering torch and directed the beam toward the end of the cellar. The blackness had consumed the end of the room and was quickly advancing toward him. He forced himself to sit up and shuffled back into the corner, drawing his knees up to his chest while still pointing the torch at the dark fog that billowed through the room. He felt a cold sweat on his brow and the clouds of breath from his rapid breathing rose up in front of his face. The light blinked on and off and in the sporadic illumination, Steve saw a figure start to take shape in the black fog. With every strobing flash of the torch, the figure became more and more defined until Steve recognised it was one of the boys from the grave in the garden. Steve hit the torch against his hand to try and make the light stay on constantly but instead, it flickered on and off more and more frequently. To Steve's frustration and terror, the torch stayed off more than it was staying on and with every passing moment, in the split-second moments of illumination, the corpse-like apparition inched its way closer to Steve. Its empty sockets stared at him and Steve was convinced that the cadaverous figure could see him, even in the dark. Steve pressed his back up against the wall as, with every flash of the torch, the terrible form drew closer and closer. The cellar began to fill with distant whispers and as the black mist grew thicker and thicker, the walls gradually disappeared completely giving the impression of a darkness that reached out into eternity. Petrified, Steve stared at the horrific figure approaching him and just before the torch died, he was sure he saw it smile. He sat petrified in the dark, his eyes wide trying to penetrate the blackness, while his head throbbed with pain. The whispers surrounded him and the cold penetrated his flesh. Steve became aware of a strong smell in front of him. It was earthy, rotten and rancid; the smell of death. Suddenly the torch flicked on for a final second and Steve stared straight into the face of the boy, inches away from his own. The black-toothed grin on its corrupted, putrefied face filled Steve with a sense of horror that he had never felt before. The wasted mouth before him opened, revealing a gaping cavity with a withered black tongue. Steve let out a shriek just as the torch went out for the last time and he felt death take him.

Bob had made it to the first floor. He was out of breath, disoriented and scared out of his wits. He had no idea where Steve and Frank had gone. One minute they were there in the chapel with him and the next, they had disappeared. Had they been taken? Did they escape? He didn't know. What he did know at that moment was that he needed to get out. Standing at the top of the staircase, surrounded by blankets of falling black ash and billowing clouds of darkness, he paused to get his bearings. He thought back to the map he had made of the site and remembered that to his right, the building had collapsed. To his left were the dormitories and the washroom. An idea suddenly came to him. He could climb out of one of the windows of the dormitory and, hanging from the window ledge, drop down to the ground below. It wasn't that far to fall. He was only on the first floor. So long as he fell straight down, bent his knees on impact and rolled onto the ground, he would probably be alright. In any case, it was a significantly better option than staying in the house. He turned to his left and started along the corridor, sweeping his torch from side to side as if to cut a path through the black ash that rained down from above. Confident that he knew where he was, he began to jog along the corridor until he came to a wall in front of him. Realising that this was the wall of the washroom, he turned his torch to the right to find the corridor that ran the remaining length of the building and where he would find the dormitory doorway a short way along it. He edged slowly with the wall close to his side, feeling along it with his fingertips until he found the corner he'd been looking for. Turning into the corridor, he transferred the torch to his left hand and reached out to the opposite side to find the doorway. The moment his fingers curled round the old doorframe, he heard shrieks and screams from behind him. He spun round but saw nothing. Quickly, he turned and went into the dormitory. The darkness was not as absolute in the large room and though the black ash still fell softly and silently, obscuring his view, he could just make out the walls and black windows on the far side. He walked into the room, making his way to the windows at the front when he heard a gurgling laugh behind him. He wheeled round on the spot and saw the decomposed form of a boy standing where he had just passed. He tottered backward, turned and started to run to the far end of the room, trying to put as much distance between him and the hideous figure of the boy. He reached the end wall and the window in the middle of it. Looking out, he saw only darkness but he knew the world was still out there. Ultimately, he had no other choice. He would have to go out the window to escape from the demonic form that was still chuckling behind him. He leant on the window sill and glanced back over his shoulder. The boy was gliding toward him, one of its withered arms outstretched and its decayed hand reaching for him.

Come with us.

The voice was clear but horrific. The rasping, whispered command echoed in Bob's head. He looked back at the window and, grasping the frame on each side, hauled himself up onto the ledge. Just as he was turning to lower himself down, he felt two claw-like hands grabbing at his ankles and yanking his feet from under him. He slipped back off the ledge but the upper half of his body fell forward. Bob cried out as he toppled forward out of the window and fell into nothingness. A split second later and the darkness vanished to reveal the earth that rapidly came up to meet him. Bob landed head first on the ground outside the hall and the weight of his body bent his neck to such an angle that it snapped his spine with a sickening crunch. Death was instant.

23

"Okay. That's brilliant. Thank you so much." Wendy called out of the window as the breakdown recovery man closed the bonnet of the car and gave her a thumbs up through the windscreen. It had only taken him half an hour to identify what the problem with the car was and fix it. It had however, taken just under an hour for him to arrive from the time when Wendy phoned for help.

"Okay. We're good to go." Dillon said as he fastened his seat-belt. He was aware that Bob, Frank and Steve must have already arrived at Trevalling house and they had probably already been there for at least an hour. He was worried they would have either started the ritual before he and Wendy arrived or that they were waiting for them to get there whilst who knows what was there with them. He didn't know which he preferred. Either way, he was nervous of what the day might bring. But he was also hopeful that the ritual Bob had received from Jackie would put an end to the horrors of The Fallen.

"Yup. Let's go." Wendy said as she revved the engine, put the car into first gear and pulled away, giving the recovery man a final wave.

Although they were already late, the deteriorating weather conditions hampered their progress further. The spray thrown up from the road by other vehicles made it difficult to see, even with the windscreen wipers on full speed. The volume of traffic decreased, however, once they reached the moors and the bleak hills rose up to meet the cold, steel-grey sky. As before, once they had turned off onto the road that led to the Hall, they were completely alone. Their only company were the black, skeletal trees that stood as sentinels with their branches waving in the wind. Not even the crows and rooks could be seen. The landscape was dark, barren and threatening. It therefore felt something of a relief to turn off into the woods that surrounded Trevalling Hall and, although the old driveway made their progress particularly bumpy and difficult, both Dillon and Wendy felt a sense of relief at having some sort of canopy above their heads and the sturdy trunks of trees to offer some protection from the elements.

"Look." Dillon pointed through the windscreen as Wendy rounded the last bend of the drive. "There's Bob's car. Pull up next to it." Wendy nodded and drove slowly along the last few hundred yards, coming to a halt next to Bob's car. She switched off both the headlights and the engine and the pair of them sat in silence for a moment, looking out of the window at the Hall.

"It's quiet." Dillon said. "Do you think they heard us coming or not?"

"I don't know." Wendy replied. "Probably not. I would have thought if they heard us, one of them would have come out to meet us."

"Yeah, like Frank maybe?"

"Exactly. Come on. Let's go see." Wendy opened her door and climbed out. Dillon followed and the pair of them stood for a few seconds, listening.

"I can't hear anything." Dillon said.

"Me neither." Wendy closed her door and walked around the front of the vehicle to Bob's car. She pulled on the handle of the passenger door. The door opened.

"It's unlocked. They must still be here then." Dillon concluded. "Are the keys in the ignition?"

"No." Wendy replied as she leaned in and studied the steering column. "It's cold in here too. The car's been sitting idle for a while."

"They must be somewhere inside." Dillon said as he started toward the steps.

"Wait." Wendy snapped. Dillon stopped and turned to look at her. She gently closed the door of Bob's car and stared up at the building. She frowned as she looked from one window to the next.

"What's the matter? What's wrong?" Dillon asked.

"I don't know." Wendy bit her bottom lip and continued to study the front of the Hall. "It just feels…"

"What? Is it different to before?" Dillon asked. He backed away from the steps and walked round Bob's car to stand next to her.

"Yes. It is. But I can't explain why. I just feel like there's something very bad here and I really don't want to go inside."

"Okay." Dillon said. He turned his attention to the windows of the first floor and scanned them in turn, hoping that he could pick up on whatever feeling Wendy had sensed. There was no denying that the building looked menacing. But no more than it had done previously. Although the rain and morose atmosphere did make it appear even gloomier, even darker, it was still the same building as before. Dillon felt he was almost becoming accustomed to it. Nevertheless, try as he might, he couldn't sense the bad feelings that Wendy had obviously picked up on.

"Maybe we could walk around the outside?" Dillon suggested. Wendy nodded slowly but didn't take her eyes off the building.

"Okay, let's go this way first." Dillon pointed to the end of the Hall that had collapsed. Wendy looked and then gave Dillon a smile. She pulled the scarf higher up around her neck and pushed her hands into her coat pockets. For a second, Dillon hoped she would have reached out to hold his hand but he knew that it was too much to wish for and in any case, this was neither the time nor the place.

Dillon let Wendy lead the way. He walked slowly by her side, but half a step back so he could see both the Hall and Wendy. As they made their way round he end of the building, Dillon examined the ruin and devastation where the roof and upper floor had collapsed. He thought that, in comparison, ancient Roman or Greek ruins on the continent seemed a lot tidier. This looked more like a bomb had gone off. Rotten wood of old floorboards stood upright in some places, tall jagged splinters piercing the ground. Elsewhere, the old, broken planks were intermingled with lumps of masonry that littered the derelict interior. In some places, brambles and other weeds had taken hold, making the most of the opportunity to grow within the shelter of the walls but still exposed to the light above. Bob had been right to ignore this end of Trevalling House and not bother investigating it. It would have been far too dangerous to even set foot into the shell of the ruin and explore. Twisted ankles, cuts and grazes, debris falling from above. It just wasn't worth the risk. Although, that's not to say that there wouldn't have been any spirits in those destroyed rooms. Dillon wondered for a moment if the ghosts who haunted this end of the building could see it as it is, or as it was during their lifetimes when they wandered the rooms and hallways. He remembered the old soldier whom Jackie had spoken with in the dormitory. He was still waiting for his sister. Perhaps he had mistaken Jackie for one of the nurses. In any case, he was obviously still walking the house as it had appeared when he was a patient there during its time as a hospital and where he later died.

"Look." Wendy said as they rounded the back corner of the building. She stopped and pointed at the fountain. Dillon paused by her side. They stood watching the fountain as if they expected it to suddenly burst into life and send showers of water cascading over the structure. In truth, it wasn't the fountain itself that they were staring at. It was the four metal poles and line of plastic blue and white Police tape stretched between them that had captured their attention. In the centre of the square was a pit with a mound of earth and grass to one side. It was a stark reminder of what they had found, what they had released and what was now haunting them.

"Come on." Dillon said decisively. "Let's head round to the front and see if we can find the others. He looked at Wendy. She continued to stare at the pit in front of the fountain but she nodded her agreement. Dillon turned to double back and retrace their steps when Wendy caught hold of his arm.

"Where are you going?"

"Round the front to find Bob, Steve and Frank."

"We can carry on this way." She nodded her head in the direction that they had been heading.

"Are you sure? I didn't think you'd want to go near the fountain?"

"No, it's fine. We'll just continue past it to the far end and go round to the front that way."

"Okay. If you're sure." Dillon replied. Wendy smiled. It was the kind of soft smile that said 'thank you'; thanks for agreeing with me and thanks for being here with me as well. For a fraction of a second, Dillon forgot where he was and why he was there. He lost himself in Wendy's smile and the warmth of her hand on his arm through his coat sleeve. He gave her a reassuring smile back and she took her hand away. They carried on walking until they passed the fountain and reached the far end of the building. Along the whole length of the back of the Hall they checked each window, both on the ground and upper floors, looking for any sign of Bob, Steve and Frank. They saw nothing. Not even the flickering of torchlight in one of the empty rooms. They didn't hear anything either. They didn't want to admit it out loud but they were both becoming increasingly concerned for their friends.

Wendy walked out further onto the grass at the end of the building. She turned to see the two cars parked at the front and the fountain at the back. Dillon wandered over to join her, resenting the wet grass soaking the bottom of his jeans. Suddenly, his whole body shook and his stomach somersaulted as Wendy let out a piercing scream. Dillon's heart raced and his wide eyes fixed on her. She was staring, pale faced and wide-eyed at one of the upper floor windows. He turned quickly and looked up. The horror made him cry out and he almost fell over backwards from the shock. His breath caught in his throat and for a moment he felt like he was going to throw up. He tottered back to where Wendy was standing. She grabbed his arm with a vice-like grip and slapped her other hand over her open mouth. Tears were already clouding her vision and as she blinked rapidly to see more clearly, they rolled down her cheeks.

"Jesus..." Dillon mumbled, his voice quaking with fright. His unblinking gaze was fixed on the three figures who stood in the end window of the front dormitory. It was unmistakably Bob, Steve and Frank but at the same time, it wasn't them. Bob stood in the centre with Steve on his left and Frank on his right. His head was lolling on one side to such a degree that his ear was resting on his shoulder. Dark lines of blood had trickled from his mouth and nostrils and dripped onto his coat, staining the fabric black. His skin was bone white and his eyes were clouded like a slaughtered sheep. Steve was equally as pale and his mouth was hanging open as though his jaw had been dislocated. His tongue, ripped and torn was hanging loosely from one side and his throat had a ragged gaping hole as if it had been torn open by a rabid animal. Although like Bob, he was looking down at Dillon and Wendy from their higher vantage point, his eyes were missing. Deep, bloody scratches surrounded his eye sockets and the flesh hung in ripped shreds. The black holes where his eyes used to be ran with dark, viscous blood as though he was crying tar. On Bob's other side, Frank stood awkwardly, his arms hanging limply by his sides. His face was screwed up with an expression of agony and, like Bob, his eyes were opaque. His chin was painted in dark crimson as though he had either vomited or coughed up blood that had then sprayed down his front. In the middle of his chest, his clothes were torn and bloody around a gaping hole that went completely through his body. His abdomen was stained red from the profuse bleeding that had followed his body being skewered.

"Bob! Steve! Frank!" Wendy cried out, her voice high pitched with panic and grief. "No!"

"What the...?" Dillon started and then froze rigid as he saw three black columns of mist form in front of Bob, Steve and Frank. The columns merged as the mist thickened and began to take shape. Suddenly, the three child corpse manifestations of The Fallen stepped forward from the darkness and stood by the window, looking down at Wendy and Dillon with an eyeless stare. Their decomposed faces filled Wendy and Dillon with a new level of horror and as the black mist enveloped and consumed their three friends, a voice drifted down to them.

Come with us.

Wendy screamed and started to run, stumbling and tripping over the uneven ground as she went. Dillon quickly followed and the pair ran as fast as they could back to the car. They got in and as Wendy fumbled with the keys, sobbing uncontrollably, Dillon saw the three cadaverous boys standing just inside the front door of the old ruin.

"Go. Go. Go!" Dillon said urgently as he fastened his seatbelt. Wendy turned the key in the ignition, slammed the car into gear, grinding the gearbox as she did so and reversed back away from the front of the Hall. She braked hard and swung the car around. As she stamped on the accelerator, the back wheels spun, sending a shower of gravel and mud up like a wave behind them. Leaving a grey cloud of exhaust in their wake, the car raced and bumped toward the driveway. Wendy navigated the potholes through the tears filling her eyes while Dillon braced himself in his seat with one hand on the dashboard and the other holding tightly onto the door handle. He turned in his seat as the car rounded the first bend into the woodland and looked back out the rear window toward the old manor. There was no sign of the three cadaverous boys or of Bob, Steve and Frank. He turned back again to look out of the windscreen as Wendy raced round the bends of the driveway and a sense of relief that they'd escaped flooded through his body.

Wendy cried the whole way back to Exeter. Dillon could offer no words of comfort or reassurance. He was in no state to speak at all. Neither of them were. Dillon stared straight ahead with a vacant expression at the white lines on the road that passed quickly under the bonnet, his cheeks and lips pale and bloodless. His hands rested on his thighs and trembled, partly because he was so very cold and partly because of what he had seen. His mind was filled with flashbacks of the horror he and Wendy had witnessed. The images of his three friends replayed through his head in slow motion again and again, and each time, he relived the terror anew. When they finally arrived at Wendy's place, they sat outside in the car with the engine still running. Wendy had stopped crying. Somehow, just being back in the city with its familiarity and people going about their everyday, normal lives seemed to distance them from their horrific experience. As the comforts of reality began to slowly take a hold, the events of the previous hours started to feel more and more like a dream. Nevertheless, they were both still in a state of severe shock and neither really knew what to do next.

"We should call the Police." Wendy said quietly.

"I don't think they'll believe us." Dillon replied, not taking his eyes from the rear number plate of the blue Ford Fiesta they were parked behind and that he had been staring at for the previous five minutes.

"Well, we can't do nothing. We can't just leave them like... that." She turned to look at Dillon. He felt her gaze on him, pleading for help. He turned his head and looked at her. Her cheeks glistened from all the tears and her eyes looked sore, red raw and bloodshot. He sighed and shook his head.

"Even if we did tell the Police and they believed us, what good would it do? I don't even think Bob, Steve and Frank are still there. All the Police will find is Bob's car parked outside but no sign of anyone."

"What do you mean you don't think they're there?" Wendy asked. She frowned.

"You saw them." Dillon said softly as he gently shook his head. "They're dead, Wendy. There's no two ways about it. They're gone. And do you remember those columns of black that appeared right before those demon children did?" Wendy nodded as fresh tears ran from the corners of her eyes. "I think Bob, Steve and Frank were taken by that mist. I think The Fallen have taken them."

"No...Don't say that. It's not true." Wendy stuttered and her voice faltered. She grimaced as she unsuccessfully tried to fight back the tears.

"I'm sorry Wendy. I really am. But they're gone."

"No. They're still there. They've got to be. Sophie was found. They found Sophie didn't they?"

"Yes. Yes, they did." Dillon sighed and dropped his gaze. "But there was something different about this time. The Fallen took Bob, Steve and Frank. They wanted them. Did you hear what they said? That hideous voice?" Wendy nodded.

"Come with us." She said coldly.

"Exactly. I have no idea why Sophie was left behind or Jackie survived but there's no doubt in my mind. They're after us. Maybe it's because they still want a sacrifice. I don't know. But it was a sacrifice that brought them into our world in the first place. Maybe they've got a taste for it now? We were the ones who released them from their grave and broke whatever spell Curwen-Oakes had placed on them to keep them imprisoned in the corpses they occupied."

"And now they want us?" Wendy asked.

"Well, it's the only thing I can think of. And unfortunately, we don't have any way of stopping them now that Jackie and Bob are gone and the binding curse has gone with them." Dillon bit his bottom lip and frowned. It was a predicament that he couldn't see a way out of.

"So." Wendy said as she sniffed and dabbed her eyes with a handkerchief. The grim situation they were in was dawning on her too. "What do we do?"

24

Wendy finally switched off the car engine and the pair emerged into the fresh air of the afternoon. Dillon stretched his back and took several deep breaths. The sounds and smells of the city were a world away from the barren moors and the damp of Trevalling Hall. If he closed his eyes and concentrated hard enough, he could almost convince himself that none of it was real, that it was all some hideous nightmare. When he opened his eyes again, exhaling slowly, he saw Wendy opening the front door of the apartment block. She was still sniffing and wiping her eyes with her sleeve. Her hand trembled as she held the key in the lock and turned it. Dillon knew that there was no getting away from the reality that had been thrust upon them. He and Wendy were in this together but now they were alone. His mind began to race with plans, solutions, ideas and theories about how they could get out of the mess they were in. He needed to come up with something. But what? He was the least experienced of the team. This was the first investigation he had been on. He didn't know about all this supernatural stuff. But had the team ever experienced anything like it before? He doubted it. None of them had ever mentioned anyone ever being hurt before. Let alone killed. This was supposed to be a hobby. A shared interest in finding out if there was anything that came after death and gathering evidence to show the world. Dillon thought about the possible motives behind Bob and Steve's fascination with the subject and collecting evidence. Did they recognise the risks involved? Was it all just for their own personal interest? Or was it to specifically challenge accepted ideas and religious doctrines? Perhaps it was both. But whatever they hoped to gain, it had ultimately cost them their lives. And that was a price surely none of them would have been willing to pay.

"You coming in?" Wendy asked meekly. Dillon snapped out of his daydreaming and saw her standing in the open doorway, leaning against the door.

"Yeah, sure." Dillon replied with a smile. He stepped forward and walked in past Wendy. She closed the door and checked it was firmly shut before brushing past Dillon and starting upstairs. Dillon followed her up to the first floor and to the door of her apartment which she opened and held ajar for him. Dillon instinctively stopped just inside the flat and removed his shoes. Wendy gave a slight chuckle as she watched him.

"No one's ever done that before." She said. Dillon looked up at her from his kneeling position and saw that she was smiling. Sunlight from a room behind her was illuminating her outline and fine wisps of hair were lit up like a halo. He said nothing but continued to remove his shoes.

"Mind you, I don't have many visitors." She added thoughtfully before slipping off her coat and hanging it on a rack mounted on the wall in the small box-shaped hallway. She turned and walked into a lounge dining room and Dillon followed. He didn't know what he might have expected from Wendy's apartment but the soft pastel colours, fluffy cushions and blankets were certainly not beyond what he would have guessed Wendy's tastes in home furnishings to be.

"Tea? Coffee?" Wendy asked.

"Erm, tea please. No sugar, thanks."

"Same as me then." Wendy smiled and disappeared through another doorway into what Dillon could see was a small galley kitchen.

"Sit down. Make yourself comfortable." Wendy called back as the sound of the kettle grew louder.

"Thanks." Dillon replied and walked over to the large, white sofa. He could easily see which spot was Wendy's preferred to sit. The cushions were arranged at one end of the sofa in the corner and a pastel blue blanket was draped over the back, ready to be pulled down with a single stroke. That end of the sofa was also closest to the small, circular glass coffee table and faced the television straight-on. Any other place to sit in the room would have meant watching the television at an angle. Not that there were many other places to sit in the lounge anyway. There were two armchairs and a small dining table with another two chairs. Wendy certainly hadn't gone out of her way to cater for lots of guests. The one thing that Dillon noticed as he sat down was the absence of clutter. There were no unnecessary ornaments or lots of pictures on the walls. And then he realised that there were no photographs either. Not of Wendy or her friends or her family.

"Here we go." Wendy said as she emerged from the kitchen and placed the two mugs of tea on the coffee table. She sat in the corner of the sofa where Dillon guessed she would and curled her legs up beside her. She looked significantly happier just to be back in her own home. The real world could be kept at bay beyond the door and the horrors of reality could hammer all they liked against the walls but inside, she was safe.

"This is a nice place you have here." Dillon said, casting his eye around the room as if he had only just noticed. Wendy blushed slightly, smiled and reached forward for her tea.

"Thank you. That's a nice thing to say." She raised the mug to her lips, blew gently over the top of the hot tea and took a sip.

"It would be good if everything could just go back to how it was before any of this started." Dillon added. He watched Wendy for her reaction. She nodded, sighed and placed the mug back on the table.

"Yes. Yes, it would." She said solemnly.

"I really don't know what to do." Dillon continued. "All this paranormal stuff is new to me and I would have never thought things could be so dangerous or that it could ever actually hurt anyone."

"Me neither." Wendy said. "I know you're the newcomer to the group but believe me, there has never, ever been anything like this before. There are plenty of stories about demons and dark entities and all that kind of stuff that you see on television but honestly, we never encountered anything like that. And definitely nothing like this." She shook her head slowly. They sat in silence for a few moments. "I don't know what to do either." She said finally.

They talked for the rest of the afternoon and into the evening. Not wishing to venture outside again, especially not in the dark, Wendy offered to phone for a pizza delivery. Dillon insisted on paying. The talking and pizza helped to lift their spirits, even if they hadn't come up with any course of action. By half past eight, Wendy was beginning to tire and Dillon stood to make a move to leave.

"Wait!" Wendy said suddenly. Dillon looked at her. She was wide-eyed and had a look of terror on her face.

"What? What's the matter?" Dillon asked.

"You're not leaving are you? Please don't leave. I don't want you to leave. Please stay."

"Well, I, er..." Dillon stumbled. He could feel his cheeks flush and he nervously rubbed his nose. "I don't want to intrude."

"You're not intruding, believe me. Please. It's just that after today, I really don't want to be left alone tonight. Please stay."

"I, er... I suppose I could sleep on the sofa." Dillon said.

"Yes, yes of course." Wendy sprang to her feet and began to rearrange the cushions into a rudimentary pillow arrangement. "And I have lots of blankets too. You won't get cold. Help yourself to anything you want from the kitchen and the bathroom is just off the hall on the left. My bedroom's on the right."

"Okay. I'll make sure I don't confuse them in the night." Dillon said and instantly blushed as the ulterior meaning of his comment dawned on him. Wendy smiled and disappeared out into the hall returning from her bedroom a few seconds later with a pile of fluffy blankets. She laid them over the arm of the sofa and stepped back to admire the makeshift bed she'd created. She reached out and touched Dillon's arm. He felt the soft warmth of her hand through his sleeve and he looked at her. She smiled at him.

"Thank you for staying, Dillon. It really means a lot to me."

"No problem." Was all Dillon could say in response.

"I'm going to turn in, but if there's anything you need, please just shout." Wendy said. Dillon nodded and Wendy turned to leave. Dillon listened for her bedroom door closing before he took off his shirt and jeans, keeping his t-shirt, boxer shorts and socks on. He lay down on the sofa and tugged a couple of blankets up over him. It was only when he rested his head on the cushions that he realised how tired he was and with Wendy's sweet scent that had been infused into the fabric of the cushions in his nostrils, he soon fell asleep.

The smell of mildew was almost overpowering. Straining his eyes to see through the gloom, Dillon could make out the grey damp-stained walls of the Trevalling Hall chapel. He looked up behind him. There was no light coming in through the large window but a strange, eerie electric-blue glow filled the room, casting faint shadows and showing up where the plaster had fallen away from the walls. All around him, a fine mist swirled and billowed. Pinpoints of light seemed to dance within the fog and as they passed close by, he heard them whisper. He didn't feel any fear. He was intrigued by what these orbs were trying to tell him. The faint blue glow was strangely comforting and warm. Every so often, he would feel a reassuring hand brush against his or rest upon his shoulder. He felt himself smile and he turned around on the spot, swirling with the mist. Unseen hands placed themselves in his palms and held him as he danced. The whispers grew louder and just as he was about to make out what they were saying, the mist, the orbs and the blue light vanished. In a fraction of a second, the temperature plummeted and Dillon could see his breath rising in front of his face. He stood still, all senses on edge, watching and listening to the darkness. From his side he heard a noise. He turned immediately to face the direction where the sound had come from. What was it? A snarl? A groan? It was faint but he certainly hadn't imagined it. There was definitely something there. He kept his eyes fixed on the side of the room where he had heard the noise, waiting for any sign of movement when another noise came from behind him. He spun round. There was no mistaking the sound this time. It was still quiet but it seemed to echo around the chapel. And then he heard it again; the sound of a child laughing. Another laugh came from his side toward the front of the room. He still couldn't see the source of the laughter but by now, he had a good idea who it was. His heart began to race and his subconscious mind began to fill with one thought; run. He tried to take a step forward in the direction of the doorway but his feet wouldn't move. The laughter came at him from all directions in sequence and then in unison. Three sickening, malevolent laughs. He could feel the malice in their tone. They were taunting him. Playing with him. And he couldn't get away. Just as a small, dark form came into view at the front of the chapel, his head filled with a piercing scream.

Dillon sat upright and the blankets fell from his chest. For a few moments he was disorientated and he looked around to work out where he was. The second he realised, he heard another scream. He leapt to his feet, almost knocking over the coffee table and spun round to sprint toward the hallway. As he left the lounge, he felt how cold the air was. Another scream and he turned his head to the right and the door where the sound was coming from. He flung open the door and in the dim light of Wendy's bedroom, saw her almost climbing up over the headboard of her bed. He looked down toward the end of the bed and felt a shiver run through his body. Standing at the foot of the bed was the black silhouette of a boy. He felt an involuntary gasp of fright leave his body before he instinctively ran his hand over the wall to his side until he found the light switch. He flicked it down and the room was suddenly filled with light. The silhouette vanished and the cold chill began to subside.

"Are you alright?" Dillon asked, rushing forward toward Wendy. She didn't reply but flung herself at him and wrapped her arms around him. He felt her body shake with violent sobs and her tears quickly soaked through his t-shirt, mixing with his cold sweat. He held her tight and rested his cheek down onto the top of her head.

"It's okay." he whispered. "It's gone."

"We can't stay here." Wendy said, pulling herself away from Dillon's embrace. "They know where we are now. They'll come back."

"How did they know where to find us?" Dillon asked.

"I don't know. They must be linked to us in some way. I mean, we were the ones who released them from their grave. It's not like they're going after anyone at random. There must be some kind of bond between us." Wendy replied, looking around the room. Then, she turned and stared straight into Dillon's eyes.

"What? What is it?" He asked.

"I think I've got it." She answered. "I was dreaming and then they showed up. Were you dreaming and then they turned up as well?"

"Yes. I was in the chapel at the hall and then everything went black and then I heard them."

"What did you hear?"

"Laughter."

"Me too. I wasn't in the Hall though, I was at work. But suddenly everyone disappeared and it all went really dark. I know I was still in the office but I couldn't see anything and I couldn't move from my desk. And then I heard it. The laughing. It came from all around me and it got closer and closer. And then I woke up and saw..." She broke off and pointed to the end of the bed where the apparition had stood.

"We can go back to mine." Dillon suggested. Wendy nodded.

"Okay. Get dressed and bring only what you need."

25

Dillon woke with an aching back. His sofa hadn't been half as comfortable as Wendy's to sleep on. He rolled on to his side with a groan and pushed his coat off of him. In the absence of comfy cushions and blankets, he'd had to make do with sleeping with a couple of rolled up jumpers for a pillow and his winter coat for a duvet. He glanced at his watch. It had just gone seven. The first glimmer of the imminent sunrise had barely appeared over the horizon but there was sufficient light in the room for him to see what he was doing. He stood up, stretched and yawned. Since they had fled from Wendy's at around half past one in the morning, it had taken him until around four to finally drop off to sleep again. It was a good thing that they'd had an early night the previous evening. He tugged on his jeans and pulled on one of the jumpers from his makeshift pillow. As he went through to the kitchen to switch on the kettle, he heard the bedroom door open.

"How are you feeling?" Dillon asked as Wendy appeared in the doorway. She looked like she had barely slept a wink since they had reached Dillon's flat. Her hair was tousled and her complexion was pale.

"Honestly?" She croaked.

"Actually. Don't worry. If it's anything like me, then it's not great."

"Yeah. Not great."

"Here, I made some tea. I don't have a lot in stock but there's a cafe in town that do a good breakfast for a pretty reasonable price."

"Sounds good. Give me a couple of minutes to shower and freshen up and make myself more human." Wendy caught sight of her reflection in one of the glass-fronted kitchen cabinets. "Actually, make it ten." She groaned.

After breakfast, they walked by the river-side. Their full stomachs, the tranquillity of the river and being amongst other people calmed their nerves. Dillon didn't want to say anything but as they walked, he had been wondering what the next night might bring. After all, they couldn't stop themselves from dreaming. And if Wendy was right and if they dreamt, The Fallen would find them again.

When they had fled in the early hours of that morning, Wendy had left her apartment with only the clothes that she was wearing. She knew she needed to go back home to collect some clean clothes and toiletries.

"It shouldn't take too long." She said. "I just need to pop in, grab a bag, throw some stuff in and leave."

Dillon could tell that she wanted him to go with her. From the look in her eyes, he also guessed that she probably wouldn't want to stay in her flat for another night. At least not yet. Why else would she need to collect toiletries?

"Listen." He said softly. "Collect what you need for a few days. You're more than welcome to stay at mine until you feel ready to go back. Or when we know what we're going to do."

"Thank you." Wendy said with a huge smile that, in the sunshine, made her face glow.

Wendy's apartment was located on the opposite side of the city centre from Dillon's flat and they walked along some back streets from the river in order to bypass the busy city centre. Along one quiet road, they had just passed a row of small independent shops when they heard a shout from behind them.

"Wait! Stop!"

They both turned to see a woman in her mid-fifties with long, wavy purple hair and wearing a long emerald green dress jog after them. She caught up with them and although she hadn't jogged very far, because of her rather generous figure, she was gasping for breath.

"Oh, my dears." She said with a pained expression on her heavily made-up face. "I saw you from my shop window and I knew I just had to catch you before you disappeared."

"I'm sorry, do we know you?" Wendy asked with a polite smile.

"No. No you don't. But please, come into my shop and tell me all that ails you."

"All that ails us?" Dillon replied with a confused frown as he picked up on the woman's lyrical tone and strange choice of words.

"Oh, yes. What ails you. I could see it in your auras as you walked by. You are marked. There is something that is looking for you. Something that it would be for the best were not to find you." Wendy and Dillon looked at each other in disbelief and then back at the woman who gave them a comforting smile.

Dillon looked around as the woman led them into her shop. Around the small shop-front were tall glass display cases filled with a multitude of colourful minerals, crystals and rocks. In the centre of the shop, a couple of tables and back-to-back bookcases were full of books about Guardian Angels and Crystal Healing. Dillon wasn't at all surprised that there were no customers in the shop.

The woman led them past the front desk, through a multi-coloured beaded curtain and into a small room with half a dozen chairs arranged in a circle. She waved her hand and nodded to beckon Wendy and Dillon to sit down. Once they had taken a seat, she sat down opposite them and placed her hands in her lap.

"My name is Serena." The woman started. "And I am a psychic." She paused, almost as if anticipating a round of applause. She smiled at both of her bewildered guests. "I saw you walk past my window and I saw the great sadness and shadow that follows you."

"What do you mean?" Wendy asked. "You said we are marked. What does that mean? What did you see?"

"Yes. You are marked. And I know not just by seeing but what I can feel as well. The moment I saw you walk past, I saw shadow surrounding you. There is something that exists in the darkest shades of existence that is looking for you. The shadow is your mark. And whatever is looking for you will find you by following that mark."

"And what was it you felt?" Dillon asked. He was highly sceptical of Serena, if that was indeed her real name, and he was intent on looking for any weakness in her story before she tried asking for money.

"Oh, I felt many things." Serena replied with a look of pity on her face. "But most of all, I felt emptiness and sorrow. You have lost people, friends, who were very dear to you. I fear that the emptiness is what took them and the sorrow is the grief you now feel."

"Yes. Four of our friends were taken from us recently." Wendy said. Dillon looked at her and saw her bottom lip quiver.

"I will try to help in any way that I can." Serena said, leaning forward and placing a hand on Wendy's knee. "But please, tell me all. From the very beginning. Tell me everything."

180

It took over three quarters of an hour for Wendy and Dillon to recall all that had happened, from the first visit to Trevalling Hall right up to the events of the previous night. By the end, Serena had tears running from the corners of her eyes. She hadn't interrupted once and had listened intently but her expression had grown more and more solemn as Wendy and Dillon told their story.

"I knew Jackie." She said finally. Wendy and Dillon stared at her. "Well, when I say I knew her, it was more a case of knowing of her. You can't be a psychic in this part of the world and have not heard of Jackie. She had an extraordinary gift. One of the most talented, so I understand. I never had the opportunity to meet her but everyone in this particular field knew of her. It's such a shame what happened to her. I must visit her in hospital and see if I can reach her."

"What about the others?" Wendy asked. "What about Sophie, Bob, Steve and Frank? Can they be reached?"

"I don't know, my darling. I don't know." Serena pursed her lips and slowly shook her head. "From what you have said, these entities that were released are from a very, very dark place. I don't know where. But I may be able to find out for you. If you come back this evening after I have closed the shop, I will ask my spirit guide to help us. She may have some answers."

"Spirit guide?" Dillon asked. He frowned. It sounded too much like mumbo-jumbo to him. And he wasn't in the mood for anyone trying to take advantage of the situation that he and Wendy were in.

Dillon looked both ways along the street to make sure nobody was watching and then knocked on the door. Although there were no lights on in the shop and a 'Sorry we're closed' sign was hanging in the door window, he and Wendy were not just potential customers or passers-by. They were expected. They had been invited. After having left the shop earlier in the afternoon, they had collected clothes, toiletries and a few other things from Wendy's flat in order that she could spend a few more nights at Dillon's. All the while, they talked about Serena and her offer of help. Dillon was cautious. He found it difficult to believe that some random woman whose only qualification for being psychic was her personal testimony would, out of the blue, offer to help them. He was more than anticipating there to be a catch. In fact, he was almost certain of it. Maybe she would ask for money. Maybe she wouldn't. At least not until later. Not until she had gained their trust and they were hanging on every word that she said. He could imagine Serena airing excuse after excuse to fob the pair off when her psychic sessions failed to produce any results. Maybe her spirit guide wasn't in a talkative mood. Maybe the stars weren't aligned correctly. Maybe her aura was feeling a bit flat. Oh, but don't worry. Just give her fifty quid and everything would magically work next time. Except it wouldn't. Ever. Because it was just a scam. Wendy, on the other hand, was more open to the idea of using Serena's psychic abilities to find out what they were up against. As always, she tried to see the good both in everyone and everything. Finally, after much deliberation, Dillon agreed to go along with the plan. His agreement was ultimately based on the fact that he didn't have an answer for the one question Wendy posed that pretty much clinched the debate in her favour; 'what have we got to lose?'

They stood in silence for a few moments and then Wendy nudged Dillon with her elbow as she saw movement at the back of the shop. The beaded curtain fluttered and Serena appeared, hurrying toward them. She smiled through the window as she unlocked the door and then held it open as Wendy and Dillon entered.

"Oh, I'm so pleased you came back. I was worried I may have scared you off or come across as a bit, how shall I say, weird?" She chuckled and closed the door, locking it and steadying the sign that was gently swaying from side to side.

"Come on through. Everything's ready." She said as she led the way through the shop and through the bead curtain. Dillon surveyed the small, dark room and was momentarily lost for words. Serena had erected a collapsible table in the middle of the circle of chairs, covered it with a green velvet cloth and adorned it with a ring of strange crystals and jewels. In the centre of the circle stood three small white candles surrounding a larger one. The candle flames flickered as the three moved around the room and took their seats. There was a sweet smell in the air from two incense cones near the candles that burned slowly. Two curling blue-grey columns rose up from the cones and the candlelight illuminated a cloud of aromatic smoke that was gently undulating by the ceiling.

"How does this work?" Wendy whispered as she nodded toward the crystals and candles.

"Well," Serena said as she placed her elbows on the table and clasped her hands together. "My spirit guide I mentioned earlier is called Helen and she was a worker in a mill here in Exeter during the reign of Queen Victoria. She was tragically killed in an accident when she was caught up in the mill machinery and crushed to death. The poor lamb, she was only seventeen. It's very sad. She never knew her parents. She was sent to the mill straight from the orphanage the moment she was old enough to work. So she's never experienced the love and companionship of a mother. And that's what drew her to me. You see, if you have certain abilities or a gift, as we like to say, then spirits are attracted to you. It's as though you shine like a beacon that shows up in their realm. I like to think of it a bit like the Northern Lights. The glowing aura of someone with the gift here in our realm can extend beyond the boundary and just as with the Northern Lights, those on the other side are drawn toward it. These candles help to light her way so she can find me easier. For her, where I am changes every day, even though in our realm I am here in the same room. The dimensions beyond the veil are in a constant state of flux, always changing, always moving. So Helen has to look for me. The candles help. Their light, combined with my aura, help her to come to me in a more reasonable time. Remember that time has no meaning in other realms. It's only here that the flow of time can be felt. If I didn't have the candles, it could take days for her to find me. As it is, the candles have been burning for almost an hour already since I closed the shop."

"What about the crystals?" Dillon asked. "Aren't they like the ones for sale in your shop?"

"Yes, they are. Other crystal healers can purchase them or I can order specific minerals that they can't easily get hold of. I have some very specialised suppliers. While the candles are lighting the way, these crystals provide the energy for the spirits to pass through the veil that separates our realm from theirs. There must always be a source of energy for them to harness or else they will not be able to make it through. The nature of the crystals and their arrangement in synchrony with each other is very specific to maximise the energy. Every crystal has its own energy signature and the skill lies in combining them together to generate enough energy to open the doorway."

"Is that a bit like the energy from the ley lines at Trevalling Hall?" Wendy asked.

"Yes. Exactly like that. Although that's far more powerful. The level of energy that the crossing of ley lines can provide is far, far more than this. That level of energy is sufficient not just to open a doorway, but under the right circumstances a full-on portal. I have to admit that I'm not personally comfortable with trying to control that amount of energy. It would be extremely dangerous for a novice like me to even think of attempting such a ritual. Only a higher level sorcerer or practitioner of the Secret Arts should dabble with that kind of thing."

"Like Alexander Curwen-Oakes?" Dillon asked.

"Quite possibly." Serena replied thoughtfully. "From what you told me, that would make sense. He must have known about the power of ley lines and their potential to open portals. He must have also have had access to ley line maps and he must have specifically identified Trevalling Hall as the perfect site for him to contact the Beyond. I daresay that he would have spent many, many years studying the secret wisdom and looking for his perfect opportunity. The very fact that he was also willing to conduct sacrifices and spill the living essence of blood can only mean one thing."

"What's that?" Asked Wendy.

"That he must have been a Master of Black Magic. And taking that into consideration, I doubt very much that he was trying to contact the souls of the departed. No, I think his quest was for a far darker, more powerful knowledge. That was why the sacrifice was important. Blood spilled on that old ground where the ley lines cross would attract the attention of demons and elder entities who hold the secrets not just of the Universe but the entirety of existence in all its myriad forms."

Wendy and Dillon sat in silence for a few moments, staring at Serena. The fog of doubt in Dillon's mind was beginning to lift. What she was saying seemed to make sense. There were specific details that she knew which correlated with everything Jackie had said before. Perhaps Serena did know what she was talking about after all.

"Ah," Serena said finally as she glanced around the darkened room. The candles flickered and a strange static charge began to build up in the air.

"Did it just get colder in here?" Dillon whispered.

"Yeah." Wendy replied nervously.

"Don't worry, my dear." Serena said with a smile. "The drop in temperature is an indication that the energy we have provided is being used for someone to come through from the Beyond. I do believe that Helen is approaching."

"Where?" Dillon asked as he looked around.

"Sadly, we cannot see her." Serena replied. "The best I have ever glimpsed is a very vague, misty white figure. But that was only when the Hale-Bopp comet was passing by, back in nineteen-ninety-seven. And even then, I had to wait for a specific planetary alignment and make contact in the middle of the witching hour. Opportunities like that, as I'm sure you can appreciate, are very rare indeed."

"Will we at least be able to hear her?" Wendy asked.

"Perhaps." Serena said with a smile. "You possibly more than he. Remember, she's attracted more to motherly figures. You might feel her too. She may stroke your hand or your hair. But don't be alarmed. Remember, to her, I am family."

The candle flames flickered again and the wispy traces of blue smoke from the incense cones danced and curled upon themselves. Serena placed her palms flat on the table with her fingertips just outside the circle of crystals. She nodded to Dillon and Wendy to do the same and then she took a deep breath, held it for a few seconds and gently exhaled through her nose.

"Helen, my love. Are you with us? Don't be shy. I have some friends with me this evening. I have told them all about you and what a darling you are. They would love to meet you. Would you like to come and speak with them?"

Dillon could feel the charge in the air prickling his scalp and his arms. It felt as though his hair was standing on end. Suddenly, Wendy twitched and as Dillon looked at her, she glanced back at him, her eyes wide with surprise.

"I just felt her run her fingers through my hair." She whispered. She looked at Serena who smiled back and gave a knowing nod.

"Helen, I would like to introduce you to Wendy and Dillon. Would you like to say hello to them?"

"Jeez." Dillon gasped as a cool breath of air passed through his body from one side to the other.

"Ah, thank you my darling." Serena said, closing her eyes and nodding. She opened her eyes and looked at Dillon and Wendy. She grinned. "Helen said she is delighted to make your acquaintance and asked if you like painting? You can answer her. She can hear you."

"Hello, Helen." Wendy started, turning her head from one side to the other as if to try and see who she was talking to. "I like looking at paintings and I like to draw sometimes. But I'm not very good. Do you like drawing?"

"She said she liked to draw with the chalk that she would find in the ground. Flowers and birds." Serena said quietly. "And now that you have answered her question, she knows she can trust you. We can now ask a question in return. Helen my dear, Dillon and Wendy would like to know if you can tell them anything about who or what is looking for them?"

A few moments passed. Dillon and Wendy kept their eyes fixed on Serena. They waited. Serena didn't move. She just waited patiently for Helen to answer.

"Helen? What's the matter, my love?" Serena asked finally.

"What's happening?" Wendy whispered.

"She's afraid." Serena replied.

"Of what?" Dillon asked.

"I think she's scared of the entities that you are dealing with."

"Helen?" Wendy said. "I know you're frightened of them. We are too. But we need to know more about them."

"Am I right in thinking that you do know what is looking for my friends?" Serena asked. She waited for a response. A breath made the candles flicker and Dillon could have sworn that he heard a sigh.

"Please Helen," Wendy pleaded. "At least tell us what they are. Some other spirits we have met called them The Fallen. But we don't really know much more than that." Wendy looked at Serena and saw her mouth drop open and her eyes widen. The expression that spread over Serena's face was unmistakable. It was the look of fear.

"Helen said that the name used by those young spirits who you met at the house, The Fallen, comes from the Bible lessons they received. They believe that these beings are the Fallen Angels who tumbled into oblivion along with Satan when they were cast out of Heaven by God. But that's not true. Their understanding was purely based on what little information they had available that they could apply to the unknown. Helen says the truth is much worse."

"So what are they then?" Dillon asked.

"She doesn't know for certain. They have always existed. In the deeper, darker realms. But she does know one thing."

"What's that?" Dillon whispered.

"They were never angels."

"That's not good." Dillon mumbled.

"Helen also said that even though she doesn't know what they are, she can show you."

"Show us?" Wendy repeated. "How?"

"She can share visions with us. It's a bit like Astral Projection only in reverse. Instead of us leaving our bodies to travel somewhere, the vision comes to us."

"How do we that?" Asked Dillon.

"Take my hands and close your eyes. Helen will use me as a conduit to share her vision and you will see it too. It won't be amazingly clear, a fuzzy outline at best, but it will give you a fair idea of what these entities are."

"I'm scared." Wendy murmured.

"Oh, my darling." Serena smiled. "Don't worry. You're perfectly safe here. The moment it becomes too much, just let go of my hand."

Wendy and Dillon reached out and took one of Serena's hands each. They closed the circle by holding each other's hand as well.

"Now, just close your eyes, breathe slow and deep and open your mind."

Dillon closed his eyes. The candlelight was just about perceptible through his eyelids. He waited and then heard Serena whisper.

"There. There's something coming through."

Dillon could see an image forming in his mind. It felt the same as if he was thinking back and recalling a memory but this time, there was no effort on his part to form the image. It just seemed to develop and grow in his brain. At first, it consisted of nothing more than a dark grey fog but then, after a few minutes, it began to brighten in the centre as though he had tunnel vision. He could make out movement in the fog but it was difficult to see what was moving. Whatever it was, it seemed to be swimming through the dense mist with an effortless gliding motion. Then Dillon noticed that there was more than one. They were still too hidden for him to make out their form, hidden behind the fog. But slowly, one came closer and its form began to take shape. It seemed to know that Dillon was there and it came forward to see him. As the fog dissolved around the shape, Dillon could finally see the full horror of The Fallen. And Helen was right. It was no angel.

The body was pale, bloodless, smooth and shiny like it was moist. Black lines that resembled blood vessels full of black blood covered its surface. It displayed some humanoid features in that it had a recognisable head, neck and trunk but that was where the similarity with humans ended. From all over the body, a dozen or more slim, whip-like tentacles waved and danced as though they were underwater. The end of the body tapered off into another long tentacle-like appendage. Two thin, multi-jointed limbs reached upward from the upper portion of the torso, like emaciated arms reaching and grasping around the head. Where there should have been hands, there were only claws, snapping and clawing at the fog. But the ovoid head was the most horrifying spectacle of all. There was no face. Instead, in the centre of where a face should have been was a large hole. It resembled a swirling, black vortex and the grey, moist skin shimmered as it seemed to cascade into the void. It looked as though the whole head would be sucked in on itself through the hole but it didn't. Ripples ran from the vortex over the head like water being sucked into a whirlpool. This was an entity that consumed darkness and took it to a place where even the blackest soul would be driven to insanity with fear.

Dillon flinched as the hideous figure suddenly lurched forward. The two arm-like appendages reached out for him, writhing around as the claws snapped closer and closer. The tentacles whipped more vigorously and Dillon could feel the menace, the malice and greed of the creature. It was reaching for him. To consume him. To extinguish him. He opened his eyes and the vision disappeared. His mouth dropped open as he saw the candle flames flickering wildly and the crystals vibrating on the table. The plumes of smoke from the incense cones coiled and waved in the air and when Dillon looked up at the cloud of smoke by the ceiling, he gasped. The cloud was rippling like the surface of a black lake in a storm. Shapes were swimming through it, creating waves. Every so often, one of the shapes would pause and approach the surface from the other side. A hideous head would push at the smoke as if pressing against a plastic film. It would peer down at Dillon, Wendy and Serena before twitching violently as though it was trying to break through. Then it would retreat back into the smoke. Serena heard Dillon's gasp of surprise and she opened her eyes. She followed his gaze up to the ceiling and saw the myriad creatures trying to break through into their world.

"They've found us!" She exclaimed. She leapt to her feet, leaned forward and swept the crystals off the table. They clattered onto the floor as she blew out the candles. A terrifying, high-pitched scream filled the room as they were plunged into darkness. And then everything was quiet.

"Oh my goodness." Serena gasped. Dillon heard a match strike and the room was again filled with light as Serena re-lit the largest of the three candles. Dillon saw that she was pale and beads of sweat had formed on her brow.

"Oh my goodness." She mumbled again as she slumped back into her seat, reached into a pocket of her dress and pulled out a paper tissue. She dabbed her forehead and panted for breath.

"At least we know what's after us now." Dillon said glumly. His heart was pounding in his chest and his arms were covered in goose bumps. He looked at Wendy. It was obvious she was in a state of shock. The vision of the things that were after them was just too horrific. She looked at Dillon and then at Serena.

"What are we going to do?" She asked. Her voice cracked with emotion. "I mean, how can we defeat these things and go back to our normal lives?"

"I..." Serena started. "I don't know." She shook her head and then placed her palms back on the table.

"Helen, my love." She said. "If you're still here, please let me know." She waited and then a breath of cool air floated over the table. Serena smiled. "Can you help my friends? Can you tell them how they can defeat these creatures of the abyss?" Serena closed her eyes and waited. Then, her head nodded forward and a tear spilled from the corner of her eye.

"What is it?" Wendy asked. "What did she say? What can we do?"

Serena opened her eyes and looked up at Wendy and Dillon with a look of pity on her face.

"Run."

26

Dillon suggested that they go for a drink. Wendy agreed with a slow nod although Dillon wasn't sure that the question had fully registered in her mind. From the moment they left Serena's shop, she had been quiet and staring blankly at the pavement in front of her as they walked. She almost bumped into a couple of people and only recognised that they were there when they swerved to avoid her or if Dillon took hold of her arm to gently manoeuvre her out of the way. She said nothing and the fingers of her left hand that hung limply by her side were trembling. Dillon took hold of her hand and felt how cold she was. They walked slowly back to the riverfront and to the pub where Dillon had first found the flyer for the ghost walk. As they entered, he glanced at the noticeboard. The flyers and posters were all different from before but he found his mind wandering, reminiscing about how he had first seen Wendy when she gave him the leaflet for the Exeter Society for the Paranormal. And then he thought about Bob, Frank, Steve and Sophie. And Jackie. He felt a sad numbness well up inside him. How could it have come to this? Four of his new friends in Exeter were dead and Jackie was in a deep coma from which she may never return. The horrors he had witnessed were overwhelming and he wished that he and Wendy could just walk away. Except they couldn't. Because those things from the darkness beyond were still looking for them. They were marked. They were being hunted.

"Here." Dillon said softly as he placed a pint on the table in front of Wendy. While he had been at the bar, he had watched her sitting at the small round table by the window. Her outline was illuminated by the lights outside that lined the river path and, even in the warm glow of the pub's lighting, her face was pale and drained of expression. She sat, staring at a beermat on the table until Dillon placed the pint on it. Then, she looked up at him.

"Thank you." She said weakly. Dillon gave her a smile and placed his hand on her shoulder. He rubbed gently to reassure her that everything was going to be alright. Even though he didn't believe it himself.

"What are we going to do?" She asked, her eyes full of desperation and filling with tears.

Dillon sighed and lowered his head. "I don't know." He replied.

"We have to do something." Wendy reached out over the table to him. Dillon looked up and saw a solitary tear run down her cheek. He lifted his hand and placed it in hers. She gripped him tightly. "We can't go on living in fear." She added as she shook her head.

"Well," Dillon started. "Serena, or rather Helen, said that the only thing we can do is to run." He shrugged. He wasn't convinced of running as a course of action. But what other options did they have?

"It makes sense." Wendy whispered. "If these things are looking for us, then if we're on the move all the time, they'll find it really hard to find us. We could even evade them for the rest of our lives."

Dillon pondered on Wendy's last few words. 'The rest of our lives'. Did she mean that they would stay together, forever? His mind filled with thoughts of the two of them travelling the globe, seeing new places, experiencing new things. America, India, Africa, China. And all the while they would be one step ahead of those horrific creatures. More importantly, they would be together. Suddenly, going on the run didn't seem so bad.

"Okay." Dillon said. "We can do this. I can work independently as a web consultant. I can do that anywhere in the world, no matter where my clients are. As long as I've got a laptop and access to the internet, I can design and set up websites. That will provide us with enough revenue to support us. And if we don't have a fixed abode, we won't have rent or bills to contend with." He smiled at Wendy and saw a light brighten in her eyes. A light of hope. "It might just work."

"We can start making preparations tomorrow." Wendy said and the excitement returned to her voice. She wiped her eyes on the back of her sleeve and smiled. "Where shall we go first?"

"Well, I don't know." Dillon replied, stroking his chin as though he was deep in thought. "I've got plenty of savings so we could go anywhere. Where do you fancy?"

"The Caribbean." Wendy said with a wide grin.

"Whoah, whoah!" Dillon said. "I was thinking more of Norwich or Edinburgh!"

"Don't tease!" Wendy said with a giggle.

"But now you've put the idea of the Caribbean in my head... I must admit it does sound tempting. How about Saint Lucia?"

"Oh, yes!" Wendy exclaimed.

"Then we'll look into it first thing in the morning. I'll check some flight websites and start making some plans."

Wendy let go of Dillon's hand and clapped her hands together. Dillon grinned and picked up his pint.

"I would like to propose a toast." He said, holding his glass out over the table. "To a long and happy life, living the jet-set lifestyle in wonderful places, far and wide."

Wendy raised her glass and clinked it against Dillon's.

"To a long and happy life." She said with a twinkle in her eye. "Together."

Dillon slowly opened the door of his flat. He and Wendy stood outside for a few moments, listening. He reached in around the door and flicked on the light switch. Again, they waited and listened. The apartment seemed quiet. It appeared just as they had left it. Slowly, they stepped inside and peered in each of the small rooms. Nothing seemed out of place. Only after they had carried out a thorough sweep of the flat, did they sit on the sofa and relax.

"It's late." Wendy said as she yawned.

"That it is." Dillon mused, stifling a yawn himself. He glanced down at his watch and had to concentrate to read the time. The two pints he had at the pub were affecting his vision and reflexes. Not enough to make him feel drunk. Just enough to make him feel as though he was coming round from an anaesthetic. Wendy rested her head on his shoulder. He breathed in the scent of her hair and closed his eyes.

"I need some water." She said after a few moments and she pulled herself to her feet. Dillon watched as she walked, slightly tottering toward the kitchen. He smiled. She had got through two pints in half the time that it had taken Dillon and as she had started to relax and loosen up, she'd insisted on a couple of gin and tonics.

"I think I need to go to bed." She said as she returned from the kitchen with a glass of water.

"Okay." Dillon said as he slowly raised himself up from the sofa. "I'll sleep here again and you can have the bedroom."

"No." Said Wendy. "I don't want to be alone tonight. Not after what happened before."

Dillon paused and stared at her. He didn't know what to say.

"Please stay with me tonight." Wendy added. Dillon's mouth opened and closed but no sound came out. Wendy smiled and walked over to him. She gently placed her hand on his upper arm.

"Don't worry." She said. "Nothing's going to happen. Those gin and tonics I had have made me feel a bit squiffy. Even if we were to have sex, I don't think I'm able to feel anything at the moment. I'll probably be asleep before you've even taken my clothes off." She raised the glass of water to her lips and sipped slowly, peering at Dillon over the rim of the glass.

"Besides," She said as she lowered the glass and began to make her way to the bedroom. "There's plenty of time for that." She looked over her shoulder and winked before disappearing into the bedroom.

Dillon looked up from the green velvet tablecloth. At first he thought he was alone in the small room, illuminated only by the glow of the three candles in the centre of the table. But then he noticed that each of the other chairs, arranged in a circle, had a black cloth that stood upright like a shroud covering a person. He looked from one black shape to another. They didn't move. There wasn't even a sign of breathing against the fabric. He heard a rocking noise and looked down at the ring of crystals surrounding the candles. They were shaking and rotating round in a circle. Gradually, one by one, they lifted up off the table and hung in the air a few inches above the green cloth. The candle flames flickered and turned red. He looked up and saw the thick grey cloud of incense smoke rippling and undulating. Things moved through the smoke. He saw tentacles whipping as bodies swam up and down, side to side. He wanted to get up and leave but his palms were stuck to the table. No matter how hard he tried to move his hands, they stayed firmly in place, his fingers outstretched. He quickly turned his head to his right to look behind him as he heard a noise. It was faint and difficult to determine what it was but then he heard it again, from his left this time. Just like in his dream in the chapel at Trevalling House, it was the sound of a child laughing. The high-pitched giggle was full of mischief, taunting him, playing with him. He craned his neck to look behind him and realised he couldn't see the walls of the room. As he peered into the blackness, it dawned on him that there were no walls. The dark extended beyond the circle of chairs with their unmoving, shrouded occupants, out into infinity.

He tried to stand up from his seat but found that, like his hands, he was unable to move his legs. The crystals, hovering in a ring around the red flames, were rotating faster and faster, spinning until they became a coloured blur, encircling the candles. They began to give off their own faint glow; a pale blue light that combined with the red of the candlelight to cast a shimmering purple iridescence on the table. He looked round as he heard the laughter again. It seemed closer this time, almost right behind him. But then he heard it from the opposite side of the table and as his head spun round, he thought he just saw the outline of a boy before it melted back into the darkness.

He looked up at the undulating cloud of smoke and instinctively ducked his head. The cloud seemed to have descended closer to him and the shapes swimming through the grey were circling round and round. The smoke was forming a spinning vortex and the centre was rising upward like an inverted whirlpool. He gazed up into the black void and it reminded him of the gaping maw of the creatures in the vision that Helen had shared. He could feel a pull on his body as the vortex began to suck the air up into it and Dillon became aware of a pungent smell. It was the smell of damp, mould and earth. But there was something else. A sickly sweet smell permeated the other odours. A smell of rotting meat.

His attention was gripped by the fluttering of one of the black shrouds on a chair to his left. He screamed as the shroud slid away and was whisked upward into the vortex, revealing the glassy-eyed, bloated and decomposing body of Bob. A menacing grin spread over Bob's face as trickles of black fluid, the tarry essence of putrefaction, spilled from the corners of his mouth and down his rotting chin. The swirling air was filled with children's laughter that came at Dillon from all sides. He turned his head in every direction but only glimpsed shadows running and vanishing into the dark. Dillon leaned back in his seat as Bob reached his decaying arms forward and placed his palms on the table top with his sickly pale fingers outstretched.

Another breath of air was swept up into the vortex above and a second black shroud flew upward, this time on his right, revealing another partially rotted form. Dillon recognised it immediately and he yelped as the head turned toward him. The grimacing face of Frank stared at Dillon with the same clouded eyes as Bob. He too reached forward and placed his hands on the table with his fingers outstretched. Both Bob and Frank kept their dead gaze upon Dillon as he looked at the three remaining shrouds on the other side of the table.

A cold shiver ran through him as a freezing blast of stagnant air was drawn upward. It carried two of the three shrouds at the same time, one to the left of Bob and one to the right of Frank. They revealed the bodies of Steve and Sophie. Both of them, in a similar state of decay to Bob and Frank, grinned at Dillon. Their unblinking, glassy eyes remained fixed on him as he gasped for air and his heart thumped against his ribcage. As he watched the final shroud, he saw three shadows appear behind it. They glided forward and gradually came into view. The red, blue and purple light did nothing to soften the hideous features of the three boys who Dillon recognised from Trevalling Hall. They approached the table and flanked the final shrouded chair.

"Come with us." The voice didn't seem to come from the decayed, grinning mouths of the boys. Instead, the rasping, gurgling sound felt as though it formed in Dillon's head. He tried again and again to free his hands but with no success. Then, the boys reached out and took a hold of the final shroud. They stared at Dillon with sickening smiles as their laughter filled his head. With a single, collective sweep of their arms, they pulled the shroud away and Dillon screamed as he looked into the dead face of Wendy. She smiled as black liquid ran from her mouth and she leant forward to place her hands on the table. The air filled with a horrific, high-pitched scream and the vortex above the table reversed, sending a column of twisting smoke down into the centre of the floating ring of crystals. Illuminated by the red flame at its heart, creatures swam down into the tornado, twisting, reaching and shrieking as their claws snapped at the surface of the column. Dillon looked past the swirling, dark mass at Wendy who sat grinning opposite him. She winked one white, clouded eye and ran her black tongue over her broken lips.

"Come with me." She said in a sickeningly muffled, gurgling voice as though her lungs were filled with water. "We can be together, forever."

Dillon screamed and sat bolt upright in bed.

"Jesus..." Wendy said as she woke up and propped herself up on one elbow beside him. "Are you alright?"

Dillon didn't answer. He couldn't answer. His mind was still filled with the horrific images of his nightmare and he was breathing too fast to speak. Wendy reached out and placed her hand on his chest. She immediately pulled it back and sat up, looking at him as best she could in the dark. His t-shirt and boxer shorts were saturated with sweat. He could feel the cold trickle of sweat run down his spine and the sensation brought his mind back to the present. He turned his head to face Wendy.

"Sorry." He panted. "A bad dream."

"It was them, wasn't it?" Wendy asked.

"Yeah. It was them." Dillon licked his lips. His mouth felt dry. He reached over for the glass of water on his bedside chest of drawers and saw the time on the digital alarm clock. It was just before five o' clock.

"Well, you're okay now." Wendy said comfortingly. "You're safe here with me. You can tell me about the dream in the mor..." She stopped mid-sentence and they both turned their heads to face the corner of the room where they just heard a faint chuckling sound. They sat absolutely still in complete silence, holding their breaths so they could listen. Dillon's heart was still pounding in his ears but it didn't block out what he heard next; a clear, distinct laugh.

"Shit!" He exclaimed as he threw off the duvet and leapt to his feet. The air in the room was cold and as it came into contact with his sweat-soaked skin and clothes, he felt freezing. "Christ almighty! It's freezing in here!" He yelped.

"They've found us!" Wendy shrieked. They heard another laugh and Wendy crawled over the bed and jumped to her feet. "Quick. Grab some clothes. We've got to get out!" She bent down to pick up her clothes and Dillon did the same. They ran from the bedroom into the lounge where they quickly dressed. Flinging on their jackets and shoes, without stopping to tie their laces, they ran from the flat. Dillon paused to lock the front door and they carried on running until they had reached the centre of town.

Dillon placed the empty cup of coffee next to the first he'd had already. The only place that was open at that time of the morning was the McDonald's restaurant in the middle of the city. They didn't have much of an appetite when they got there. Their stomachs were still churning from the experience they had fled from. It took a while for them both to calm down and stop shaking but the warmth and light inside the restaurant certainly helped. As did the couple of cups of coffee.

"How are you holding up there?" He asked. Wendy sighed.

"I'm okay now." She replied with a nod. Dillon felt as though she was trying to convince herself more than him.

"But I don't think I can carry on like this for much longer." She added. She looked him straight in the eyes. "We need to get away. Far away. As far as we can from here. Then we keep moving. Outrun them. It's the only way."

"I don't know." Dillon said with a soft shake of his head. "I've been thinking. There was something that Serena said that's been playing over in my mind."

"What?"

"She said that on the other side, time is meaningless. So therefore, decades for us could be a matter of seconds for them. They'll keep hunting us until we drop dead or until they catch us. And another thing she said was that the Beyond is in a constant state of flux. Always moving. Always shifting. So our location here in this realm would mean nothing to them. They're not fixed to one spot like we are, in the here and now. They just have to see where our mark shows up and make a bee-line for it. They don't have to cross oceans and continents like we would just to outrun them. We could see them in London for example, and then jump on a flight to California and they'll show up the same night. I don't think that distance is going to slow them down. All they have to do is follow our dreams. Just like they did with me last night."

"But Helen and Serena said we could run." Wendy said, her voice quivering with uncertainty.

"I know that's what they said. But neither of them really know what these things are or what they're capable of. I just think there must be another way."

"Like what?"

"It's a thought I've had before and it follows on from Jackie's idea to conduct a Binding Spell to trap these spirits in one place. Now, I know we don't have Jackie's spell and that threw us for a while but that doesn't mean the spell is not out there somewhere. It, or something like it, has been used before."

"When?"

"After Alexander Curwen-Oakes realised what he'd done and trapped The Fallen in the bodies of the children who he then buried in the grounds of Trevalling Hall."

"But we don't have that either." Wendy said. Dillon could sense the frustration building in her voice.

"Not yet. But again, it doesn't mean that it's not out there somewhere, hidden in some old book in a library somewhere. The positive thing is, we know the one that Curwen-Oakes used worked. Until we came along, dug up the bodies and broke the spell."

"Where do we start looking?"

"Well, Alexander Curwen-Oakes is where we start. He was a real person. He existed. He has a birth certificate, death certificate. There are probably documents and records of him from his time as Headmaster of the school at the Hall. All we have to do is piece together his history and work backwards. Find out where he was. Where he lived. Where he would have visited to obtain materials and research for his studies of Black Magic. If we can piece his life back together, we may find the spell that he used. I'm not saying we have to become a master of the Dark Arts ourselves. All we need is that one spell and the resources and opportunity to carry it out."

Wendy stared at him as she considered his proposition. It did make sense. It was unlikely that the ritual Curwen-Oakes used was a product of his own mind. So that could only mean that the spell must be written down somewhere and during his studies and training, Curwen-Oakes discovered it. But there was something that was making Wendy feel nervous and unsure. It would be like looking for a needle in a haystack. What if the document trail ran cold? What if they couldn't find the right document? For how long was Dillon prepared to keep looking? And every day that they were engaged with their search, The Fallen would be looking for them.

"What do you think?" Dillon asked.

Wendy leant forward and reached out across the table to him. She took hold of both of his hands and looked him straight in the eyes.

"It all just feels too risky. Too uncertain." She said. "There's no guarantee that we'll ever find anything. And we'll be hunted every step of the way. Let's just run. As far away as possible. At least for a little while. Then we can rethink. I have an aunt who moved to Australia back in the mid-nineties. We could go and stay with her."

"I..." Dillon began. He winced and squeezed Wendy's hands tight. "I just feel like I need to fight this. To finish it. For us and for Bob, Frank, Steve and Sophie. It needs to end. It can't carry on. I can't let it carry on." He looked into Wendy's glittering eyes. "I think I love you, Wendy. And I cannot bear the thought that these monsters are going to haunt you, haunt us, for the rest of our lives. I need to stop it."

"Oh, Dillon." Wendy sighed. She leaned over the table, lifted his right hand up and kissed it tenderly.

"You go to Australia." Dillon whispered. "Stay with your aunt. I want you to. Really I do. I don't want you to be here in danger. And I have no doubt that it is going to be dangerous. I have no idea where I'll need to go, what I'm going to find or the kinds of people I'm going to meet. I'm guessing if they're into Black Magic, then they're not going to be the friendliest people on the planet. I don't want to risk losing you, Wendy. So go to Australia. I'll call you every day and let you know how I'm getting on. And then, when it's over, we can be together and not be afraid anymore."

Wendy stood up from her seat, walked round the table and leant over Dillon, wrapping her arms around him and holding him tight.

"Okay." She whispered in his ear. "I'll go and stay with my aunt for as long as you need to put an end to this nightmare. But promise me you will be safe. I will wait for you. And when it's finally over, we can be together." She pulled away from him and looked into his eyes. "Because you know what, Dillon? I think I love you too." She leant forward and kissed him and for a moment, every shred of fear in Dillon's mind seemed to evaporate.

27

Dillon stared out the window of the seventh floor flat he had recently rented. He'd had no trouble in negotiating a pittance for the rent for just a couple of weeks because in the truest sense of the term, the place was an utter shit-hole. On the near horizon, three similar grey tower blocks stood, a blot on the landscape, corrupting the crimson hue of the sky as the sun set behind them. Not that there was much of a landscape to ruin. Steel fences, topped with razor wire surrounded ramshackle single-storey industrial units with rusted, corrugated iron roofs. Dirty white transit vans motored and bumped along the pot-holed roads between the units and in one enclosed yard, a battered JCB was moving piles of scrap metal that had been harvested from the almost unrecognisable remains of cars. Most of the flats in the block Dillon was temporarily staying in were empty. And that was because in a couple of months, the whole block would be demolished. It was perfect. It was just what he had been looking for.

A long and tiring year had passed since he had waved goodbye to Wendy as she boarded the National Express coach from Exeter to London Heathrow. Since she left, they had spoken every day of course and Wendy delighted in showing Dillon her aunt's house in Carrickalinga, to the south of Adelaide, through the magic of Skype. Although she was on the other side of the world, he could still see her on his phone or laptop and imagine she was actually there with him. Dillon was happy to see Wendy so pleased with her new life in Australia. Over the course of a few weeks, her skin had tanned to a gorgeous brown and the Sun had lightened her hair, creating streaks of blonde. Dillon teased her, saying she looked like a surfer-chick and she had laughed in her beautiful musical way. She certainly looked happier and healthier though. As though the weight of all the fears and worries that she suffered in England had been lifted from her shoulders. And it wasn't long before she got a job in Adelaide working on a reception desk in an office. Her experience with Customer Services back in Exeter had helped her to secure the position. And the salary in Australia was far more than she would have made back home. She looked like she had really taken to a new life in Australia. A new life. A new beginning.

Dillon on the other hand was alone, pale, tired and not eating very well. He suffered recurrent bouts of heartburn and a packet of indigestion tablets was never too far away. He'd spent the year travelling the country on a mission. And every step of the way, The Fallen were never far behind. Dillon would rent rooms in a bedsit for a few days or a couple of weeks, knowing that he wouldn't be staying in one place for very long. As soon as he felt The Fallen had found him he would leave and move to another location. The sound of their laughter constantly plagued his mind, even when he was awake, like a demonic tune that played on a loop in his head. Sometimes, the only way to quiet the sinister, malicious giggling was to medicate with vodka. And sometimes, that was the only way he could sleep through the night.

Dillon had started with the records from the prison in Exeter where Alexander Curwen-Oakes had spent his last few weeks before taking his own life. Dillon reasoned that if he hadn't killed himself and was put on trial, he probably would have been found guilty of a number of charges of child abuse, maybe even manslaughter or murder, which would have resulted in him being hanged anyway. Nevertheless, the prison records did contain some personal details about the man including a photograph. Dillon felt a chill run through his body every time he looked into the eyes of the black and white portrait. There was a coldness there. A smart, calculating, evil presence. Dillon kept a copy of the photo hidden in an envelope in a portfolio of evidence that he was collecting and only looked at it rarely, when he needed to try and understand the man behind the image.

The evidence portfolio grew larger the moment he started to investigate the background of Curwen-Oakes as Headmaster for the school at Trevalling. Dillon also came across records of Alexander's wife from that time and the newspaper clippings and documents soon outgrew the folder he was using to collect his evidence. He eventually decided that, to keep a chronological record of all the events and the research notes he was making, he should buy a journal. He spent many hours in coffee shops and bars in quiet contemplation and reflection as he diligently recorded everything he had witnessed. Some of the pages caught his tears as he wrote about his friends whom The Fallen had taken. It was a difficult task, but necessary. Every experience, every observation, every infinitesimally tiny nugget of information could be useful in helping to stop The Fallen.

He moved from place to place, following the paper trail. From Exeter, he went to Bristol where Curwen-Oakes and his wife had lived for a while, probably biding their time before they could sweep in and take over the school in Exmoor. Looking back through the places where Curwen-Oakes had lived, Dillon began to see a pattern forming. They were old cities. And old cities had old libraries and museums. From Bristol, Dillon visited Oxford, then Cambridge, London and finally Edinburgh.

One of the most striking revelations that Dillon found was that Alexander Curwen-Oakes had no formal qualifications. The documents and experience that he produced to get the Headmaster's position at the Trevalling School were entirely fabricated. It was a means to an end. By the time he'd moved to Bristol, Curwen-Oakes must have already identified the old Hall as a perfect place for his Black Magic rituals. From there, he could watch and wait for an opportunity to move into the school. He must have been overjoyed when he learned that the old Headmaster was retiring. It must have felt like a gift. And by the time he moved to Exeter, his research and skills as a Master of the Dark Arts were complete. But it was in Edinburgh, when Curwen-Oakes was a young man that his interest in the Occult and the supernatural first took hold of him and blossomed.

Edinburgh was the ideal place for Curwen-Oakes to immerse himself in the paranormal. The history of grave robbers and murderers such as the infamous Burke and Hare coupled with the haunted vaults and graveyards would have provided ample stimulation and intrigue for the young student. The only piece of information that Dillon never found was how Curwen-Oakes had developed his interest in the first place. What was the trigger? What was the spark that ignited his passion for the dead and the realms beyond? It didn't really matter too much that Dillon never found out. He was after all, only going through the man's history to try and find the source material of the binding spell that he used.

Even without knowing how Curwen-Oakes had started along his dark path, Dillon recognised Edinburgh as a place of significance in accelerating him along it. It was in Edinburgh that his studies took on a whole new level of intensity. Records from his old school showed that he was failing in all subjects and he played truant a great deal. He even stopped attending church along with his parents. No doubt, he was using his time to study Black Magic. Like Curwen-Oakes, Dillon found scores of old texts dating from the nineteenth century to as far back as the mediaeval period in the libraries of Edinburgh. Some, specifically concerned with the Occult Sciences would have provided the young student with valuable information on talismans, symbols, spells and rituals that he could have tested and refined in the graveyards of the city. One specific text still had a scrap of paper tucked into it, covered with scribblings and notes. Dillon wondered if this was the hand of Curwen-Oakes himself and, suspecting that the notes may be significant, he secreted the sheet in his own journal.

Eleven months passed and Dillon had amassed a wealth of material about Curwen-Oakes and his likely studies. He had gathered page after page of symbols and magic diagrams, written in obscure, ancient texts. He had recorded spells and rituals designed to make contact with spirits of the dead. He made note of the necromancy rituals that Steve had mentioned were the specialism of John Dee. He found passages on how to open portals to the Beyond, how to command demons and then finally, he hit the jackpot.

The ritual on how to bind a spirit to something in the living realm was surprisingly simple. Very few materials were needed and the spell itself was short. The hardest part for Dillon was translating the text from the original Latin into English so he could understand what it was saying. He learned that the spirits from the nether realms, once conjured and questioned, could be bound not just into a sacrificial body, but into inanimate objects as well. And that gave Dillon an idea.

Dillon walked slowly from the window into the bedroom. He didn't bother to switch on any of the lights. The darkness was necessary. Any lights could attract their attention. He didn't want The Fallen finding him before he was ready. He paused just inside the doorway and glanced around the room. Even in the dim light from the lounge behind him, he could see the sheets of white paper that he had covered the walls and ceiling with. On each was drawn a large magic symbol that all together, created a space where the power of The Fallen would be diminished. Around the room, at strategic places marking out the points of a compass, Dillon had nailed wooden five-pointed stars. They were made from a range of different trees with magical properties; Yew, Willow, Oak and Ash. Most he had managed to purchase, but some, he had made himself, including the star that marked the North. By infusing his own spiritual essence into the star, he had provided it with additional powers. He closed the door and ran his fingertips over the sheets that covered the inside before he secured the deadbolts. Now, in total darkness, he closed his eyes, turned round and took a few steps toward the bed. He knew exactly what he was doing. He had practiced the moves several times that very afternoon. He leant forward and felt the soft duvet on the bed. He swept his hand to one side until he found the candle that he had placed there earlier. Reaching into his jeans pocket, he took out a lighter and struck the flint. The flame lit up the room and the symbols that surrounded him seemed to come to life and dance upon their pages. He held his breath as he lit the candle, extinguished the lighter and sat on the bed. Then he waited.

Several times over the following few hours, Dillon could feel himself starting to nod off. But he shook himself awake and hummed a tune to himself to prevent sleep from overwhelming him. He had to fetch two new candles from under the bed as the flame burned the wick almost to his fingers and his back was starting to ache from sitting on the edge of the bed for so long. At just after midnight, a strange sensation overcame him. It was like a static charge from the screen of an old fashioned television and it crept over his body like prickly fingers caressing his skin. He knew what it meant. He stood up. All thoughts of sleep disappeared from his mind. His heart began to beat faster and his breathing grew deeper and more rapid. He reached down beside him and picked up the journal. He flicked to the last entry he had written earlier that evening and glanced over the letter. He hadn't made it out to anyone in particular because there was no-one in particular to make it out to. Wendy was in Australia. It wouldn't be her to find him if everything went tragically wrong. He silently prayed that they wouldn't be his final words. That he would survive this. That he would go on to live another day. That he could fly out to Australia and be with Wendy. A lump caught in his throat and he quickly turned back several pages to the Latin text of the ritual. He glanced at the armchair and the three dolls he had fashioned out of corn, following an ancient pagan tradition. It was these that he planned to trap The Fallen in. And there, in that room they would remain until the block of flats was demolished and they would be buried in the rubble forever.

He gulped nervously as the candle flame quivered and the temperature dropped. He was safe inside the room though. The symbols and talismans that adorned the walls would protect him. The Fallen couldn't get in. He would have to invite them using the first half of the spell to summon them before him. Within the magic space he had created, their powers would be vanquished and he could command them as he wished. And what he was going to command them to do was to enter the corn dollies where they would remain for eternity.

He turned his head toward the door as he heard their laughter. They were just outside and he heard them scratching with their bony fingers on the wood. Then he heard them from behind him, laughing and scratching on the other side of the wall. He listened as they moved around the room, trying to find a way in. The laughter intensified and became almost hysterical. It was working. The protective talismans were holding them at bay, keeping them outside and away from him. Dillon grinned. *You thought I'd be that easy did you? You evil bastards. I'll show you. This is the end of the line for you. It's payback time for all you've done. All you've taken. All you've destroyed. I'm going to make you pay.*

He held the candle aloft in front of him and the light spilled over the open page of the journal that he was holding in his other hand. The room grew colder and the candle flame flickered and took on a bluish hue. He heard the scratching from several directions and the laughter began to change into a series of impatient growls and shrieks. Dillon took a few deep breaths, ready to read the first few lines of the spell when he was stunned into silence by a loud banging against the door. The scratching and banging against the door was truly terrifying and the hairs all over Dillon's body stood on end in fright. The door shook in its frame and the deadbolts rattled as the barrage continued. It felt as though the whole room was vibrating. Dillon knew he had to hurry and he glanced down to read the spell when he heard the shrieks and banging suddenly stop. He looked at the door. It was still. For a moment, there was silence and Dillon wondered if The Fallen had gone. But then he heard the laughter again. It was quiet at first but grew steadily louder. This time, it sounded different. It was still malicious and mischievous but there was a new emotion that struck fear into Dillon's heart; it was the sound of victory.

By the time Dillon noticed that a corner of one of the sheets on the wall next to the door had come loose, it was too late. The glue holding the sheet had lost its adhesiveness as the wall was shaking when The Fallen were banging violently on the door. Dillon turned to face the wall and held the candle closer. He gasped as he saw the patch of wall revealed by the drooping corner of paper turn black with a viscous, oily sheen. The blackness began to slowly pour into the room as a dark fog, crawling over the floor and up over the walls. Dillon stepped back into the centre of the room.

"No! No! No!" He cried out and the journal slipped from his hand and fell to the floor. As he shuffled backward, he kicked the journal under the bed with his heel and when the back of his legs bumped against the edge of the bed, he stopped. He stood, looking around the room as the black mist crept up every wall, obscuring the symbols that were supposed to offer him protection, rotating the stars until they were upside down and plunging him into the middle of a dark void. Panic filled his mind. He was supposed to summon them, taking away their power in the process. But they'd found their own way in. And now he was the one who was powerless. He brandished the candle with both hands like a dagger and spun round to locate the door where he could make his escape. But the door was gone, hidden by the darkness.

"Leave me alone!" He cried out and spun round as he heard laughter from behind him. As he peered beyond the glow of the candle, he saw shadows moving in the fog. Slowly, they came closer and emerged from the mist to stand before him. Dillon's legs wobbled and he sat down on the edge of the bed. Now he was at eye-level with the creatures, he could see their horror lit up by the flame. The three boys stood before him, the black mist swirling around behind them as though it was emanating from their hideous forms. The clothes were dirty rags, barely covering the putrefying flesh and exposed, discoloured bones beneath. Their faces were somewhere between a grinning skull and the visage of a rotting corpse. They stared at him with empty, black eye sockets and then he heard their collective, gargling, rasping voices in his head.

"Come with us."

"No! Never!" Dillon yelled at them and he waved the candle in their faces. They didn't flinch but instead held out their emaciated and skeletal arms, their hands open with palms turned upward.

"Come with us." The voice in Dillon's head was insistent but cold and emotionless. Dillon's heart sank and he felt tears well up in his eyes.

"What do you want? Why are you doing this? Why can't you just leave me alone?" He cried out. The three figures didn't answer. They just stood with arms outstretched, waiting for Dillon to give in. But that wasn't something he was going to do lightly. He felt a flood of rage rush through his body and he gritted his teeth and stood up.

"You're not going to take me! You hear? I'm not going with you fuckers! Go back to Hell where you came from!" He held the candle out closer to his tormentors and they all simultaneously lowered their arms and looked at the flame. Dillon held it still for a moment, conscious that he had distracted their attention. And then the boy in the middle leant forward and with a cold, stale breath, blew the candle out.

Dillon gasped as he was plunged into cold darkness. He quickly fumbled in his pocket for the lighter and tried repeatedly to strike the light. It didn't work. With each flash of the flint, he saw the three figures before him, waiting, watching.

"Come on you bastard!" Dillon cried as he tried again and again to strike a flame. In his haste, he dropped the candle and rather than bend down to retrieve it, he gripped the lighter with both hands and struck the flint again and again. As the sparks lit up the room, he saw the figures start to move apart from each other. The movement, captured in the split-second flashes of light was jerky, like the images in a flick-book but Dillon was aware that The Fallen were surrounding him on three sides. In between strikes, when the dark was absolute, Dillon heard them laughing. The sound seemed so distant, like an echo, even though he could smell the rotting flesh of the boys both in front of him and to his sides. He struck the lighter vigorously but then suddenly, the wheel popped out from the metal clasp and the flint was catapulted into the air by the spring. And then everything was deathly quiet.

Dillon waited. He didn't dare move. He knew the three figures were right next to him. He could sense them. He could smell them. He could feel their coldness. His breathing was rapid and his heart pounded in his ears.

This is it. He thought. *This is the end.*

He yelped as he felt two ice-cold bony hands grab each of his forearms with a vice-like grip. Freezing cold swept up through his arms and filled his body. He gasped as he felt his heart flutter and stall. As a burning pain filled his chest, he felt the face of one of the figures right in front of his own and then, as his lungs ceased to ventilate and he slumped to the floor, its hideous voice filled his mind.

No. This is just the beginning.

*   *   *   *   *

Two days ago, I heard them again.

Although it's been nearly a fortnight since they last found me, I recognised their laughter immediately. No matter how far I run, or where I go, they always manage to find me.

At first, they seem distant; far away. I wasn't sure if I could really hear them or if my mind was playing tricks on me, replaying haunting memories just to torment me. But when I heard them, I knew it was time to leave. And quick. I wouldn't risk another night.

But this time is different. I won't run anymore. I'm ready for them now. I know how to defeat them. I let them get closer and closer. I want them to find me this time. I want them to feel like they've won. And so gradually, like a leaking tap in the darkness that, for a tortured mind, seems to grow louder with every successive drip, their laughter has become closer and louder.

Now they're with me all the time.

But I'm ready.

I know that they're there in the darkness. Watching me. I can feel them. I can hear their quiet, rasping breaths. I can feel their cold presence but I cannot run any longer. I'm not going to run any longer. There's no escaping them. I'm so tired. I simply cannot go on. I have to finish this. I have to end it.

It's our own fault. We set them free. We released them.

And they came looking for us.

We thought we were breaking new ground, charting new territory, broadening the horizons of our own understanding. We were reaching out to another world, making contact, writing a new chapter in the history of parapsychology. We just didn't know the world we were trying to peer into should have been left well alone.

For our own sake.

The others have gone. They were found. They were taken.

But I will defeat them. And I will stop them from taking me too.

I hope that these will not be my final words.

I hope that my plan will work and I will banish them.

I hope that I will live on and can spend the rest of my days with Wendy.

I hope that I will see her again.

But if I do not succeed, I cannot leave my friend's tragic story untold.

So I have recorded everything that happened before. Here, in this journal.

I had to leave a testimony of what really happened. The truth. Unbelievable as it may be. Of course, there were investigations into what happened to the others. Suicides and accidents. At least that's what the coroner's inquests concluded. They never linked the deaths together. But how could they? How could they know the horrors that really happened? Would they want to know?

If I had my time again, I wouldn't want to know.

But I do.

So it has fallen on me to tell the whole story. From the very beginning.

To lay the souls of my friends finally to rest.

And when the time comes, my own too.

God help me.

28

The hot, salt breeze blew gently through Wendy's hair. She closed her eyes and felt the heat of the late evening sun on her face as the sound of the ocean washing up and down the beach filled her being. She sighed and breathed in the fresh air. The smells of the sea, the vegetation on the sand dunes behind her and her own skin, warm from the heat of the sun blended into the sweet scent of happiness.

And she was happy. Life in Australia for the past year had been better than anything she could have ever hoped for. She felt relaxed, more confident and healthier than she had ever felt before in her life. Especially considering what she had escaped from back in England.

Living with her relative, her own flesh and blood, was great. They had always been close since she was a young girl. Her aunt, being her mother's sister, had practically shared raising her and she would stay at her aunt's house for the weekend whenever she could. She could remember with fondness each and every day trip and visit to the seaside with her. The rides on the pier. The ice cream and packets of chips. They were happy memories. And she had been devastated when her aunt moved out to Australia. They hadn't seen each other for around twenty years. But the past year had made up for all of that. It had felt like a long-overdue holiday. But a holiday that would never end.

Wendy wiggled her toes in the sand. The grains flowed over her feet and she felt the coolness of the sand below the surface on her soles. She giggled to herself as the sand tickled in between her toes and then she glanced along the beach in both directions to ensure no one had seen. She smiled as she marvelled at the beauty of her surroundings. Pure golden sand stretched away along the coast for as far as she could see. A few sea-birds wheeled in the air high above her head, riding the breeze one last time before the sun would set. The long leaves of grass on the dunes rustled, a gentle swishing sound that accompanied the wash of the sea over the sand. Although the small settlement of Carrickalinga was just the other side of the dunes behind her, there were no sounds of traffic or aircraft flying overhead. It was the quintessential definition of Paradise.

Wendy felt a surge of longing well up in her. It was all very well her enjoying this idyllic new life but she was still alone. She missed Dillon. Although he had kept her up to date with all the progress he had made in tracking Alexander Curwen-

Jakes' life and studies, he was still half a world away. She was cautiously optimistic when he had told her that he'd found a Binding Ritual and that he had a plan on how to use it. She had to fight the urge to get on a flight and return to England to help him. When she had offered, he had point blank told her not to. He said it would be too risky and he didn't want her in any danger. She trusted him and told him to be careful. But that was over a week ago, just before he was going to move location again. For the last time, she hoped, before he could fly out to Australia to be with her.

It did seem strange that she hadn't heard from him in so long. Normally, they would speak over the internet every day. There had been a couple of times when she hadn't heard from him or couldn't make contact but when they did catch up again, Dillon would normally say it was because he was on the move or there was no signal where he was at that moment in time. But over a week was a bit long. She knew better than to worry however. The first time she didn't hear from him, she panicked. When he called the very next day, she felt foolish for getting so worked up and on subsequent occasions when he missed calling her, she just told herself that it would be fine and she'd hear from him tomorrow. But she'd been telling herself that for over eight days now.

The bottom edge of the sun gently touched the horizon. The sky was turning shades of orange, red and purple with the dark, inky-blue of approaching nightfall behind her. The air began to chill as the sun lost its strength and Wendy folded her arms across her chest, pulling her dress tight to her body. She watched as the sun slowly dipped further and further beyond the ocean, turning redder and redder with each passing second. Then, she felt a cool breeze behind her as though someone had just run past. She instinctively turned her head but there was no one there. She frowned. The gust was colder than anything else she had felt that evening and it came from the opposite direction that the breeze had been blowing. She waited a few seconds to see if it would happen again and when it didn't, she turned back to continue watching the sunset.

A noise from behind distracted her. She turned round fully, expecting to see someone on the sand dunes. There was nobody in sight and the plants were still. She stood motionless, scanning the dunes for any sign of an animal scurrying across the sand but when nothing revealed itself, she turned back to see the last, upper quarter of the sun dipping below the horizon. As the light began to fade, she felt the temperature drop and a strange static sensation tickled the skin on her bare arms. She began to feel nervousness take over and she rubbed her arms to get rid of the tingling feeling. The hairs on her arms were standing on end and just as a cold breath of air caressed the back of her neck, she heard another noise. Spinning round, she quickly looked for the source of the sound. She was completely alone and it was getting darker and colder. She became aware of a strange smell that wafted toward her. It was a sickly scent. Damp earth and rotting meat. She began to shake with terror as wide-eyed, she scanned along the beach for any hint of what she feared was out there, watching her. And then she heard something that she recognised. A sound that she hoped she would never hear again. In that moment she knew that Dillon was lost. And so was she.

From somewhere just beyond the dunes, she heard the rasping, gurgling sound of a dead child laughing.

End.

Printed in Poland
by Amazon Fulfillment
Poland Sp. z o.o., Wrocław

55263962R00121